24.09.13   1 7 SEP 2013   10/-

0 3 DEC 2018

Please return on or before the latest date above.
You can renew online at *www.kent.gov.uk/libs*
or by telephone 08458 247 200

CUSTOMER SERVICE EXCELLENCE   **Libraries & Archives**

00884\DTP\RN\07.07   LIB 7

D1343677

WICKED AUTUMN

A Max Tudor Novel

G.M. Malliet

CHIVERS

British Library Cataloguing in Publication Data available

This Large Print edition published by AudioGO Ltd, Bath, 2012.
Published by arrangement with St Martin's Press

U.K. Hardcover   ISBN 978 1 4458 8676 3
U.K. Softcover   ISBN 978 1 4458 8677 0

Printed and bound in Great Britain by
MPG Books Group Limited

This book is dedicated to the members of the National Federation of Women's Institutes (NFWI) and to the memory of Mrs. B, who loved detective stories.

CONTENTS

ACKNOWLEDGMENTS 9
CAST OF CHARACTERS 11
"I SING A SONG OF THE
    SAINTS OF GOD" 15

The Women 17
The Vicar 27
The Village 41
Out 48
. . . and About 63
Help Us 72
Harvest Fayre 84
Harvest Fayre II 96
Grim Reaper 112
Law and Order: Pod People 125
Baptizing the Teddy Bear 135
Legend 157
Medicine Man 172
Temptation 184

The Baker 196
The Major 203
At Home 225
The Antiquarian 234
What's Cooking 251
Miss Pitchford Disposes 270
Goddessspell 291
Quandary 316
St. Edwold's 333
Acolyte Down 347
After the Funeral 360
Revelations 380
At the Horseshoe 389
Jolie Laide 408
Epilogue 418

ACKNOWLEDGMENTS

With sincere thanks to Vicky Bijur, Karyn Marcus, and Marcia Talley. And as always, Bob.

CAST OF CHARACTERS

WANDA BATTON-SMYTHE — The formidable and much-feared head of the Nether Monkslip Women's Institute. Her stewardship of the annual Harvest Fayre netted her many enemies.

LILY IVERSON — Owner of a local knitting and textiles business, timid Lily was much put-upon by Wanda.

SUZANNA WINSHIP — Lily's champion and sister of the local doctor. The vampy, ambitious Suzanna often felt restless in the small village.

ELKA GARTH — Owner of the Cavalier Tea Room and Garden, and mother of the feckless Clayton, she was pressured by a relentless Wanda to donate her services for the Harvest Fayre.

AWENA OWEN — Owner of Goddessspell, the village's New Age shop. Down-to-earth Awena predicted cosmic consequences if Wanda were not brought under control.

11

MAXEN "MAX" TUDOR — A former MI5 agent turned Anglican priest, he thought he'd found a measure of peace in the idyllic South West English village of Nether Monkslip — until murder invaded his Garden of Eden.

GUY NICHOLLS — Chef and restaurateur, he was also dragooned by a persistent Wanda into donating his services to the Fayre.

DR. BRUCE WINSHIP — An expert in general ailments, he reveled in theories of how the criminal mind operates.

MAJOR BATTON-SMYTHE — Wanda's long-suffering husband, he claimed to be quite fond of his wealthy wife.

TARA RAINE — A lithe, attractive yoga instructor, she rented studio space at Goddessspell.

FRANK CUTHBERT — Local historian, author (*Wherefore Nether Monkslip*), and husband of Mme Lucie Cuthbert, who was proprietress of La Maison Bleue, Frank clashed with Wanda over his beloved books.

MRS. HOOSER — Max's housekeeper at the Vicarage, and the mother of Tildy Ann and Tom.

NOAH CARAWAY — Wealthy owner of Noah's Ark Antiques and of Abbot's Lodge, site of the fatal Harvest Fayre.

CONSTABLE MUSTEILE — An officious man,

he was the first official on the scene of the crime.

DETECTIVE CHIEF INSPECTOR COTTON — The kinetic DCI was dispatched from Monkslip-super-Mare to investigate a most suspicious death.

DETECTIVE SERGEANT ESSEX — DCI Cotton's assistant.

MISS AGNES PITCHFORD — A retired schoolmistress, prim Miss Pitchford was a walking cross-indexed repository of all village gossip.

JASPER BATTON-SMYTHE — Absent son of Wanda and the Major, and a talented young man with a burgeoning artistic career.

LAWRENCE HAWKER — Jasper's friend-turned-enemy from his school days.

LYDIA LACE — Acolyte at St. Edwold's, she knew she was not just seeing things when she spotted a killer.

"I SING A SONG OF THE SAINTS OF GOD"

And one was a soldier, and one was a
 priest,
And one was slain by a fierce wild beast:
And there's not any reason, no, not the
 least
Why I shouldn't be one too.
> ~ *Hymn lyrics by Lesbia Scott, 1929*

CHAPTER 1
THE WOMEN

Wanda Batton-Smythe, head of the Women's Institute of Nether Monkslip, liked to say she was not one to mince words. She might add that she was always one to call a spade a spade, and that what more people needed was simply to pull their socks up and get on with it. She was saying these things now — calling on all the resources in her cliché lineup, in fact — to a captive audience of approximately thirty-five women who, to a woman, were wishing themselves elsewhere than in the Village Hall, sitting on orange molded-plastic seats that might have been rejects from an ergonomics study, on an otherwise peaceful Saturday night in September.

Reports of members present and apologies for absence received (Miss Pitchford had a head cold) had already been swiftly recorded. The women had stood to sing the traditional "Jerusalem," if at a somewhat

17

faster tempo than was customary. Still, they had reached this night a deep, throaty trill on "Bring me my chariot of fire!" — for so many, a favorite line, unifying the straying or hesitant warblers into a mighty whole — before the effort collapsed again at "I will not cease from mental fight."

Finally, reports from the Flower Show and Guy Fawkes committees had been rushed through in unseemly haste, lest they detract from the main event: Wanda Batton-Smythe's address to the troops.

The men of the village, upholding a time-honored tradition in the division of labor, were of course safely ensconced amongst the gleaming brass and cheery glow of the nearby Hidden Fox pub.

"I am, as you know, not one to mince words, and you can always count on me to call a spade a spade," Wanda reminded them, her voice filling the room like a sonic gun. "The preparations for the annual Harvest Fayre are in an absolute *shambles*. We have all *got* to start pulling our socks up."

Calling on her knowledge of public speaking, newly refreshed by a rereading of the 1983 classic *Grabbing Your Audience by the Throat: Tips and Tricks for the Successful Orator,* Wanda paused, her unblinking gaze

18

panning the crowd, gathering eyeballs like so many marbles into her rhetorical basket.

"A shambles," she repeated, a doomsday prophetess. "It's an absolute disgrace."

Lily Iverson, rightly assuming part of this condemnation to be aimed starkly at her small head, began a stuttering apology, but in such a small voice as to be easily drowned out by Wanda's stentorian tones. It was a bullying technique nicely honed during Wanda's time in the trenches of the parish council meetings, where skirmishes over the proposed redesign of the coat of arms had become the stuff of legend. The name Wanda Batton-Smythe indeed was often invoked by young parents in warnings aimed at keeping their offspring in line, for she had become for many an embodiment of fear, a veritable bogeywoman.

Wanda now stood before the group, marshaling her resources for further onslaught, her broad, still-handsome face framed by a starchy collar over a dark summer wool dress that Cotton Mather would have approved. Her hair was a helmet of hardened curls, like rows of teeny brown snakes highlighted and poised to strike, living testament to the efficacy of Final Net, and her bosom was tightly bound in some unmoving modern wonder fabric that rendered her body rigid and unbowing, much like her mind. The gray eyes again scanned her audience like an advance scout awaiting the approach of enemy forces. Altogether she looked, as always, more like a woman gearing up for battle than the leader of a group of well-intentioned if somewhat loopy volunteers. Much of her life with her husband the Major, as well as her own service in the Women's Royal Army Corps, had rubbed off.

"Wanda, I don't think —" began Suzanna Winship, the willowy blond sister of the local doctor, coming to the defense of Lily, whose lower lip had begun to tremble around her adult braces. Wrapped in a fluffy white mohair dress of her own design (Lily owned a local yarn and knitting business), her hair clipped short around protuberant ears, she resembled a Chihuahua puppy abandoned in a snowdrift.

Wanda pounced.

"You have not asked to be recognized, nor have you been given permission to speak."

"Permission to speak?" Suzanna spluttered, looking round her: *Did anyone else find Wanda ridiculous?* They did, but no one had the courage to indicate so by word or deed, at least not to Wanda's face. Suzanna was new to the village. She'd learn.

Elka Garth, a grandmotherly woman in her fifties who owned the village bakery-slash-tearoom, did exhale a soft little sigh, adjusting her thick glasses and wishing the Reverend Max Tudor would hurry up and marry so his wife might take on the role traditionally allotted to those in her position. A palace coup, as it were, was called for. But the Vicar remained unwed — despite being a rakishly handsome man whose arrival in the village three years ago had had much the impact of a Hugh Grant exiting the elevator as Aretha Franklin sang "What you want, baby, I got" (Elka was a movie buff). His advent having utterly galvanized the female population, he remained, it was felt, *stubbornly* unattached despite the concerted best efforts of every woman in Nether Monkslip to corral him for either themselves or a relative. Over time, he tended to be thought of as "more in the mold of Tom Hanks," which only leant more to his appeal, and to the frustration of what came to be called, with linguistic inaccuracy, the Anglican Yenta Corps.

Only slightly daunted, Suzanna now stood up in her sexy, slip-on heels, her hair artfully tousled, a cruel if unintentional contrast to Wanda's battened-down façade. Aware that most women hated her on sight,

21

or at least regarded her with deep suspicion as having the potential to quickly develop, without careful monitoring, into the village hussy, Suzanna had cultivated in self-defense a genuinely warm and disarming persona. The others watched in awed silence as they realized she was going to engage. It was like watching a sacrificial virgin preparing to fling herself into the mouth of an active volcano.

"It is not Lily's fault that the vendor let us down," Suzanna said loudly, anticipating Wanda's air-raid siren shout-down. When roused, Suzanna could give as good as she got, and in defense of someone already as downtrodden as Lily, Suzanna could be formidable indeed. Besides, she knew there lingered among the members of the Women's Institute some unresolved feeling, however unwarranted, from the debacle that was the "All about Mixing Cocktails!" program of earlier in the year. Suzanna, who had suggested the scheme, and felt some ground had been lost in the sound-judgment department, was anxious to shine here.

"The Fayre this year apparently has been a cock-up all round compared with previous years, but perhaps we could focus efforts on what we should be doing to be ready anyway in one week's time."

Wanda, who had drawn a deep, shocked breath on the word "cock-up," had not otherwise disturbed the loaded silence of the room. Mme Cuthbert, who operated La Maison Bleue wine and cheese shop with a polished élan, allowed herself a small moue of approval in Suzanna's direction. The others stared straight ahead, like zombies in a bad sci-fi movie.

Finally, Awena Owen, the village's self-proclaimed New-Agey Neopagan, for want of a better description, was emboldened to speak, pushing back her thick dark hair, striking because of its single streak of white over one brow. She stood, feet solidly planted, a vital, comely, and charismatic figure who, although essentially other-worldly, managed to operate her New Age gift shop on a large profit margin. She was well liked and respected by the villagers, who called her the Great White Oprah.

"I have a few extra chairs in my shop," Awena said now, "cluttering up the back room. One needs mending, is all. I'd bet the rest of us could have a look in our attics and find something there too. Save us money, anyway, and this *is* all for charity."

Wanda Batton-Smythe found her voice at last.

"I Know It's For Charity," she bit out, her tone now apocalyptic. She looked like a bishop about to consign the Maid of Orléans to the flames. "We'll have a hodge-podge of furniture in the tea tent that won't match." Her mouth, which she had barely peeled open for speech, now snapped shut in a thin line of distaste, as if Awena had suggested they all ride naked in the fete's pony ride.

"So?" said Awena, not unreasonably.

"Then that's settled," yelled Suzanna, in triumph this time. She began rootling in her handbag for pencil and paper. "If everyone would put down their name and the number of chairs they think they can provide. We'll need tables, too, of course. Now, as to the Bring and Buy . . ."

Lily swiveled a brief, grateful glance in her direction, but overall Lily's round brown eyes remained fixed on Wanda's face. It was a sight not without fascination as outrage, frustration, and murderous impulse struggled for supremacy. Wanda seemed to telegraph an unambiguous *Fuck you* in Suzanna's direction, but when she spoke she had evidently decided to "Rise Above It." Cutting across the Bring and Buy chatter, she said, "As we seem to have no choice in the matter, due to the incompetence of the person in charge" (here she pointed a quivering, outraged finger in Lily's direction, in case anyone remained in doubt about who was to blame), "this poor stopgap measure will have to do." She sighed heavily, dissatisfaction puckering her lips. "As I am in charge of the Bring and Buy, there is no need for further discussion. That will come off like clockwork." The *or else* was implied, and hung in the air like sulfur following a visit from Beelzebub himself. "Now, tonight we have refreshments, provided by Elka Garth, so if there is no further business . . ." She brought down the gavel before anyone could speak.

Nonetheless, Elka had a small contribution to make.

"I've brought two kinds of biscuits — chocolate this time. As usual, one made with peanuts and one without."

Wanda nodded her approval. She was allergic to peanuts and appreciated that Elka always made concessions in this regard. There was a headlong rush toward the food-and-drinks table followed by more than a little genteel elbowing, for Elka was a superb baker.

Pigs to the trough, thought Wanda. Aloud she said, with a regal nod, in public recognition of a good and faithful servant, "Thank you *sooo* much, Elka."

Lead by example, that was the ticket. Never let it be said that Wanda Batton-Smythe was not the embodiment of gracious behavior at all times. She folded her glasses into her handbag — a handbag ever present, like the Queen's — and snapped it shut.

Never.

CHAPTER 2
THE VICAR

Not far from the unpleasantness at the Village Hall, the Reverend Maxen "Max" Tudor, object of much interest and strategic planning, sat in the vicarage study. A darkened fireplace was before him, and a Gordon setter asleep at his feet; a glass of whiskey and soda was at one hand, a pen in the other, and a writing pad atop his knees. To anyone looking in through the mullioned windows of the study, the darkly handsome man presented a picture of absorbed contentment as he worked on his sermon for the next day. The topic, James and the two kinds of wisdom, was more than normally appropriate, had he but known it: the one kind of wisdom — pure, peaceable, and gentle — came from above, but the other was earthly, unspiritual, and devilish. "You want something and do not have it; so you commit murder."

That nothing had changed from James's

time did not prevent Max from believing in future miracles, but he himself thought this duality was what made the occasional monster in the room harder to spot. People, in his experience, were always a combination of good and bad, of wisdom and foolishness. The family man, loved by his wife, friends, and colleagues, who turns out to be a serial killer — the seeming contradiction of such a nature continued to provide endless fodder for psychologists and theologians. It was a question of the extremes of good and evil, not a question of whether either existed. Max knew both did.

But it was a topic too large to contain in the minutes he allotted himself for a sermon; he was ever conscious of the moment when he might lose his congregation's mind to fretting over the shopping list, or a loose button, or what was on the telly that night. Himself preoccupied and uneasy for no reason he could discern, Max set aside the pad, and stood and stretched.

Tall and with a compact, muscular build, Max Tudor was a man physically at ease in the world, and his authoritative mien stood him well among the more fractious members of his congregation. Max, they sensed, beneath his open and welcoming countenance was not a man to be crossed. Insurrections were quelled, animosities quickly put aside, in his presence. Only the weekly struggle to the death over the church flower rota was beyond his capacity to suppress, since the desire to have more opportunities to interact with Max himself was the reason behind the infighting.

Now the whiskey and the stillness of the room were making him drowsy, yet he was determined to have the sermon put to bed before he himself slept. He decided on a rousing cup of tea; stepping carefully around Thea's luxuriant black and tan tresses, he moved toward the kitchen. Thea had earlier been fed and walked, and would have a final turn around the village before bedtime, none of which prevented her from now following him in the hope of another treat, an extra walk, or a random comment on her remarkable beauty.

Writing the sermon was one of Max's favorite duties, but this week he'd put it off, like a student late with a paper. He turned the topic over in his mind as he waited for the kettle to boil, attempting to resume the theme of duality that had so captivated James — the Dr. Jekyll/Mr. Hyde, heaven-and-hell nature of mankind. The following Sunday's sermon, much of which he had already drafted, was far easier. The topic for the day after the Harvest Fayre could only be thanksgiving for all that heaven and nature had provided: food, shelter, clothing, freedom from want.

"You want something and do not have it; so you commit murder." How much corruption, he wondered now, political and personal, came about because of greed? Out of coveting what we do not have, whether it be the neighbor's wife or the neighbor's goods, as the commandments had so neatly encapsulated men's motives?

Back in the study with his Earl Grey, he sat distractedly tapping the cap of his pen against the writing pad. It was cold enough for a small fire, he thought, and even if it weren't, he was going to rush the season. The sounds and smells of burning wood could always soothe if not inspire.

The housekeeper, Mrs. Hooser, had placed a somewhat lopsided arrangement of dried flowers in the hearth, a placeholder until the first autumn chill. He rose, set aside the flowers to open the flue, and took three of last winter's small logs from the stack, arranging them in a pyramid on top of kindling wood and crumpled paper. Soon a small blaze emerged, and he pulled his chair in closer to enjoy it. Thea hunkered down near enough to singe her coat, until he called her back. Both man and dog heaved a sigh of satisfaction.

He sipped his tea. Maybe he'd wing the sermon. It wouldn't be the first time.

The church of St. Edwold's had a small office, but Max preferred the coziness of the vicarage study. The house had been built, with uncommon foresight, along economical lines two hundred years previously. The room where he sat was effectively a study-slash-sitting room and had been the scene of many private counseling sessions with troubled parishioners, or, in some cases, parishioners with simply too much time on their hands. It was small and modern compared with what was now the Old Vicarage, occupied by Noah's Ark Antiques, the church having cashed in on rising property prices, recognizing the waste of maintaining such a large building. Everything had changed from the old days, when parsons were often the younger sons of gentry, and might themselves have private holdings. Unheard of was the stereotypical younger son choosing the church (or the army, navy, or the law) so the family wealth could devolve on the eldest. Those days had more or less gone out with the barouches of *Pride and Prejudice.*

The room where he sat was small, with

wood-paneled walls and the beautiful mullioned windows, reminiscent of an old manor house. Two walls were in fact bookshelves that stretched to the ceiling; on the third wall hung Max's collection of small seascape paintings, particularly those of a local artist named Coombebridge. A cross and a copy of Caravaggio's famous *The Betrayal of Christ* hung on the wall opposite.

The room contained many museum-quality relics, including a Bakelite phone so ancient Max was always astonished when it rang, and tended to shout into it as though, himself ancient and hard of hearing, he was calling to someone cast adrift on a raging sea. Much of the furniture when he'd arrived at the vicarage had been heavy, dark, or ugly — in other words, Victorian — and he'd had a good clearing out. Noah Caraway of Noah's Ark had taken much of it on commission.

The windows of the room were swathed by a fusty collection of curtain hangings, relicts of Walter Bokeler, his predecessor. They looked like they might have been made from Queen Victoria's cast-off undergarments. He always meant to get them changed but the money was always needed in a nobler cause. Leather chairs (his) and a skirted sofa (Bokeler's) were grouped

32

around the attractive stone fireplace.

Some of the shelves lining the walls were filled with old volumes of sermons by presumably esteemed and undoubtedly long-dead sermonizers. Most had been privately printed and were expensively bound in dark embossed leather — walls of books that should have warmed the room but instead tended to suggest that the march of history was long, gray, and deadly dull. Max had long wished to rid himself of them, along with the curtains, but who, when it came down to it, would want them? Even the owner of the new-and-used bookshop in the village had politely declined to take the volumes on commission. Repeatedly. As had Noah Caraway.

The air in the room grew close from the heat. Max walked over and pushed the casement wide, letting into the room the night scents of the plants beneath the window. He saw a sky still and clear, bright with stars. A hint of approaching autumn hung in the air, giving the garden the smell of something just washed with cold rain. Beyond his range of vision, outside the village of Nether Monkslip, were green fields turning yellow as the earth continued its slow tilt away from the sun. It would soon be the autumn equinox, long recognized under different guises and names. In the church, the feast of St. Michael — Michaelmas — had been assigned to mark this all-important shortening of days.

He decided he was hungry, but could not get excited at the prospect of whatever foil-wrapped packet Mrs. Hooser, the woman who "did" for him (and whom he had inherited, much like the curtains, from Walter Bokeler), had left in the fridge for him to reheat. It was more than likely a rubbery pasta-ish dish smothered in a sauce containing either suspect mushrooms or equally suspect-looking herbs. Mrs. Hooser cooked from store-bought packets for her own children, the extravagantly named Tildy Ann and her younger brother, Tom, which on the whole, Max felt, may have added years to the children's odds of survival.

She often brought Tom and Tildy Ann with her to the vicarage on the occasions when her own "help" had failed to materialize. Tildy Ann, a bossy little thing, as vigilant as her mother was feckless, kept Tom on the straight and narrow, held firm in her small iron grip. She was also fiercely protective of him: woe betide anyone who might try to do Tom a harm.

That Mrs. Hooser was at best an indifferent housekeeper was a fact to which Max had long become resigned. She tended to move and speak with sweeping, theatrical gestures and, as a result, many a vicarage bibelot had met a shattering fate at her hands. With bovine cunning, she would attempt to hide the evidence of the latest catastrophe — the broken crockery, the missing drawer handle — apparently never learning that Max, the most forgiving of employers, was incapable of anything but mild reproof. Mrs. Hooser, with her indifferent hoovering and her doubtful menu selections, had found secure employment at last, had she but known it — an island in the storm-tossed sea of life. She responded to his forbearance with an inflated protectiveness of her own, more or less frisking every visitor to the vicarage. As she was raising the two children alone, Mrs. Hooser had become an obligation Max felt both obliged and (more or less) content to accept.

She called him Father Tudor, and he knew without trying he'd never be able to persuade her to a less formal mode of address. He in his turn always called her Mrs. Hooser. The "Mrs." was a courtesy title she had granted to herself, he suspected. If there had ever been either a Mr. Hooser, or a boyfriend, he had long since left the field.

■ ■ ■ ■

Max Tudor had been at St. Edwold's nearly three years, a time of relative peace and respite, for himself as well as Mrs. Hooser. He had gathered from various villagers that the search to find a replacement for Walter Bokeler had not gone smoothly, particularly as three joint parishes were involved. In fact, the position had been vacant for several months.

He had been surprised to learn that many Nether Monkslip villagers had plumped for a female vicar. This seemed daringly forward, looking for what was clearly a hidebound place, even recklessly avant-garde, until someone had explained the reasoning: "You can generally get more work out of a woman." Others, of course, felt this was the thin edge of the wedge and were vehemently opposed to a female in the role.

Max also had gathered his single status had been cause for debate until, as has been mentioned, the women of Nether Monkslip got a good look at him. (What the men thought in this regard as in so many others did not really matter.) Even then, the question of whether or not he was professionally celibate and intended to remain so was an argument that had raged long into the wee hours at the Hidden Fox.

For it was a truth universally acknowledged that a single vicar must be in want of a wife. Someone to make traybakes and scones; someone to teach Sunday school. Of course there were others to fill these roles, but it wasn't right somehow that there was no one on hand to be officially landed with these jobs. And in some matters, it must be said, it was to a woman the parishioners wanted to unburden themselves. For some of the men and women of the parish, there was an element of embarrassment in confiding one's troubles to such a handsome male specimen, however kindhearted and well-intentioned he might be.

But the tide had turned, and those in the "Max Camp" had won out. Over the months leading into years, Max's genuine and growing affection for the countryside and its people had gone a long way toward wearing away the misgivings that naturally attended on any new incumbent. Max was, luckily, the kind of man also to inspire a fanatic protectiveness amongst all his parishioners, not just Mrs. Hooser. Within a short period of time (short by village standards, which tended to measure things in centuries), Max had become *their* vicar.

His enthusiasm for and willing participation in customs such as the upcoming Fayre had only helped in winning them over. The payoff for him — a sense of being vital to the community — was huge. It was nearly a 180-degree change from the frequent isolation, and the secrecy, of his former life.

The Fayre's official title was "Harvest Home: A Harvest Fayre" — Max had seen flyers posted with ruthless efficiency by Wanda Batton-Smythe throughout the village (or more likely, by whomever she'd managed to shanghai onto the Fayre publicity committee). The flyer featured an amateurishly drawn collection of apples and gourds, unconsciously phallic in composition and execution. Max gathered that every year for decades there had been great excitement over the Largest Vegetable competition ("That would be my husband," was the standard comment), which was an adjunct to the Marrow-Growing contest. Both competitions had been known to produce rather strong feelings that could linger for weeks, if not for generations, so those called to judge did not, if they were wise, take their duties lightly. The day also would feature many tests of skill like Ball in the Bottle. (There was, predictably, also a more ribald name for this event.)

Alongside the competitions, there would be produce stalls selling honey, jam, jelly, chutney, and pickles, in addition to all the usual handcrafted items and the parsley and dandelion wines that had come to typify the offerings of small English villages. Nether Monkslip — a village of professional bakers, tailors, knitters, potters, weavers, and so forth — was subjected to much less of the usual rubbish than other villages, where oddly misshapen baby clothes and jars of stuff teeming with gestating botulism were the norm.

And of course there was Wanda Batton-Smythe leading the charge of the Women's Institute, to insure that all went well — if not, they'd have Wanda to answer to.

The Women's Institute, reflected Max, settling back into his chair. That backbone of English village life, founded nearly one hundred years ago and still responsible for much kindhearted do-gooding in the world. Because of a paucity of volunteers, many other groups had died out; the WI had assumed disproportionate status, especially in such a small village as Nether Monkslip. The Fayre, along with the various Christmas festivities, had likewise come to assume monumental importance, with the responsibility for its success falling to the women and to whatever men could be dragooned into helping with the heavy lifting. Max, while aware of the stressors inherent in the situation, and somewhat ill at ease because of them, could see no way, or any real reason, to stop it.

In any event, his duties for the Fayre were not onerous, consisting of an opening blessing, judging the Largest Vegetable competition (despite his many protests, he had not been spared), and preventing various members of the choir, recruited as entertainment, from strangling Wanda Batton-Smythe to death.

Max's mouth twitched into a wry, complacent grin. It was all so predictable. All the usual harmless fun. Somehow this year's Fayre seemed to him a significant milestone, an outward sign of his successful entry into his new life. A good, solid case of "As ye sow, so shall ye reap."

He found he was actually looking forward to it.

CHAPTER 3
THE VILLAGE

The village of Nether Monkslip nestled with its narrow river beneath a high ridge called Hawk Crest. A steep and winding path led to the brow of this promontory, which was the site of the gap-toothed remains of an ancient stone circle. A visitor on first reaching the top of the Crest, as villagers called it, and seeing the village below, might catch his or her breath in wonder that anything so pristine could have survived into the twenty-first century.

At a distance to the south, just visible and twinkling like a mirage, was the sea, and on a clear day one could glimpse the Monkslip-super-Mare lighthouse. A few inhabitants commuted to this nearby town for jobs, but by and large Nether Monkslip was self-sustaining. London, two hours and more away, depending on the humor of those who ran the train, remained a remote place for "special" shopping or for taking in the occasional play, nearly as exotic and remote a place to villagers as Marrakech.

The village had cottages of stone, of timber, and of brick, in a salvaged mix of styles — Saxon, Norman, and medieval — giving it the rakish charm of a place that had evolved in periodic, spontaneous bursts of energy and affluence over centuries. These homes and shops, many with steeply pitched thatched roofs, sat surrounded by flowers in summer, jewel-like in their lush, ornate settings. It looked like every English village and like no other village on earth — a jumble of buildings sited haphazardly and expanded organically, to pleasing effect.

The High Street of Nether Monkslip was intersected by a secondary road and numerous lanes and alleyways. Buildings meandered away from the High, trickling up or down ancient dirt tracks that over centuries of use and custom had hardened into lanes, side streets, and cobbled alleyways. Most, like Sheep Lane, had names which had long since outlived their original meaning or purpose; nearly all the houses had names rather than numbers.

The High itself began well — a straight shot from the Hidden Fox, running east past St. Edwold's Church and the Old Vicarage; past the fishmonger's, the baker's, and the candlemaker's, to the one-man train station near the Horseshoe pub. At the stone bridge over the river it began to roam, as if by this point completely distracted from the straight and narrow path by the lush beauty of the countryside. By the river ranged the old almshouses.

To the southwest of the village proper lay the ruins of a Benedictine abbey (partially destroyed during a courtesy visit from Cromwell's men), which was to be the site of the upcoming Harvest Fayre. The parish church of St. Edwold's — balanced, as it were, between the very ancient abbey and the more ancient vestiges of differing beliefs represented by the Crest and its healing spring — had always seemed to villagers to act as a sort of religious fulcrum.

The region surrounding Nether Monkslip had indeed long been a matrix for religions both contemporary and long forgotten, boasting a circle of menhirs in addition to the Abbey Ruins. Its lure might have had something to do with the light — that eerie luminosity that had begun attracting artists in an organized way since the 1920s, and in a disorganized way for centuries. The light that shone like a carpet of diamonds on the distant sea. Many claimed the light rivaled anything Cornwall had to offer.

For the manorial history buff, Totleigh Hall was nearby; a bit further afield lay Chedrow Castle, actually a fortified manor house, and still home to the Footrustle family.

Tourists drawn by these sights tended to visit in summer, but since the only inn in the village, the Horseshoe, was too small to house more than two (small) couples, the village never achieved the kind of destination status that most of the villagers didn't want, anyway. In warm weather there might be at most a few visitors of the caravan-and-tent variety.

The village's isolation was reinforced by the lack of transport options, although there was a village taxi for those who could afford it, and it did have that rail station boasting a single employee. The occasional train would chug by randomly to collect and deposit mail and passengers, but with a punctuality so rare as to call for little hoots of celebration from its weary and sorely vexed customers. A bus service trundled the villagers about, particularly to and from Monkslip-super-Mare, via a winding, narrow road lined with unyielding stone walls cleverly concealed behind harmless-looking hedgerows.

In other words, you had to really want to

get to Nether Monkslip, in the worst way, and were often accommodated in your heart's desire by washed-out roads and sheep and herds of cattle making sudden, unrehearsed appearances in your path. This inaccessibility went a long way toward preserving the chocolate-box charm of the village.

The children in the population tended to grow bored and leave as soon as they were able, like raucous guests departing after a late-night party. They were sent to Monkslip-super-Mare for their schooling in the meanwhile. (The Mothers' Union had once had a small toehold in Nether Monkslip, but Wanda Batton-Smythe had pressured the young women until, out-flanked and outmaneuvered, they had either retreated, taking their prams with them, or had gone over to the enemy.)

Because of its bucolic charm and low cost of living, the village had in recent years begun to attract escaping yuppies from London. The Internet had aided this trans-formation by allowing villagers like Felicity Gates and Adam Birch to set up shop as potters and booksellers, respectively, and sell online what goods they could not sell in their stores. Even Elka Garth, the owner of the bakery and tearoom, did rather a brisk side business shipping out tiny animals made of marzipan, her ark centerpiece being much in demand for children's parties. Most of all, objects from Awena Owen's Goddessspell flew off the shelves. So to speak.

So while some traditional trades — malster and blacksmith, saddler and wheelwright — had declined or vanished, they had been replaced by others, many of them efforts New Agey, Back-to-the-Land, and Save-the-Planet in nature. The villagers quickly had discovered that city dwellers would pay almost any price for a product labeled "organic" or "handmade."

It helped tremendously that most of these shop owners were able to draw on pensions and savings accumulated during their (in some cases) rapacious careers in London, so that a dry spell in sales didn't matter. The parish was wealthy in comparison with most, although the drives for repairs to the church roof were never-ending, and proceeds from efforts such as the Harvest Fayre were a definite boon.

There *was* a fly in this sweet-smelling ointment: apart from Maria Delacruz, who owned the thriving Our Ladies of Perpetual Help maid service and worshiped at St. Mary's in Monkslip-super-Mare, and Mr.

46

Vijay, who ran the Maharajah Restaurant and Takeaway, Nether Monkslip was noticeably lacking in ethnic and religious diversity. The unsightly little Methodist chapel, defiantly plain and squat, had long ago fallen into disuse.

Preparing to charge into the midst of this bucolic scene was a further sign of underlying discord and imbalance: Wanda Batton-Smythe.

CHAPTER 4
OUT . . .

Wanda sat in front of her computer at Morning Glory Cottage. Having once again gone over her to-do list for the Fayre, now mere days away, she was idly checking headlines, a rare lapse in her otherwise tightly stacked day. Reminded by one tragic headline or another of a recent, keenly felt disappointment in her own life, she navigated over to the online bookstore she occasionally used when she couldn't get into Monkslip-super-Mare to the chain booksellers. (She had long ago feuded her way into a permanent rift with Adam Birch, owner of The Onlie Begetter, vowing never to set foot in his shop again. His evident relief at her declaration of war still rankled.)

But now: the last book she had ordered online, a much-lauded Booker Prize winner, had arrived with a cover ever-so-slightly dented at one corner, despite the seller's extravagant use of Bubble Wrap. *Someone* would have to pay for this negligence. In truth, Wanda had found the book, a novelization of the lives of the Mitford sisters, rather heavy going. In no year, in fact, had she enjoyed reading any of the Booker winners, but she felt honor-bound to read them, and to drop into conversation the fact that she was reading them. Navigating over to the page for the book, she gave it, anonymously, a one-star review, writing a brief, maundering, and venomous note that explained, at least to her own satisfaction, her unhappiness. Satisfied with her work for the day, Wanda hit the submit button and logged off the computer. She'd return the book once she'd finished reading it. That way she only had to pay for postage. She looked at her watch, a small diamond-studded affair she'd inherited from her mother: still a while before the Major returned home from whatever occupation he'd ginned up for himself that morning. He'd said something about the golf course. Golf was a hobby Wanda regarded as nothing more than a costly waste of time involving thrashing about with expensive equipment. But at least, she thought, it gets him out of my hair for part of the day.

She tapped the fingers of one hand against the desk. Normally, Wanda was invigorated by the kind of exchanges she'd had recently with the various denizens of the village, and the chance to vent her spleen over the damaged Mitford book had helped a little, but now she felt a slight soreness in the muscles of her neck. No doubt the tension of having to handle everything for the Fayre herself, she thought. The best management advice suggested delegation, but when one was surrounded by imbeciles . . . Really, it was too much for one human being to bear. If you want something done right . . . Now it was all giving her a headache. If only she had someone to talk to, but it was too early in the day . . . Rubbing her forehead, she went to find the aspirin.

She had had the bathroom of Morning Glory Cottage specially renovated into something suitable for a modern-day Cleopatra, knocking out two walls to create a single room of sumptuous proportions, and destroying much of the character of the old house in the process. She'd mounted an enormous mirror over the sink; arranged all along its sides were globe lights, such as an actress might have backstage in a West End theater. She'd also removed the claw-footed bathtub, an act of vandalism that had broken the heart of Noah Caraway, the local antiques dealer, especially as he had not had the chance to retrieve the item before it was removed by the rubbish collectors.

In its place was a faux-marble fitted tub "suitable for bathing an extra large porpoise of no taste or discernment," so Noah, still bitter, had been heard to say.

Now Wanda scrambled for the aspirin in the newly installed cabinet that ranged across one wall. She pushed aside a stack of new, pink Turkish towels and a set of hot rollers, in the process dislodging two auto-injectors of epinephrine. They skidded onto the floor and Wanda, swearing under her breath as she stooped to retrieve them, returned the lifesaving injectors safely to a top shelf. It was the one terror in her otherwise fearless existence, that she might accidentally ingest peanuts and be stranded without recourse to the injection that would almost certainly save her life.

After swallowing the aspirin, she paused to peer at her gray eyes in the mirror, for the first time noticing that she may have overdone it a bit with the new eyeliner. Dampening a ball of cotton with lotion, she wiped away the errant traces of Midnight Vamp. She stood back to enjoy the effect. Hers, she knew, was a strong face of good bones, and she enjoyed studying it from all angles. As she prepared for bed each night, her hair done up in twists with hairpins, applying Pond's cold cream followed by one of the new antiwrinkle creams from Boots, she would study her image critically in the mirror, defying any new wrinkles to appear. The Major, waiting for her in the marital bed, proof of the tenacity of hope over experience, more often than not fell asleep.

She adjusted the pearls at her neck, wishing anew that she had a daughter to leave her jewelry to. Sons were less satisfactory in some regards. She leaned into the mirror. Was that a new wrinkle? *Dab, dab* went the eye cream.

Just as she was taking a brush to the thick corrugation that was her hair, the Major came in the front door of the cottage, making his usual racket as he juggled several packages he'd picked up on Wanda's orders.

"I'm home," he shouted down the hallway, as he always did. (Then: "Damn it!" as a bag slipped from his grasp and a tin of tomatoes rolled noisily across the floor.)

Where else would you be, thought Wanda, setting down the brush with a sharp crack against the sink. Charm school?

The retirement years of the Batton-Smythes were not going well. These golden years somehow failed to give off the glow promised by the ads promulgated by retirement planners — ads where trim, well-preserved couples played golf together, merrily chortling as they ran their cart over the greens; where they took cruises to exotic ports in intrepid, devil-mind-the-cost fashion; or skipped playfully down sunlit beaches before returning home to the mega-mansions their carefully planned retirements had earned for them. Arthritis and other debilitating diseases were nowhere on the horizon for these sprightly, laughing millionaires with their costly dental veneers. For Wanda and the Major, the tiny irritations of a lifetime instead were on full display, proximity exacerbating them into character flaws of Shakespearian proportions, a tube of toothpaste squeezed the wrong way the catalyst for hours of huffy silence. Wanda, who had never counted patience as a virtue, was less qualified than most women to trot peacefully along in marital harness to the grave. In truth, she had long regarded the Major as little more than a buffoon, and she seldom troubled to hide her disregard from him or from her adoring (she imagined) public.

She also felt keenly the loss of status that seemed to accrue these days to military men, especially retired ones. Things were not as they once had been, when an officer, however incompetent, was automatically accorded some respect.

This was *not* how she had envisaged spending her golden years.

That night she would prepare the Major's dinner with packets from the Marks and Spencer in Monkslip-super-Mare, and dream of a new life in Paris or Rome.

And why not? she would ask herself. She could afford it. *She* had money — and she'd made very sure to keep it in her own control.

Half an hour later, Wanda Batton-Smythe was going about her business, and an odd sort of business it was. Wanda, who had too much time on her hands for anyone's comfort, was known frequently to draw from her quiverful of clichés the one about not knowing where the time had flown, when in fact her day was no more than a round of visits to shops or meetings where her approach was viewed with a kind of instinctive dread, like the sighting of a pirate ship.

The days leading up to the Fayre had showcased Wanda in her busybody element to perfection. Built for warfare — low to the ground, wide at hips and shoulders — she altogether gave the impression of a German WWII tank rolling through a French village as a speechless and demoralized peasantry looked on.

Many noted (with a desperate roll of the eyes) that she seemed particularly rejuvenated this year, with a youthful spring in her step as she pounced on some unsuspecting volunteer or potential "extra pair of hands" to set up tables, sort things, and haul things about, only to have to haul them back again when Wanda changed her mind.

Having taken extra care with her makeup, she had also embellished her dress with an atypically chosen scrap of antique cloisonné jewelry pinned to an armored, rigid bosom, likened by more than one to the prow of a ship, parting the villagers as it sailed. The pink and red decoration clashed slightly with the print of her belted, crisply pleated skirt — again, that clash was atypical, for Wanda tended to dress in conservative fashions from the same catalog that might have been used by Buckingham Palace, had its inhabitants been given to ordering from a catalog. Her accessories tended to be safe choices, never remotely flamboyant; her shoes generally were Wellies or flesh-colored pumps with round toes and one-inch heels. The ever-present string of pearls, however, a wedding gift from her husband, was wrapped securely around her neck. People believed that she slept in them.

On her feet today, in a concession to the extra yards she would walk in the name of "rallying the troops" (her term), were sturdy brogues, suitable for mucking out a stables; she had tied up her hair in a large patterned scarf, such as the Queen might wear to walk the corgis at Balmoral.

The strain of responsibility for the Fayre was showing, it was whispered, as Wanda flitted loudly from pillar to post, and shop to shop, a busy bee collecting pollen. She lingered only at the village's single cashpoint, where a queue had collected behind old Mrs. Barrow, who as always was befuddled by the machine's operation but too distrustful to allow anyone to help her withdraw her twenty-pound note, then moved on for a brief stop at the newsagent's. She rushed through her usual shopping chores, basket swinging briskly from her arm, a woman with far, far better things to do than collect the cod from the fishmonger's and the tomatoes from the greengrocer's.

"Here comes Her Majesty," the candle shop owner murmured apprehensively to his assistant, on sighting Wanda's approach. But Wanda's first purposeful stop was instead at the Cavalier Tea Room and Garden, carefully chosen as a site of potential uprising and rebellion in need of quashing.

Years before, Elka Garth had renovated the old communal bake house into a tearoom with adjoining bakery, thereby continuing the building's centuries-old role at the center of village life. On offer were — among a dazzling array of temptations — Elka's specialty scones with strawberry jam and Devonshire cream, although she also offered gluten-free, low-fat alternatives for the health conscious.

The villagers would gather in the Cavalier (the name reflecting on the service, it was said), where news was exchanged twice a day, recalling the heyday of the Royal Mail. Coffee in the mornings (elevenses), and tea and buns and scandal each afternoon at four. Nonstop flow of information and dis-information in between, with doorstep sandwiches for reinforcement.

The seating by the windows overlooking the High was at a premium and thus much in demand, for some of the best news (no one would ever think of it as gossip) could from that vantage often be witnessed *in the making(!)*. They had a virtual, unrehearsed reality show of village life at their fingertips.

This Royal Mail efficiency applied, of

course, to men as well as women, although the men tended more toward the twin outlets of the Hidden Fox and the Horseshoe for the dissemination of news. Indeed, if the Cavalier was the source of gossip, the pubs served as a sort of surround-sound enhancement, with speakers on either side of the village to ensure efficient distribution. The hair salon and barber's, being on side streets, were a vital adjunct to the process.

A more efficient method for Wanda might have been to wait for elevenses at the Cavalier, where she could attack her audience en masse as they were trapped behind cake plates, fingers slippy with buttered scones. But Wanda, superb tactician that she fondly believed she was, thought the time was ripe for what she called (to the cringing dread of her subjects) "the personal touch." Today's target was one of the essential players in Wanda's drama: Elka Garth.

So this morning, breaking all protocol and short-circuiting the usual lines of communication, Wanda entered the Cavalier early to tackle the owner about various bits and bobs of crockery and equipment she wanted donated for use at the Fayre. Elka Garth, emerging from the back in a waft of just-baked cookie dough, would readily have volunteered both her coffee urn and her goodwill, but she was more than usually put off by Wanda's officious manner. There was a history behind this, as there so often is behind otherwise inexplicable conflicts. Elka's son Clayton, admittedly a somewhat slow-witted child, and Wanda's Jasper had been at school together, and Elka had never forgiven Wanda's tendency to boast whenever Jasper won that year's prize in finger painting, penmanship, personal hygiene — whatever it was. The more so when Elka's son began going to the bad in his teen years, culminating in a short jail sentence for drug possession. Clayton now reigned, the embodiment of scruffy indolence, behind the counter on the odd day when he could be induced to help his mother.

No one knew of his troubles at first but Wanda, who heard of them from her son, and who "happened" to mention it to Miss Pitchford, retired schoolmistress and legendary repository of knowledge of village doings, who "happened" to mention it to half the village before a month was out. Telling Miss Pitchford anything, as Wanda well knew, was tantamount to taking out an ad in the *Monkslip-super-Mare Globe and Bugle*. Mrs. Garth never forgave Wanda, nor did she feel forgiveness was required in such a situation. But as a sensible businesswoman, in the name of keeping village strife to a minimum, she was civil to her. Just.

Elka now eyed Wanda with masked disfavor from behind thick glasses and said evenly, "What time do you want it all brought round, then?"

"Oh, have Clayton drop it off by nine the day of. How lovely it must be for you to have your son at home. Such a help to you, I'm sure." Wanda gave her a beam of fierce good cheer, knowing full well that thirty-year-old Clayton lived with his mother not out of preference — his or hers — but because he was both untrainable and unemployable and had little choice in the matter. What little assistance he was able to offer his mother in the tea shop was more than offset by the cost of broken crockery and customer complaints.

He had been a late, much-hoped-for child, so his later disappointments were the more keenly felt and were exacerbated by the early death of his father. Elka's good-natured face, as round and pudding-like as some of her tearoom offerings, now creased into a vinegarish expression. It was as if she had slipped on an ill-fitting mask.

Wanda's usual braying confidence faltered, but only for a moment. Elka's good-will — or, failing that, at least her full participation in the bake sale stall — was crucial to the success of what Wanda thought of as "her" Fayre. Softly, softly, then. Swatting away the mosquito of Elka's displeasure, Wanda added gushingly, "I have always thought him a most handsome lad. It takes some of them time." Here a rueful, all-girls-together shrug. "Don't I just know it!"

"Clayton will be there," Elka replied, smiling the smile of a woman whose jaw has been wired shut. "And on time. I'll see to it."

"Oh, one more thing," said Wanda.

"Ye-e-ess?"

"More fairy cakes!" said Wanda brightly, as though it were a thought newly minted, rather than part of a carefully staged campaign. "They were wonderfully popular last year. Oh! And more biscuits like we had at the meeting the other night — people liked those so much. Need I remind you: it *is* all for charity."

If there was one reminder of which Elka was by now thoroughly sick, one reminder she did not need, it was that her free labor, outlay, and expense were all for charity.

"Yes, I know." Again a form of smile, lips

taut as wire pulled back from still-gritted teeth. Elka, who tended to sample her own wares when under stress, pulled a cranberry muffin from the display. She began chewing, jaws slowly working over the muffin as she kept a watchful eye on Wanda. Elka did not offer her a sample, and Wanda (wisely, for once) decided it was best to choose her battles.

There was a mirror in back of the pastry case over which they talked. Wanda, catching sight of herself, patted one spring of her tightly wound hair back in place under her scarf. Apropos of absolutely nothing, she said, "In my youth, people told me I looked like Joan Crawford."

Elka might have been wondering who Joan Crawford was, or trying to peg the resemblance (which, it has to be said, was extremely slight. One might grudgingly have admitted they shared a heavy hand with the dark eyebrow pencil). Her own brow creased, Elka said, "Was there anything else, Wanda? Because if not . . ."

Wanda, never one to take the hint or to realize one was being offered, said, "Just be there." She gave Elka something between a gracious nod and a saucy toss of her head, and took herself off.

CHAPTER 5
. . . AND ABOUT

A master of the surprise overland attack, Wanda, exiting the Cavalier, made a sudden, unexpected detour in the direction of the greengrocer's. Spotting her too late, Guy Nicholls, who owned a restaurant in Monkslip-super-Mare but did his shopping for fresh produce in Nether Monkslip, had attempted to nip back into a small alleyway between two shops, but to no avail.

Lily Iverson, seeing this, herself ran for cover into a lane beside the greengrocer's. The Vicar, emerging from St. Edwold's, also had a near miss. Lily, peering around the corner, thought she could almost see the hand of a merciful God emerging from the clouds overhead: Wanda at that moment had eyes only for Guy Nicholls. The Vicar had been spared.

Guy, looking distracted, seemed not to realize he was still wearing an apron, having just stepped out from his restaurant for a moment, as he thought. With a cry of triumph Wanda hailed him, crossing the High to waylay him in his tracks; with hawk-like grace she swooped, pouncing on her victim, and nearly pinning him to the wall. In a heavily flirtatious way, she began to grill him about the drinks, biscuits, and sandwiches his restaurant would be donating to the Fayre. Her message for him was the same as for Elka: *More. Give me more.*

Suzanna Winship walked by just then, on her way to take a pair of shoes in for repair. This day she wore a fluorescent blouse under a gray sweater with matching skirt, and progressed slowly in her usual sultry saunter, unconsciously or otherwise channeling the girl from Ipanema, a walking revival of the sounds of the bossa nova era. Obligingly, Guy gave her a wink and used the distraction to make a neat sprint away from Wanda — but only after having agreed to everything she wanted.

It was all done so smoothly, Wanda, admittedly not the most aware of people, didn't seem to notice she'd been given the brush-off. She gazed admiringly at his retreating back.

Awena stood at the counter of her New Age shop, unpacking the latest shipment of crystals (for once carefully packed, so as not to become a box full of glass shards). Her face reflected thoughts of the recent Women's Institute meeting, none of them happy thoughts, a frown marring the classic line of her generally serene profile. She recognized that Wanda was a ridiculous person. She also recognized that didn't prevent half the village from wanting to throttle her on occasion. It presented a nice challenge to someone like Awena, who struggled to maintain a balance and a flow in all the areas of her life.

She chanced to look up and, as if summoned, here came the devil.

"Hallo!" said Wanda, entering Goddessspell with a suspicious cheeriness, wearing one of her more regal, province-visiting smiles as she set the little bell over the door ajingle. She shut the heavy wooden door of the half-timbered building behind her and stood looking about expectantly, handbag clasped tightly in both hands. Anyone knowing her well would see the smile as the preamble to some outrageous request.

"The chairs . . ." she began.

"Oh, yes," said Awena. "I'll see it's all in order on the day. Don't you worry."

"That's as may well be, but I did want a word."

Awena, feeling the first twinges of foreboding, said, softly, "Oh?" Her mouth puckered into a frozen little circle of feigned interest.

"Do you feel it is in the best interests of the WI — such a noble institution! — for there to be outright dissension in the ranks such as we had the other day? After all, morale among the troops is paramount to a successful outcome this Saturday."

"Morale among the troops?" repeated Awena, blankly, but sensing where this was going. Next, she thought, she'll be reminding me that an army marches on its stomach. True enough, and totally beside the point.

"The failings of one sniveling idiot," said Wanda, "cannot be allowed to derail the whole process." Awena, knowing with certainty that the sniveling idiot Wanda referred to was Lily Iverson, was immediately incensed on Lily's behalf.

"Look," Awena said, trying and failing to keep an edge from her voice, "it is simply Harvest Fayre, not Napoleon's march on Moscow. It's a time of fun, and of quiet reflection. A time to enjoy and celebrate life. It is *not* time to come down on a bunch of willing, hardworking, and unpaid volunteers like a ton of bricks. Keep it up and you'll lose them for certain. There won't be a

Fayre next year if this keeps up."

Something in this had sunk into the deep recesses of Wanda's mind, something that told her the unqualified flattery she desired — nay, craved — was not forthcoming from this quarter. Her face blotched with the effort to control her considerable anger, she said, "I see." The words dripped with ice, but Awena could almost have sworn she saw flames burning behind the gray eyes. Her imagination added tiny martyrs chained to a stake. The clumsily applied eyeliner may have contributed to the effect — Wanda was not given to wearing makeup beyond the aforementioned eyebrow pencil and occasional dark lipstick.

"I really think you need to back off of Lily. She's got a bigger cross to bear than most of us, keeping the farm and her business going."

"Cross to bear? An odd choice of words for a pagan," replied Wanda. Her voice had resumed its superior and unperturbed modulation. This was somehow always more aggravating than Wanda unhinged.

"I'm not a pagan. I am —" Awena broke off. She was not going to waste her breath trying to explain the finer points of her beliefs, which encompassed most religions, so long as they were stripped of any tinges of self-righteous bigotry. Admittedly, Awena's good-hearted embrace of any positive creed led her into some muddled thinking; fortunately, she had an enormous capacity for the embrace of ambiguity.

By this point, though, Awena was nearly snarling. It didn't help that she realized she had no one but herself to blame for her temper: she had plunged, as it were, directly into the polluted waters of Wanda's World.

Before she turned, preparatory to flouncing out of the shop, Wanda said, "You needn't think you'll be needed to sell your gimcrack rubbish again at the Fayre after this year."

It was again the complacent, satisfied set to her lips that set Awena off. Wanda was always happiest when provoking a reaction. Now she waved a hand dismissively, the wave encompassing the entire inventory of Goddessspell: tapes and CDs of the sounds of the rain forest or the wind or ocean waves; jars of herbs and honey and all manner of folk remedies — St. John's wort for happiness and Mugwort for dreams; packets of seed to plant in the spring; stones for hot rock massage; massage and aromatherapy oils; dozens of teas; bunches of dried flowers, suspended from hooks in the beams of the low ceiling; charms and jewelry and other things of beauty, items that rested the mind just by a person's gazing on them, or holding them, or smelling them. Goddessspell, it was said, was like a small corner of Glastonbury brought to Nether Monkslip.

Then there were the courses and classes run by Awena and a coterie of like-minded men and women of the village. She had just moments before finished her midmorning meditation session, an exercise meant to connect her mind with the energy of the reproductive regions of her lower abdomen. She did not feel this effort had been entirely successful, which may have been why Wanda had so easily been able to provoke a reaction.

"Rubbish, is it?" shouted Awena at the departing back, resisting the ignoble impulse to run after Wanda, fist raised, and chase her down the High. "Rubbish! Well, I may just not be there *this* year, and I wouldn't care either way!" This was quite a false declaration, for Awena made a tidy profit out of her stall at the Fayre each year, despite the percentages siphoned off for charity, and it served as wonderful advertising for the store in the ramp-up to the winter holidays — herbs and candles and wreaths being in great demand. Moreover, she thoroughly enjoyed herself in the process. It was a simple pleasure, Harvest Fayre, and she knew as soon as she said the words she wouldn't miss it for anything. But Wanda was gone, and the perfectly devastating parting shot had in any event not risen into Awena's mind.

As Wanda steamed away, Tara Raine emerged, barefoot, toned, tanned, and flat-bellied, from the back of the shop, where she rented space for her yoga and Pilates classes from Awena. She had been setting up the room for her noontime yoga session. She looked with concern at the normally placid and unruffled countenance of her friend — she who was now puffing like a dragon struggling to catch its breath.

"I heard it all," Tara said. "Couldn't help it. Frightful old cow."

Awena, a true believer in karma, in speaking no ill, in "what goes round," completely lost cosmic control. It made it worse that it was Mabon, the autumn equinox, a time of reflection and Thanksgiving and peace in Awena's calendar. For Wanda to choose today of all days . . .

"Some day," she said, her melodious voice throbbing with emotion, "someone is going to give Wanda what's due her."

"A right bollocking, you mean?"

"Actually," said Awena slowly, her rosy cheeks flushed red with anger, "I had in mind something more permanent."

Lily Iverson, who had just come in through the back door of Goddessspell, on a mission to retrieve chairs for the Fayre (the Fayre Chairs as they were now being called), stood hidden by the beaded curtain to the back room. She was still trying to let the words "sniveling idiot" run off her back like water. The effort having failed, she turned and quietly retreated the way she had come. The curtain clicked softly in the breeze created by her swift departure.

She was ashamed of this visceral, cowardly reaction, but was helpless against such a primitive instinct for self-protection. She felt a surge of another reaction so foreign to her normally placid, timid small self that it was a moment before she could find a name for the emotion. And that name was hate.

Lily, quite simply, hated Wanda.

It was, at least momentarily, freeing to realize this — to be able to put a name to the roiling emotion at last.

CHAPTER 6
HELP US

As soon as Wanda's back had safely disappeared over the horizon, Awena threw on her cape and headed for the vicarage, asking Tara to mind the shop while she went for "a fireside chat," saying that it was time — possibly too late — to ask "our tousled vicar" to intervene.

She sailed along, preoccupied, something in her aspect brooking no interference from anyone she chanced to meet. Why Max Tudor had been her first thought as someone likely to be able to deal with Wanda, she couldn't have said for certain. But she held the Vicar in the highest regard, despite what she saw as the difference in their approaches: her practicality and earthiness versus his good-hearted otherworldliness. It was not that she thought him useless, by any means (an opinion she reserved for his predecessor), but while Max would comfort the dying, she was one of those he would call to make sure the afflicted had someone to come in to clean and visit the shops for them. This unofficial arrangement had somehow sorted itself in the early days following his arrival.

She would have been amazed to know that Max, in his turn, considered Awena to be bighearted but hopelessly impractical, her head always in the spiritual clouds.

Max had just returned to the vicarage from the church, where he'd gone to meet with a contractor following Morning Prayer. The man had submitted a bid that only made sense if he were planning to repair St. Edwold's roof using melted-down gold and rare pearls. Max had been hoping to talk him down. To no avail: it became stunningly clear the bid was honest. What was less clear to Max was where to find the money to pay for the repairs. How many more times could he hit up his parishioners before they completely tuned him out?

There at least had been a satisfying crowd at Morning Prayer. On the "if you build it" principle, Max had begun promoting weekday attendance at the service. Saying Morning Prayer was part of his duties as a priest, in any event, although there was nothing to require that he do this outside his study.

For the first week or two of the experiment he had recited the words in splendid isolation, but he carried on, regardless.

From those early isolated days, the celebration now had grown steadily in attendance, due in no small part to the coffee service afterwards — Max had come to an agreement with Elka Garth that benefited both her tearoom and the church. People now seemed not only to recognize the frame the service gave to their day, but to welcome the sense of community engendered by this simple daily commitment to themselves and others. In some cases, it provided a much-needed excuse simply to get out of the house, away from the telly, and among people — to get out of the house slippers, to see and be seen. It helped that Max encouraged the few young mothers in the parish to bring their babies with them. He had no illusions that he was making permanent inroads in the "hatch, match, and dispatch" Anglican mind-set, but it was a start in bringing people together. Social cohesiveness was as good as any other kind in creating a safety net for those who might otherwise feel they were on the fringe of village life. He made it clear at all times that all were welcome.

Attendance, having grown, had held

steady. In a small village, any absence was so much more noticed than in a town or city — the exponential power of peer pressure could never be underestimated. Besides, much of the social life of the village either emanated from the church or overlapped with its activities. Even the few holdouts who seldom attended viewed St. Edwold's as "theirs," so much was it a part of the historic fabric of the village.

Max tried, in subtle ways, to present his parishioners with an ethical worldview, asking them to assess their lives in ways meaningful to them. In studying for the priesthood at Oxford, he had found it at times too easy to get caught up in ritual, in chapter and verse. The trappings of his MI5 days had not entirely left him, he imagined. The Security Service was, after all, an organization much like a monkhood — a closed brotherhood with its own esoteric knowledge, its own secrets.

He further understood one could never underestimate the power of a charismatic priest. He had no illusions about the part his personal appeal played in the success of St. Edwold's as a center of village life; in the wrong hands, this influence could be a force for ill, as Max well knew. He viewed his role in the village with an awed and humble respect.

Mrs. Hooser announced their visitor in her usual garbled way.

"It's that one that sells them herbs and candles and suchlike."

This might have been several people in the village, but Max guessed correctly that she meant Awena, proprietress of Goddessspell and maven of all things New Age.

Awena was shown in. Not one to stand on ceremony, Mrs. Hooser said simply, "She's here," which was evident, and then shut the door loudly on Awena's back. Thea, poised for her usual rapturous leap at the sight of a visitor, remembered her training just in time: she sat hard, tail wagging so thunderously that its hip-shaking momentum threatened to topple her over. Awena paused, bending over to scratch Thea's ears.

Awena didn't appear to walk so much as swim toward him. She was given to wearing long, flowing, drapey, often heavily embroidered robes that made her look like an icon carried on a float during a religious festival. Today it was a claret, belted robe in a silhouette made famous by the Empress Josephine. The color somehow accentuated the almost purplish blue of her eyes under dark, arched eyebrows — eyes that generally held such a faraway look her real target might have been Alpha Centauri. They were of an otherworldly paleness Max associated with much colder climes — Iceland, the Scandinavian countries — clear as ice, and enhanced by the contrast with the black sheen of her hair with its dramatic white streak. The eyes of a seer, if ever there were such a thing.

But today her youthful face was flushed; he thought he might have imagined that the brows were more arched than usual, the gaze wider with alarm or concern, but he was soon proven right.

"It's Wanda," she said, without preliminary. "Max, you have *got* to help us."

"It's been nonstop, you see," Awena told him. They had settled in over coffee and biscuits, brought in with much ado and clatter and near wreckage by Mrs. Hooser. "Every day we've had a ring-around over something, to the point where I'm avoiding the telephone altogether. It's worse than when Wanda wanted to establish a civil defense early warning system using the bell ringers. Drove them all mad, and by the time she was through 'rehearsing' them, they sounded like scrap metal being dumped down a steel silo. This time it's *far* worse.

And I have a business to run — God-dessspell doesn't run on hope and prayer, no more than your church, if I may put it that way."

"I admit her techniques are a bit . . . draconian, at times."

"May the gods defend us," said Awena solemnly, "from the energetic 'do-gooder.' " She shook out a fold in her skirt; the light caught the sparkle of gold thread in the weave. "If she'd confine it to the constant nagging and wheedling, I could cope," she added. "What I cannot abide is when wheedling is abandoned in favor of more direct devices, like threats, intimidation, and humiliation."

"Under what conditions, one wonders, and in what kind of home, was the woman raised?"

"I would wonder that, if I had time, and a shred of compassion left. You are too forgiving, Vicar."

"I'm not, as a matter of fact," he said, thinking fleetingly of his days undercover when he had ruthlessly tamped down any such dangerous emotion, "but remember that it's in the job description — forgiveness."

She looked at him levelly: at the attractive crinkle of lines around his slightly down-

78

turned eyes, at the normally good-humored curve of his mouth with its lopsided, roguish grin. It was the roguishness of the grin that nearly did for the women of the village, she reflected.

"There hasn't been such a kerfuffle," said Awena, giving up on Mrs. Hooser's boiled coffee and putting the cup well aside, "since Ben Standon's goat ran amok during the Blessing of the Animals five years ago. It's been the talk over at the Cavalier for weeks now. Wanda, I mean."

Max thought of the Cavalier as the start of many a barium meal — an MI5 expression for starting a false rumor so its path could be traced. But in this case the rumors were probably based in fact. Wanda could be a handful.

"You really must have a word with her," Awena continued. "I think she'd listen to you. You may be the only one she'd listen to."

He considered inviting Wanda to the vicarage for a chat, a prospect that held all the appeal of being coated with honey and tied to an anthill. He acknowledged his own cowardice without an inward blush. He had faced down drug-addled criminals bent on revenge, or simply high on their own malevolence, but a representative from the

Women's Institute in full flood was more terrifying, particularly this representative. He thought over what little he knew of Wanda, what leverage there might be in personal data. He really only knew the gossip: she and her husband the Major had one son to whom they routinely sent money, whether as a bribe to stay away or an incentive to return home was not clear. In any event, the son was said to have made no appearance in the village since his eighteenth birthday — close to fifteen years hence. This was somehow tied up in Max's mind with Elka Garth and her son, but he couldn't have said why.

Apart from his personal feelings of inability to deal with this particular crisis was the practical question of how to get Wanda inside the vicarage undetected. Mrs. Hooser had conceived a violent dislike of her, and on the occasion of Wanda's last visit (a complaint about the sermon) had made such a commotion in the kitchen with the pots and pans he daren't, he felt, repeat the experiment. Although Mrs. Hooser was a diabolical cook and slapdash cleaner at best, it was not as if he were spoiled for choice in the village. Well-trained daily help was courted assiduously and, once won over, shamelessly coddled by the homeowners of

Nether Monkslip. He paid Mrs. Hooser what little he could afford, and tipped her even when some days it seemed to him the financial arrangement should be reversed.

"Don't you have some magic potion or other you can spray on her?" he asked, goaded into uncharacteristic exasperation. "Some ritual you can perform?"

"Don't you?"

"I mean, why me? I hardly am holding the whip hand here."

Max found that, as so often happened, he was being catapulted into the role of diplomat, mediator, and pourer of oil on troubled waters. As much as he wanted to take sides, he knew that in what was essentially an unimportant clashing of egos (or so he told himself at the time), he would be unwise in the extreme to be seen to intervene or to support one side over the other. In a case of moral certainty, he felt later, he would have known that intervention was the only choice. But this seemed trivial — one of those instances where his focusing attention on it would give it more importance than it was due. Best to let it blow over. He said this last aloud.

Awena sighed. "I was afraid you'd say that."

"I'm sorry, Awena, but —"

81

"And you are quite right, of course." She dusted crumbs from a sampled and discarded biscuit off her lap. Really, it was a wonder Mrs. Hooser hadn't accidentally poisoned the poor man. "It's just that that bloody woman does get up my nose. I guess I just wanted someone to listen while I let off some steam."

He didn't feel he could mention this to Awena, but there was a further reason that prevented Max from weighing in. In his prior dealings with Wanda, she had turned on him, quite unprovoked, a heavy-handed coquettishness, smiling a fearsome smile and waving a perfumed handkerchief about like the fading star of some forties film. It was so at odds with her usual sergeant-major approach to life and leadership as to be quite unsettling, making him doubt her sanity.

Awena paused in petting the dog, who was leaning heavily against her knee.

"Thea," she said, gazing into the sherry-colored eyes. "What a beauty she is. Short for Theadora?"

"No — just Thea."

"Ah. It means 'goddess,' you know. Which is kind of funny, when you think about it."

Max grinned. "I know. She came with the name and it just suited her somehow. No question *she* agrees it suits her."

He had not had a pet since childhood; the unpredictable schedule of his former life had not permitted it. Nearly his first act on arriving in Nether Monkslip had been to adopt the young Thea, he supposed in some outward display of his desire for normalcy, for routine.

"Anyway," Awena said, revisiting her previous refrain, "I still think Wanda might listen to you. In fact, I think you're the only one who could penetrate that almighty, know-everything façade."

Max hesitated. There were some situations — more situations than were acknowledged — where doing nothing was the better course. A patient willingness to wait was both part of his nature and ingrained from his old training in surveillance, in analysis and code-breaking — in watching and waiting for patterns to emerge.

The Zen-like approach, as he thought of it, had much to recommend it. This, he felt, might be one of those times. Provoking Wanda, after all — what good could it do? It might be cowardice on his part, but still . . .

Much later he was to wonder, more than once, if he'd been wrong.

CHAPTER 7
HARVEST FAYRE

In the week leading up to the Fayre, the Reverend Max Tudor had been kept busy doing this or that church business at this or that church in his care. Not until the dawning of the day of the Fayre itself did he think to utter a little prayer that his parishioners would behave themselves. Failing that, that a posse had not already been dispatched to take out Wanda Batton-Smythe.

With the approach of fall, the trees around the village were starting to shed their finery, dropping apples and leaves to the ground. The fields had been cut back to an ochre stubble and the harvest mice, exposed, would soon shelter in the hedgerows. The spinney atop Hawk Crest would stand out like a thinning thatch of hair on an old man's head. As it was, some trees had already been stripped bare in a recent storm; the Crest had always been vulnerable to the freak storms that had beset

Nether Monkslip from time immemorial. The equinox heralded more to come as the days began their slow creep toward winter, the austere white light of summer shading to an autumnal gray. It was the time, Max knew, that Awena Owen called Mabon: the celebration of the second harvest and the start of winter preparations.

All the same, for him and for her, and all different. The Christians had wisely chosen (in most cases) not to eradicate the pagan celebrations but to wrap them up with new paper and ribbon into a palatable offering. The solstices and equinoxes, the all-important movements of the planets, the timing of the plantings and the harvests and the full rush of seasons, the return of the sun after its long, cold, and frightening retreat — these observances wisely were not eradicated by those newly in power, but absorbed into items on the Christian calendar. The Harvest Fayre was a remnant of the old days, and still vital in modern times. The equinox had been melded onto Michaelmas, the feast of the Archangel Michael, now three days away. Time to get the harvest in and settle accounts.

Max crossed Church Street and walked over to the Fayre grounds, greeting villagers as he went. Everywhere over the past few days there had been signs of change: the monarchs, blown off their usual course and supping gracefully on the butterfly bush; the drowsing bees, so recently a menace, the cooler air taking the zip out of their movements. The green tomatoes, the gold chrysanthemums. The eerie harvest moon, which soon would hang low in the sky.

Proud of his newfound rustic ability to name a few basic flowers, Max noted with pleasure the Michaelmas daisies and the last of the yellow St. John's wort. He breathed deeply of the sweet decay that was autumn; his heart lifted as he felt on his skin the slight nip in the air that signaled the shortening of days. The marquee erected on the grounds of the old Abbey came into view. Use of the land had been donated for the day by Noah Caraway, collector of art and antiques, bon vivant, general man about Europe, and owner of Abbot's Lodge.

Approaching the tended grounds of Abbot's Lodge and the ruins of the old Abbey, Max briefly stood back to survey unobserved the essentially pagan scene. The Fayre preparations already were in full swing, even as visitors began to arrive, and from his vantage point, the villagers had the aspect of a Bruegel painting — decked out in the bright colors of autumn, reds and golds and the occasional flash of green. The smoky smells of autumn were more concentrated here, mingling with the fruits of the harvest, and there was a bank-holiday feel to the day, of cares set aside, and work delayed for pleasure. The sway of the spoilsport Puritans — they who had banned maypoles, dancing, and secular singing, and who treated this type of festival as dangerous superstition — was mercifully long over. Max thought it a wonder their humorless reign of forbidden amusements had lasted as long as it had.

Yet the stark, somber Abbey Ruins with their few remaining trefoil windows always struck him as immeasurably sad, and today were a pronounced contrast with the villagers' gaiety. By unvoiced consent, out of respect and/or superstitious fear of the violated monks, the inner areas of the ruins — the inner sanctums, as it were, especially the chancel with its "bare ruin'd choirs" — were never lightly breached. The stalls for selling the villagers' various wares thus were ranged along the outside of the Abbey Ruins, interspersed with the gooseberry bushes that seemed to thrive in this particular spot. There was a surfeit of apple products for sale, he saw at a glance — cider, of course, and jam, and wine, and both traditional and caramel apple cake with clotted cream.

A tent had been erected in case the weather failed to cooperate, but it had been universally agreed the weather would not dare cross Wanda any more than anyone else would.

As Max entered the area set aside for the stalls, he noticed the subtle adjustments villagers seemed to make as he approached. Cheerful congregants became just that much more cheerful, children were tugged at to stand up straighter, men called out hearty hellos, and many women pretended not to notice him at all until he made a pointed hello, at which point they assumed a posture of great surprise at seeing him. Max's nascent rock star status had, as has been said, led to fierce and sustained infighting over the church flower rota. Such interest was not precisely sexual in nature — at least, not always. It was more that scraps of information about the new vicar were a commodity in high demand for gossip sessions at the Cavalier Tea Room.

On his arrival in the village, rampant speculation over many an afternoon tea had included that he was MI5 — Military Intelligence, Section 5 — and posted as a special guard to Queen Elizabeth. No, said someone: MI5 weren't used for that — he was posted in Iraq, some top secret mission thingie at the highest level. No, said someone else: they only used MI6 for those foreign le Carré–style missions, not MI5 — everyone knew that. But he was wounded somewhere, that was definite. Where? demanded another. His leg, I think. There's nothing the matter with his legs, either of them. Besides, I meant, where in the *world* was he wounded? Oh, in Iraq, wasn't it?

His days as an MI5 officer had not been wreathed in glory. The nature of the business was of course that things happened behind the scenes, the route of history altered minutely, with no one to thank or blame when the mission was over — whatever his part in the mission had been. He had been recruited by a talent spotter while an undergraduate student at Oxford, where the cold fog off the Isis leant itself to those kinds of mysterious goings-on, and had joined MI5 at the age of twenty-one — such a baby's age he could hardly credit that they thought him worth troubling with. Perhaps his youth made him malleable, and that was what they most needed, that malleable quality.

No doubt that was it.

They called them Spooks, these members of Her Majesty's Security Service, the men and women of MI5 or simply Five, devoted to ferreting out internal threats to the safety of Britain.

He had had perhaps a dozen aliases in the course of his career, so many legends to remember — a legend being the make-believe history and background that people had to be convinced to believe, and that he himself, most importantly, had to believe. He'd be grilled on this legend by his handlers, repeatedly asked the same questions in different ways until he had the story down pat. He'd generally be issued records showing he'd been born in a country where no official birth records were kept — millions of children born worldwide went undocumented, and he'd simply, temporarily, joined the ranks of these stateless unfortunates. His curriculum vitae was a list of spurious jobs at no-longer-existing companies — there being a never-ending supply of defunct companies for MI5 to appropriate to its purposes.

False IDs were a part of his life, and he quickly began to master the ability to lose himself completely in his various roles. It was the only way to keep it all straight in his mind. He wondered sometimes if he'd missed a career on the stage. But the incentive to maintain a false identity was so much more than matinee entertainment, and the driving force, the need to stay alive, was incentivizing in the extreme. He'd played the roles of bank manager and schoolmaster, of politicized student and cagey estate agent and dodgy car salesman. No one had suspected a thing. He still wasn't sure whether to be proud or ashamed of that.

A job with Five was often boring, often heart-stopping, most often requiring an ability to wait endlessly. September 11 raised the stakes considerably. In response, they now had SOCA, the Serious Organised Crime Agency, Britain's version of the FBI, an organization, merged from others, whose priorities were drug trafficking and organized immigration crime. Terrorists were not a stated target, but it was generally impossible to differentiate dirty money from the unclean uses to which it was put.

It was interesting work on some days; mostly, it was just his job. The way other people worked at a dry cleaners, he went to work for MI5 every day. He might have gone on forever had it not been for the Russian.

■ ■ ■ ■

His approach now never went unnoticed, and he reveled (modestly, he hoped) in the happy greetings and the goodwill of the people he had promised to serve. The fresh air, the beguiling smoky smell of early fires hanging over all, the camaraderie . . .

It was a peaceful scene, only now broken by a loud noise, as of a loud trumpeting . . . surely not — yes —

Wanda's foghorn voice could be heard, as if from a great distance. Moses rallying the Israelites.

"Come *on,* people! For the love of *heaven!* We don't have all day! Shift it! Shift it! Oh, hello, Vicar. Just in time. We need a big strong man like yourself to . . ." Eyelashes working overtime, she launched into a tedious and complicated request having to do with trestle tables and a placard advertising the location of the tea tent. Today she again wore her brogues, and another outfit that might have been issued by the Palace, this time in deep violet. A large, old-fashioned brooch representing a bumblebee seemed to crawl toward her left shoulder. Max good-naturedly allowed himself to be volunteered, if only to keep her quiet for a moment, and give someone else a respite.

She plowed on to other fields of endeavor, ignoring anger or opposition as they were encountered, occasionally bending an ear to the urgent request of an underling. She was bold and decisive in her decisions, or so her self-satisfied expression suggested, apparently missing the looks of bafflement and frustration she often left in her wake. She paused in her supervisory duties on one return pass only long enough to lean in confidingly and say, "Would you believe it, Vicar? Mrs. Percy has dropped out of the rota for the Pickles and Preserves table. 'Death in the family,' she says." Wanda sniffed. It was clear that no death in Mrs. Percy's tribe would be cause for protracted sorrow. "That could wait, couldn't it?" she demanded. "I mean, they're not going to get any *warmer* if she drops everything and races to the bedside, are they?"

Max, taken aback, allowed as how they probably were not.

"Still . . ."

"Still nothing!" Wanda blared. "Besides, funerals are for the living. Now that's interesting . . ." She seemed to change topics, distracted by something seen in the distance. Her eyes took on the cast of an old sailor seeing a mythical, long-sought-after whale. "Well, well," she said slowly. "*Someone* will need to be told."

"What's that?" asked the Vicar, himself distracted by a splinter that had found its way painfully into his thumb.

"Oh, nothing to bother you with, Vicar, at least not yet." Here she turned on the spigot marked "Flirtation with Handsome Vicar" and fiercely batted her eyes. He noticed she once again had lined her lashes, with none too steady a hand, using some murky and dark substance, like the leavings found in a coal scuttle. "I have to follow the dictates of my conscience, I suppose," she added. But she frowned, as if for once she was not sure what her conscience might dictate. Then, recalling that she had a Fayre to run, and no doubt an insurrection or two to quell, she visibly composed herself, adjusting the fingers of her cotton gloves one by one, pressing the cloth into the valleys between her pudgy digits.

Max had returned to his assigned chores when, some minutes later, Wanda shot briefly into view again. "Time to man the braces!" she cried. Max, who had never expected to hear anything like that outside of a Horatio Hornblower novel, grinned across the trestle table at Guy Nicholls, a new fellow recruit in Wanda's War, as it was now being called.

"Don't fire until you see the whites of their eyes," muttered Guy under his breath.

Max shook his head.

"Wrong battle."

"Do you think she makes a distinction? All life's a battle. She seems to meld the different branches of service, too."

Wanda briefly disappeared down the side of a small hillock, a faint cry trailing her like a flag: "I swear, you lot couldn't run a whelk stall without me!"

No doubt this was true. It was strange, Max reflected, how this truth didn't go very far toward endearing her to those who hastened to do her bidding.

CHAPTER 8
HARVEST FAYRE II

Max had to credit Wanda in this much: the Fayre was an enormous undertaking, and as it got underway, the seams involved in putting together such a large display virtually had disappeared.

Stalls seemed in the past half hour to have exploded in number. Those selling home produce predominated, as farmers came in from miles around for this event. There were also stalls selling knitwear (Lily's offerings putting all others in the shade) and children's wear. Teas and coffees and herbs were available in sweet-smelling abundance, and secondhand toys and games changed hands for probably the fifth time in a generation. There were displays of wrestling and tests of strength for the men, and antiques that verged on rubbish for sale, and rubbish from attics that might include a pirate's treasure — one never knew. The siren call of the undiscovered hoard hung thick in the air, and Noah Caraway —round, balding, ebullient — reigned in that department, offering lamps with mismatched lampshades, rusting garden equipment and furniture, tablecloths with three matching napkins, dog-eared books and photo albums of the long-deceased — sadly, with no relative left to claim them, these studio portraits and snapshots became mere curiosities, reduced for quick sale.

Max gave Noah a friendly wave as he passed. He had his own rubbishy things to unload, and was afraid of collecting someone else's, like lint, if he came too near. In the distance, the church choir was launching into "You'll Never Walk Alone." This song never being one of his favorites, Max veered left and walked on, walked on with hope in his heart, until he came face-to-face with Wanda's soul mate: the Major.

The Major was in theory manning a stall (he seemed to be selling ball bearings, but Max felt overall that that couldn't be right), but in actuality he was reading a book as he perched on his ubiquitous shooting stick, pointedly ignoring all inquiries of passersby as to his wares. But as Max approached, he made an exception, for the Major approved of the "New Padre," as he always called him. "A fighting man to his fingertips; you can always tell," he would say. In the Major's estimation there was no higher tribute: it was as if Max could fly.

"It's a biography of King Æthelfrith," he told Max now, flipping the book over to display the cover. "Mighty warrior — gave the Britons a jolly good trouncing. Interesting note for you, Padre: at one point he killed the monks who were helping the Britons by praying for them. Hah! Æthelfrith. Not a name you'd want to attempt with a lisp, eh?" In a typical non sequitur, he added, " 'Don't ask, don't tell' — what a load of American codswallop."

The Major was a great rumbling bear of a man given to using words like *trouncing* and *balderdash,* as if he were forever starring in some drawing-room comedy of the 1930s. Rather than say, "Where are you?" he would demand to know, "What are your coordinates?" But he was almost a Dickensian character, wearing brocaded waistcoats in all seasons and with a Rudolph-like red nose that could nearly light the way in the holiday pageant. He had dark eyes, close-cropped white hair, a flourishing mustache, and a somewhat gray complexion. He was still able to wear the belts of his youth, only now they hugged the underside of a prominent paunch rather than circling a waist rendered taut by daily sit-ups. Today's wide belt, slung low on his hips, gave him the appearance of a portly gunslinger.

It was a source of some consternation and puzzlement to the Major, if not to Wanda, his wife, that he'd never seen "action on the front lines," as he put it. But a senior officer had summed it up, succinctly if obliquely, in one of the Major's official evaluations: "The object of any campaign being to avoid a complete rout, it is recommended Major B-S be confined to a behind-the-scenes role — very behind." There was always an air about the Major of someone self-important, who was aware if baffled by the knowledge that the rest of the world did not share his self-assessment. Listening to him on any subject quickly made one conscious that time was not always fleeting, but could move at a tortoise-like pace. Max often felt sorry for the man — for his evident fall from what he had believed to be a position of influence in the world.

Sensing one of the Major's more predictable tirades coming on, Max gave him a neutral smile, struggling to hide the "all is lost" look of dismay in his eyes.

"Æthelfrith wouldn't have stood for it, I can tell you that," continued the Major. " 'Don't ask, don't tell' — Pah! But you wouldn't have to ask nowadays, would you? All of them pouring out of the closet, in tights and spangles. What this country's come to. Sad end to an empire, what? Learned nothing from the Romans or the Turks, did we?"

Max again made no response, although he was rather wondering what the Turks had to do with anything. The Major's right-wing views were too well known for Max to wish to invite a reprise by showing so much as a blink of interest. He noted, not for the first time, that the Major was excessively loquacious when his wife was out of range. Probably it was the only chance he got to talk uninterrupted.

"What we need," the Major was saying now, "is what your St. Augustine would call a 'just war.' "

Max, surprised by the reference, thought there might actually be something more going on beneath the Major's buffoonish, pukka sahib-ish, drag hunt–loving exterior. A thought dispelled by the Major's next comment.

"Of course, not 'just' any war qualifies. 'Just war.' Get it?"

Max pretended to spot a long-lost parishioner in the crowd. With murmured apologies, he hared off, just as the Major was getting started on the hallucinogenic waywardness of elected officials.

It was an escape, however, from the fire into the flames. Max ran, in his panic, straight toward a stall manned by a lone local author. Too late he noticed the rabid eye of Frank Cuthbert (husband of Mme Lucie Cuthbert, who operated La Maison Bleue). Frank was offering an unwary public his self-published book — a long, rambling, crackpot pamphlet, really — on the history of the region, spliced with dubious, hand-drawn maps of local walks that, if followed closely, could land the user miles from civilization. Since the book had been published ten years previously, and everyone within a thirty-mile radius had already been strong-armed into buying a copy, it was hard to justify the winsome smile of anticipation and optimism on the author's moonish, apple-cheeked face as he sat surrounded by half a dozen boxes of unsold copies. He wore his usual tweed sports jacket over a dark shirt open to a cranberry cravat. His black beret perched at a rakish, authorly angle, he twinkled at the Vicar from behind, literally, rose-tinted glasses. Everything about him, including the biblical white beard, seemed to be an unconscious parody of the stereotypes of the literary genius. That his books sold by the handful rather than the thousands diminished his belief in his destiny not one jot. With Frank, bookselling was a blood sport.

Now smiling at Max, Frank emitted something like a high-pitched chortle that made him sound quite mad. It was widely felt that Frank *was* more than a little mad, but in that harmless way of many writers with a book to sell. At his feet sat Sadie, a beautiful bichon frise whose spotless white coat gleamed in the sunlight. She seemed to offer living proof of the breed's good and loyal nature, for she clearly adored Frank, who was seldom to be seen, walking about the village with his bowlegged gait, without her.

Max, resigned to giving at least the appearance of renewed interest, picked up a copy of *Wherefore Nether Monkslip.* As Max recalled, the Arthurian legend also featured prominently in Frank's recounting, with Arthur recast as a lost pilgrim resting his horses at the Horseshoe on his way to Glastonbury. Max had a suspicion that this gratuitous reference had been worked into the narrative because the owner of the pub had agreed to keep copies of Frank's opus on sale at the bar in case of passing tourists with ties to the world of London publishing.

Max idly flipped the book over. On the back dust jacket, beneath a photo of Frank at least twenty years out of date, one Jack Ralston-Fifle, Historian and Author, was quoted as finding the book "fascinating." That, Max felt, certainly raised the question of what other books Ralston-Fifle had read, overriding the key question of who in hell Ralston-Fifle was in the first place.

"You've read it already, haven't you?" Frank asked him now.

"Oh, yes, and I thoroughly enjoyed it. It was just really . . . good. Quite good." God forgive me for being the liar I am, Max thought.

His words had a noticeably galvanizing effect.

"Yes, I felt there were parts, at least, that were extremely good in capturing the spirit of the various ages," Frank said, eyes alight. "Pushing the historic envelope, as it were. You thought it successful?"

"Oh my, yes."

Max, now feeling both guilty and moved to pity, ended up buying yet another copy of *Wherefore* to add to his growing collection, thinking he could pass it along to some distant relative or other at Christmastime. As he started to walk away, he saw Frank push yet another copy of his book into the hands of a passing woman, simultaneously asking if she liked reading history. Max gathered this was a much-rehearsed technique, but the woman stared at the cover like Queen Victoria being handed a pamphlet on early contraceptive techniques. She shook her head and walked away. A woman made of sterner stuff than I, thought Max. He walked on and into the swirl of the Fayre, stopping briefly at the stall overseen by Lily Iverson. Lily was one of his Sunday regulars, but was not one of his Morning Prayer attendees: the requirements of farm life understandably interfered. Today Lily wore a Breton blue-and-white-striped sweater. He complimented her on it, assuming rightly that it was another of her own creations. She blushingly told him it was called the "Hey, Sailor!" model. A woman approached, waving a checkbook and asking if Lily also sold her creations in the shops. Together the two women fell into an excited gabble.

Someone at the next stall was selling corn dollies, each a work of art, traditionally platted from the last sheaf of corn harvested, a symbol of luck to be held for the next year. These looked to be made from barley. They were another harking-back to pagan times, when successful harvests were literally a matter of life or death. Max picked one up, turned it over. It looked like a child's toy, but much too finely crafted to be entrusted to small hands.

A small girl of perhaps seven walked by just then, dressed as a milkmaid in cap and apron, handing out flyers advertising the sale of goat cheese fresh from her family's farm.

He came to the stall of Adam Birch, the cardigan-wearing owner of The Onlie Begetter, a shop selling new and "antiquarian" books. Adam was rumored to be writing a novel — to have been writing the same novel, in fact, for many years. He hosted the local writers' circle, and had by now read versions of most of his book aloud several times to its glassy-eyed members. Adam himself had the eyes of a basset hound with a lifetime of bad decisions behind him, but he was in reality as sturdily optimistic as his fellow scribe and writers' circle member, Frank Cuthbert. Frank held frequent book signings in Adam's shop, neither man discouraged by the complete lack of foot traffic these events produced. The literary life, Max gathered — and the chance at the brass ring — was all.

The books on offer from Adam today consisted largely of tattered copies of works by authors as disparate as Janet Evanovich, Julia Child, and Agatha Christie. He browsed through several of the Christies, happily lost in the memories of Dame Agatha's ingenious plots . . . He was just leaving Adam's table with an extremely old copy of *Crooked House,* purchased for fifty pence, when he overheard a female voice say, "Have you seen Wanda?"

He turned and spotted Awena Owen and Tara Raine behind the Goddessspell booth, a gauzy affair of twinkling lights and scented candles, of herbs collected by moonlight and the promise of magic.

Awena, her expression normally serene, was looking a bit the worse for wear. She didn't seem to notice that her sleeve was caught on the "Make an Offer" sign atop the boxes of tarot cards until she'd tipped it over. Setting it aright with a sigh of frustration, she said, "No, and that's not like her. At all."

"I should say not," replied Tara. Her long red hair today was out of its usual yoga ponytail and pinned to the top of her head; a colorful scarf circled her face. Her complexion was its usual mix of year-round tan and freckles — Max gathered she spent a great deal of time near the water in Monkslip-super-Mare. "She's usually everywhere, or certainly does a good impression of being everywhere," Tara continued. "We're nearly out of tea. But there's more in the Village Hall — Wanda said earlier."

He saw Awena hesitate. "I know, but who's going to help you mind the stall if I start coping with things in the tea tent? Wasn't someone supposed to be handling that? They'll rob you blind, this lot, if you're not careful. And we don't want Wanda chugging along to ask why the takings are so lean."

Max stepped up. "I'd be glad to help."

Awena, turning, clutched at his arm like a drowning woman.

"Oh, would you, Vicar? I'd be ever so."

"Just tell me whereabouts to look."

"There should be supplies left out on the table in the Village Hall kitchen. They'll be in an upper kitchen cabinet, if not."

"Is it locked?"

Awena shook her head. "Shouldn't be."

The two women sighed at Max's retreating back.

"Bloody waste of a man that is," said Tara. "I need to get on to my niece to get her out here for a visit. Too bad I'm otherwise engaged myself." She smiled, straightening the boxes of Tarot cards. "But that could change."

■ ■ ■ ■

Wanda, unseen by all but a few pairs of interested eyes, had minutes before stomped her way over to the Village Hall. Anyone who didn't know her well would have said she skulked over, in fact, a mode of locomotion not often in her repertoire. In any event, on reaching the door, she definitely looked over her shoulder to see if she had been observed. Which was odd in itself, for nothing could be more normal than that Wanda Batton-Smythe should enter the scene of many of her greatest triumphs.

The Village Hall was typical of its type — perhaps better than most, since it had been richly endowed at its beginning. It had been solidly built between the two world wars from local stone, and the whole enlarged in years past via the munificence of a local squire, who had also given the St. Edwold's tower its clock.

Wanda entered the main room and crossed over to a south-facing window, where she peered out cautiously from behind the net curtains. She adjusted the position of a figurine that sat on the ledge, a representation of a shepherdess — a decorative prop left over from a drawing-room play, a prop that had never been returned to its rightful owner. It was made of plaster of Paris and amateurishly painted, the shepherdess's hectic expression suggesting a facelift operation gone wrong, the receipt of a telegram containing bad news, or the irretrievable loss of her flock.

Wanda sighed contentedly, a secret smile playing at her lips. She had recently had confirmation — if any more were needed! — that her organizational skills were superb, second to none, and would be in much demand in the business world. Surely she was wasted here, hiding her light under the provincial bushel that was Nether Monkslip? She would need up-to-the-minute training, of course, but that was easily done. Possibly there was a course she could take through Denman College, the Women's Institute's adult education center in Oxfordshire. But then, those courses trended toward subjects like hen keeping and stump-work embroidery. Perhaps what was needed was a *proper* degree, a longer course, with diplomas and exams and things. Her heart gave a thrilling little surge at the thought.

If not Denman, then, certainly she could do something via the Open University. Business or hospitality management or some such. Yes, as soon as the Fayre wrapped up, she would look into it. There was money to hand . . . Again, her pulse quickened at the thought of her new, glamorous, rewarding life.

The sounds of celebrating villagers reached her ears, as of a far-off ocean wave, or the muted blare a telly makes when no one's watching it. A whoop of pleasure, perhaps a cry of recognition as old friends from neighboring villages seized the chance to catch up.

Really, everything was going quite well. The Fayre was a personal triumph. At the thought, an expression of exultant satisfaction curled her thin mouth. She opened the door into the kitchen and practically twirled her way girlishly into the room, like someone in a shampoo ad.

Yes, it was a tragic waste of her talent to continue on as she had been, year after year. Didn't the easy success of all her undertakings in Nether Monkslip just demonstrate that? Undoubtedly. The village was becoming too small a stage for her triumphs. It always had been so. And she was too young to waste any more time with th—

A sound interrupted this reverie — a slight rustling, and the creak of the main door opening. Wanda frowned: that useless Maurice had once again failed to oil the hinges.

But she turned, her body tense with energy and awareness, a cautious smile of greeting on her lips.

CHAPTER 9
GRIM REAPER

The men of Nether Monkslip had learned
their assigned tasks when it came to the
Fayre, even before the accession of Wanda
Batton-Smythe to the throne of the Wom-
en's Institute. These tasks included hauling
supplies that had been stored over the
preceding weeks in the Village Hall to the
grounds near the Abbey Ruins. The kitchen
of the Village Hall was used as an additional
staging area for various provisions for the
tea that was served throughout the Fayre,
the kitchen of the nearer Abbot's Lodge
having quickly reached capacity.

Walking past the marquee entrance, where
Constable Musteile stood self-importantly
on duty, Max literally ran into Guy Nicholls,
who was just emerging from inside. Guy
("Rhymes with 'High,' " as he had told Max
at their first meeting), a well-set-up man in
his early forties, fell into step beside him.
He had an open countenance with aquiline

112

features and a smooth complexion, now, like Tara's, lightly tanned and freckled from the summer sun. He was a relative newcomer to the area, operating a trendy restaurant in Monkslip-super-Mare, and the men had formed a bond of sorts over their mutual newness and outsider status. Max welcomed Guy's easy friendship, framed as it was by the man's shrewdness, his sense of humor, and a worldliness that called to Max from his pre–Nether Monkslip days. Guy wore his sandy hair cropped in seemingly haphazard fashion by someone wielding an axe, but in fact in slavish (and expensive) devotion to the spiky fashion of the day. Max noticed the suspicion of a colorful hair dye on the tips, growing out from some previous experiment; chefs, in recent years having achieved a fame to rival that of pop stars, had become more concerned with being adventurous in their appearance, as well as in their menus. In voguish-swashbuckler style, Guy wore a small gold hoop in each ear.

Guy greeted him in the fashion which had become a routine between the two men.

"Villagers haven't tarred and feathered you yet, I see?"

"I've escaped so far," Max answered.

"Wanda still have you running hither and

yon today?"

"I will be much in demand later on for my services as a fine judge of turnips," Max told him. "But right now, I've been dispatched by Awena to see where the rest of the tea rations have gone."

"Can I help?"

"Probably. Best if you're seen to be doing something rather than enjoying yourself, if you follow. I'd enjoy the company in any event."

The two men loped in companionable silence away from the Fayre and toward the Village Hall, which was wedged on the High Street between various shops and the Hidden Fox pub. They were similarly tall and rangy, with Max being the slightly taller of the two. Their steps took them past Raven's Wood, which in the spring would be home to waves of bluebells, and on into St. Edwold's Road. They walked past the ancient Plague Tree in the churchyard, said to have been planted over a mass grave of plague victims. While some disputed the truth of the legend, the name had stuck, no better explanation having been put forward for the unusual, small hill over which the tree cast its shade.

"We are lucky in the weather," said Max. They generally were. The southwest of

England generally enjoyed more temperate climates than the north — cooler summers and warmer winters.

Guy shot him a winning smile. "Do you really think Wanda would have allowed it any other way?"

Max smiled in his turn. "Funny you should say that."

It was strange when one thought about it: it was believed Wanda not only controlled village affairs, but the very heavens. As the two men chatted about the prospects for the coming winter, which was predicted to be an unusually cold one, Max noticed, not for the first time, that Guy's melodious voice had a trace of a French accent. He said "you" as "ewe" — more a matter of the pursing of the lips than the pronunciation. Not the accent of the native-born French speaker, Max didn't think, but the accent of someone who has acquired an overlay to his English after months or years of immersion in a foreign culture. For MI6 operatives who spent so much time overseas, in particular, it went with the territory.

Max asked, in typically roundabout British fashion, "How are you settling in, then? Learning the local customs?"

Guy grinned. "As you know, it takes a while to be accepted, even though we've both been here quite a while now. Nether Monkslip seems to have its own rules about these things. But the restaurant is starting to fill up without too much print advertising required — good old word-of-mouth is saving the day. Always the best way, anyway."

"Glad to hear it. In fact, I've heard the good reports myself."

"You'll have to stop in soon. Let me know ahead of time when you're coming, and we'll whip up something special for you."

By this point they had reached the heavy wooden door of the Village Hall. Max was unsurprised to find it unlocked, as Awena had predicted. It was the Nether Monkslip way of doing things. Besides, what was there inside worth stealing, really, apart from moth-eaten costumes and props willingly cast off by their owners?

He pulled the door open and stepped aside to let Guy enter.

Max realized he had not been inside the Village Hall for some weeks, when he'd dropped in on the local whist drive, new to the pastime but willing to learn. Nothing about the place had changed, but then, one wouldn't expect it to: it was as enduring and static as the Albert Memorial. Some still mourned the days of the traveling cinema when it came to the Hall, but transport had changed much of the complexion of village life. Still, the whist drive never dimmed in popularity.

The much-maligned orange plastic chairs had been stacked on one side, so as to leave the center of the large room free for ballroom dancing and the like. The area was uncarpeted, the wooden floors polished smooth by decades of use. Windows ranged along one side, curtained in what looked like Irish lace, although he suspected these were acrylic. Between two windows stood a large commode, used for storage, on top of which was an enormous cup — perhaps used to represent the Holy Grail in a Nether Monkslip Dramatic Society presentation on the life of King Arthur (Frank Cuthbert's portrayal of a superannuated Galahad was still spoken of with some puzzlement), perhaps a trophy from some long-ago sporting event, perhaps both. Figurines stood on each window ledge, a shepherd and his shepherdess. He recognized them as having been used in a production of *Lady Windermere's Fan* — a year ago now that was, or was it two? The place was littered with such artifacts from amateur pageants and plays, awaiting storage or disposal. One figurine seemed to teeter too close to the window ledge.

"What is it we're looking for again?" asked Guy.

Max swiveled his attention back. "Tea."

"Bags or loose?"

Max blew out his cheeks. "Good question. Dunno. I forgot to ask. Let's grab what we can find and hope it's right."

"In the kitchen, then." And suiting action to the word, Guy walked over to push open the door to the room opposite the stage area. One wall of the kitchen had a serving hatch that could be opened to sell refreshments during performance breaks, but the pass-through was closed. Max noted a padlock had been applied to it.

Guy's voice reached him from the other room. "Maybe we should —" he began, and stopped.

"Maybe we should what?" Max, on his heels, came up beside him. But Guy flew from his side. He was suddenly kneeling over a prone figure, his head bent to the victim, for victim it was — of a stroke? A heart attack? A body that had ceased to breath on its own — that much was clear.

Max's old training instantly kicked in. Just the presence of a body seemed to charge the air around him, as if one of his old instructors stood in the background, saying calmly, *What do you see?* Max was once again in a classroom, images being flashed across a screen, one scene after another, as he was tested on his ability to eyewitness a scene of carnage, and the moments leading up to it, and the faces in a crowd. There, there in a corner might be the young man, one of dozens of young men and women with the usual backpacks, wearing the usual jeans and jackets and with wires to their music running out of their ears, only this man was different. His body also was taped with wires and explosives and a detonator and surely, yes surely, his eyes shone with the crazy bloody-minded will to take his own life, and to commit the senseless murder of dozens more, as his handlers watched and waited for news from a place of safety.

Max's heart rate slowed now, his breathing slowed, and he began coolly, robotically taking in the scene around him, his brain dividing the room into sections, his eyes taking mental snapshots of every wall, every corner. Like a camera lens, his eyes recorded the ordinary kitchen, with nothing out of place, everything lined up and looking spotless, bags of tea, bags of coffee, everything put away except for these, except for the plates of food, biscuits and cakes, covered in cling film, that waited for collection on the counter. A leather handbag rested there, too.

Guy had tilted the victim's head back, pinched the nostrils, and began breathing several times into the mouth. Then settling back on his haunches, he placed one hand over the other and pushed, hard, against the chest. "One, two, three, four . . ." He counted aloud to fifteen, his voice loud and ragged with stress. Max, beside him, saw that the chest wore a bumblebee that rose and fell with these efforts, but it was the artificial rise and fall produced only by Guy's efforts. Guy was giving mouth-to-mouth to a figure in dark violet. He was trying to save Wanda. But he clearly was far too late.

"You work on her heart while I try to get her breathing," Guy said. He sounded determined now — settled into the situation, as if he'd done this often, as perhaps he had. Mouth-to-mouth was probably part of the training for working in a restaurant.

Max knew it was no use — the staring gray eyes and the waxy sheen of her skin told their own tale. She had been dead some time, perhaps as much as half an hour. As much to humor the man as to ensure they really had done all they could, Max placed the heel of one hand on Wanda's lower chest. Locking the fingers of both hands together, he took over the chest compression, pressing rhythmically down with his palms, as Guy continued to try to administer the breath of life. They worked in the desperate silence of the minutes, focused only on the body, on the lungs that refused to respond, until Guy, reluctantly, looked frantically back at Max and said, "It's no use."

Max gently helped Guy to his feet and looked closely at the body.

Wanda seemed to look straight ahead with wide, disbelieving eyes: *This can't be happening.* Her lips appeared swollen, and her hands were clasped loosely near her neck, as if she'd been choking, and had made an instinctive, ineffectual grab for the afflicted area. He could see the scratch marks where she'd clawed at the white, soft skin. In honor of the day, she'd painted her fingernails, which shone glossy pink against her neck.

Even as he took in the details, a *No!* seemed to pinball about inside his skull: *This can't be happening.* Not here, not here of all places. I came here, I became a priest, I came *here* to get away from senseless death, from too many deaths, deaths caused by me, deaths I was helpless to prevent.

But even as the horror ricocheted inside his head he continued automatically to register every detail. He looked again at the handbag. It had to Max the look of something Wanda would own, black and prim and squared off at the bottom, snapped closed at the top. In fact, he realized he'd seldom seen her without a similar bag, either slung over one arm or with the handle clutched to her waist with both hands.

Then his focus returned to the body itself. What was different here? Ignoring those eyes, staring, accusing, filled with silent outrage, he took in the violet dress, the pin, the sturdy brogues on her large feet, which splayed out at the ankles. She wasn't wearing the body armor — was that it? And her hair — her hair had been loosed from its Final Net death grip, and stood out in a sort of halo around her head, as if unleashed by humidity and the force of wind.

There were marks on her wrists. Bruises? A struggle of some kind, then, or simply her struggle for air?

She had clipped a small black velvet bow to the side of her finely shaped, curly head, and this ornament remained in place. It was too small a device to be anything but purely decorative, which Max found immeasurably sad. Vanity might be a "sin" according to some lights, but he thought in measured doses it was one of life's allowable little pleasures. It helped everyone get through their days. A simple thing like a velvet bow: Wanda worried about looking nice on her big day.

"Let's get some help in here," he said, turning his attention back to Guy, who had moved away, averting his eyes from the corpse. "Do you have a mobile? I left mine at the vicarage. Mrs. Hooser had instructions to send Tildy Ann and her brother to fetch me if there were a need."

"Mine was nearly out of power earlier," Guy replied, looking rather gray. "I'll try standing by a window to get a signal. You know Nether Monkslip. We could be on the moon."

He walked into the next room and stopped near one of the windows. Max followed close behind, his eyes swiftly cataloging the details of the space. As Guy powered up his mobile he reached out to touch the figurine of the shepherdess on the ledge.

"Don't touch anything," Max said sharply.

Guy dropped his hand quickly away, but said, "Whyever not?"

That was quite a good question, thought

Max. There was something about the setup that bothered him. That was all he could have said in truth.

"I just think it would be better if you didn't touch anything," he said firmly.

Guy gave the mobile a frustrated shake. "This is hopeless. I'll go myself and fetch Constable Musteile. Should I?"

Oh, God, thought Max. That oaf. He supposed there was no hope for it, though. Constable Musteile was the local bobby and the natural source for official help — rather, the most direct route to officialdom.

"Yes," said Max. "He'll need to ring in someone from Monkslip-super-Mare. Better the request comes from him. You go and look for him — he's standing by the entrance to the marquee, looking important, last I saw. I'll wait here and make sure no one comes in here accidentally. We don't want anyone to see her looking like that."

He paused, then added, "I suppose you'd better tell him: I think it's a crime scene."

CHAPTER 10
LAW AND ORDER: POD PEOPLE

By the mysterious process of instant village communication, word had leaked out that something was up at the Village Hall, and a sizable crowd gathered almost at the same moment the police arrived and began setting up cordons of blue-and-white crime-scene tape. The villagers and many Fayre visitors from farther away stood outside the Village Hall, a chaotic buzz of hushed conversation floating over their heads like a cartoon cloud. Nether Monkslip, Max had often reflected, was the original social networking site.

The arrival of the police car from Monkslip-super-Mare had been excitement enough, as it careened up Church Street to the High, spewing dirt and gravel, and quickly followed by its smaller brethren. (The police sitting in these tiny, new, energy-efficient cars looked like they were sitting in roller skates, which detracted somewhat from the gravitas of their mission.) "They must've come to take over the investigation," the whisper went about. "Must be something serious, then." Normally the village had to be content for "real" police presence with periodic appearances of the Community Contact Vehicle, a special-built Fiat Ducato, looking much like the Perambulating Library that similarly visited small villages in the area.

It was felt that the arrival of the local constable, madly peddling on his bicycle, was in the nature of an anticlimax, but since Constable Musteile was not greatly loved by the villagers, this in itself was a welcome and entertaining spectacle. Sensing that his arrival might have been an occasion for ridicule, Musteile, after first propping up his bike, pulled a mobile phone from his hip pocket, viciously punched in a few numbers, and, forgetting to announce himself (he was connected to his home's call minder), barked a couple of "Right"s and "Will do"s into the device, concluding with, "Roger that. I'm on it. Over." He flipped the phone shut with a practiced, one-handed flick of the wrist and swaggered toward the Village Hall, where he was promptly curtailed by an enormous, immovable constable from Monkslip-super-Mare.

The above-mentioned erection of cordons by the new arrivals from Monkslip-super-Mare had, however, prompted more than a bit of resentful comment ("What do they think we are, to herd us about like this? A load of football hooligans?" "It's *our* Village Hall. This is still England, isn't it? I think I know my rights." Etc.) and a palpable swell of excitement. Nothing had happened like this in Nether Monkslip since . . . well, since no one could quite say when. Certainly since time out of mind. Tongues wagging, they pressed against the barriers, a tight knot of people craning to see and looking like a many-headed hydra. But to their frustration, the windows of the building were too high and narrow for them to look inside.

Some enterprising soul should have brought a ladder and sold tickets to *this* event, thought Max, who was the excited center of attention once it was learned — again, via that mysterious jungle drum telepathy — that he had actually been *inside* the Village Hall and made some sort of Discovery, and it couldn't be good, could it, if the police were here now? Max, attempting too late to extract himself, looked around for Guy Nicholls, but he, wise man, seemed to have vanished. That or been swallowed whole by the crowd, avid for a first-hand account.

For Max, politely ignoring the avid curiosity, but curious himself, there was an eerie sense of déjà vu, as he watched the police engaged in their sad business of collecting and photographing. The scenes-of-crime officers would be inside dusting for fingerprints, and collecting DNA samples, going about the grim business of death, codified over time into a ritual of rules and procedures, much like a religious service, the aim being to bring to justice the person or persons who had gone rogue, and had violated one of mankind's primary rules and agreements: *Thou shalt not kill.*

Someone was taking Max's opinion that it was a crime scene very seriously.

Time passed, and the crowd grew less agitated, more willing to wait for news on something as big as this. Several people were sent by their families to bring food from the Fayre, lending some sense of a fun outing to the occasion.

But the removal of Wanda's body was something else entirely — with that came a shift in mood. A somber silence descended such as no one in the bustling village could recall. Death was not unknown in Nether

Monkslip, but everyone sensed there was something different about this death. No one had been as alive as Wanda, although "indestructible" was the word most often evoked.

But they recovered themselves quickly, recalling their duty to inform. As the news made its way up and down the High, the few remaining villagers outside the loop of current events struggled to make an appropriate response. "Thank God" didn't seem quite right somehow — there was the Major to think of, after all, and he was regarded by many as somewhat of a pet, if an irksome one. Most of the villagers settled on verbalizing some version of "How shocking!" before settling in for a good chin-wag over possible suspects. But here, bewilderment reigned. For when you thought about it, who would "knock off" — Frank, the scribe's, phrase — a member of the WI for being perhaps a little too diligent over her responsibilities? Any other motive, however, lay quite outside the imaginations of most.

"It was a robbery, pure and simple," was the overall consensus.

"What was there to steal in the Village Hall? My gran's recipe for candied yams isn't that rare."

"People get killed these days for less.

Some of the costumes and such must have been valuable. And she'd have had her handbag with her, wouldn't she?" Here a sage nod of the head, and a finger tapped alongside the nose.

"Makes you think."

But not in Nether Monkslip. Such things just didn't happen. That was the constant refrain: not in Nether Monkslip.

It was the arrival of the mobile station much later on that let villagers know something new and noteworthy definitely was afoot. The police set up the pod next to the Village Hall in the same spot usually reserved for the Perambulating Library. Soon wires and cords trailed from the sides of this portable shell. The police were in business.

A local wag at the Horseshoe immediately christened it "the Bobby Pod." It was a name that stuck.

The news updates continued to spread through Nether Monkslip as only unexpected and shocking news could in a small village — rapidly and with mule-headed inaccuracy. For some reason, it became established fact that Wanda had been bludgeoned to death, once the likelihood of her having been stabbed to death had been dismissed as a possibility. It took several hours of effort by the postmistress, the fountain of most avid conjecture in the village, to help everyone sort through the speculation, summarize what little was known, and render a popular verdict of probable suicide while the balance of her mind was disturbed — a phrase many of them had come across in their reading of the newspapers.

Max had gone back to the vicarage to try (with little hope) to work on his sermon, but he had rejoined the crowd as news of the pod's arrival reached him (via the simple expedient of someone's sticking their head in the study window to announce the news in passing). Again he stood on the fringes of the crowd, watching, but in truth there was little to see. He was turning away — the sermon was going to have to be completely rewritten, after all; how could he ignore this particular elephant in the room? — when he heard a familiar voice call his name.

Max had crossed paths with DCI Cotton of the Monkslip-super-Mare police in the past. He and the policeman were at times working on opposite sides of the coin, with DCI Cotton trying to pin a crime on a miscreant, and Max presenting the reasons why leniency should be shown, especially in the case of a young offender. But neither of their devil's advocate roles struck Max as being at odds in their aims. Cotton was too professional, and too competent, for that.

Max gave him a solemn smile and stuck out a hand in greeting. DCI Cotton was a slight, wiry man who seemed to vibrate with unexpended energy, like a tuning fork just struck. He had a thatch of thick blond hair springing back from a widow's peak and the glint of a devil in his gray-blue eyes. They reminded Max of a cat's eyes in their focused concentration.

Max Tudor on first meeting had liked and trusted him.

"I say, we sh —" began Cotton.

But he was interrupted.

It was Constable Musteile — a weasel of a man. In direct contrast with Cotton, Musteile instantly had provoked Max's instinctive dislike. Not because he was dishonest — well, not precisely dishonest. He was probably incorruptible, in fact: a Mr. Law-and-Order of the type frequently drawn to the armed forces or law enforcement. He was ramrod straight, unyielding, unimaginative. Profoundly stupid, in fact. A man who followed the rules, and asked no questions as to whether each rule really applied in every situation. Respectable, moral —

132

indeed, holier-than-thou. A bit of a bully, especially when cornered. A dangerous man in every way.

"Hello," Max greeted him, civilly.

Musteile seemed to enjoy cementing his reputation as a bit of an ass. He ignored the Vicar and spoke directly to his superior.

"Clearly it will be Travelers responsible. I'll get right on it."

Cotton regarded him. "Travelers?"

"You know. Gypsies."

"You've spotted a caravan site of Gypsies, have you?"

They were joined briefly by Detective Sergeant Essex, who handed Cotton a report of some type, then walked on. Max had briefly seen her, as well, outside a courtroom in Monkslip-super-Mare. Tiny and extremely fit, with her multicolored strands of hair she reminded Max of a small terrier. A blind man could see she held Musteile in the lowest possible esteem.

" 'Course not," Musteile was saying. "Sir. Only stands to reason, though." Musteile had caught some of the *Zeitgeist* in the village, and expanded on it, seasoning it with a bit of his own brand of bigotry.

Over his head, Max and Cotton looked at each other.

"Thank you, Constable. That will be all

for now."

Musteile nodded, all but clicking his heels and saluting. He turned sharply and left them.

As the constable departed, DCI Cotton seemed to reconsider. He called him back: "Actually . . . I say . . ." he began. Musteile spun on his heels and stepped smartly back toward them. "Do you know what would be useful? If you could get a statement from the local postmistress. In my experience, that's the person in a village who always knows where the bodies are buried. So to speak." Having sent Constable Musteile on this spurious mission, he turned to Max. Relief was reflected on both their faces.

Cotton said, "I've taken a room at the Horseshoe for tonight, perhaps longer. I'll be putting in some long days and I don't relish that drive home after dark."

"That sounds a sensible plan," said Max.

"Mind if I drop by the vicarage this evening? It probably will be late."

"Certainly, if you think I can be of help."

The look Cotton gave him was quirky.

"Help? You started this ball rolling. I'd like to hear your reasons," he said, adding: "Not that I disagree with you."

134

CHAPTER 11
BAPTIZING THE TEDDY BEAR

The cold descended like a sheer curtain that Harvest Fayre night. The autumn sun had quickly dimmed, and the smell of burning firewood now floated over the village in a pine-scented cloud.

Max also had a fire burning in his study, shedding its light on the gilt-framed painting over the mantel. There was a crackling noise as a log collapsed. He grabbed a poker and pushed the log back to safety.

Mrs. Hooser had long since left for home. At the rap of the knocker he went to answer the door himself, Thea close at his heels.

DCI Cotton strode in, in what was apparently his habitual mode of alertness: tightly wound and ready to strike. Apart from a jacket swinging from his shoulders that looked like it might be Armani, he reminded Max of countless men — and women — he had worked with in the past. He somehow felt in Cotton's brisk presence the push-pull of that past, and was sure that if you were teamed with a man like Cotton, he'd always have your back. Max thought fleetingly of a former colleague, and pushed the thought aside.

"We've sent Constable Musteile on a search of Raven's Wood."

Max parted the curtains and looked out the window.

"In the pitch dark? Why? Do you expect to find anything there?" asked Max.

Cotton answered him with a wry grin.

Max, catching on: "You wanted him out of your hair."

"If we've a hope of finding out what happened to Wanda, that man is best kept as far away from the scene as possible. We'll make a fuller search of the woods in daylight hours, of course. It's not completely a spurious assignment."

Cotton arranged the razor-like pleats in his immaculate trousers and sat on a chair by the fire. Max joined him opposite.

"Wanda?" he asked delicately.

"They've taken her to the police mortuary at Monkslip-super-Mare."

Max gently persisted. "Is there anything you can tell me? It goes without saying, but it will go no further than this room."

Cotton readily replied, "She does not appear to have been sexually molested in any way. And she had her handbag with her, with a few pound coins inside, her cashpoint card, and so on. Cause of death appears to be anaphylactic shock."

Max said, "I thought it must be. She was famously allergic to peanuts. So much for the passing crazed madman theory then. Sex and theft ruled out. So we're left with — what?"

"That remains to be seen," said Cotton — rather complacently, Max thought, wishing he were as sanguine. With the obvious motives ruled out, what was there left?

"The Village Hall was unlocked when Guy Nicholls and I went there," he told Cotton. "It was left unlocked all day, I would imagine."

"Probably. At least, we are going for now on the assumption that the building was kept unlocked for the day, since access would be needed by so many people — yourself included. Even had it not been unlocked, prying open a window would be easy as winking."

"No sign of that, though?"

"None whatsoever. But of course Wanda, in the normal course of events, would have a key. Whatever she was there for — to pick up some forgotten or left-behind item, perhaps — it also seems unlikely in the extreme that she would bolt herself inside, doesn't it? Whatever for? So anyone could walk in while she was there, surprise her . . . Anyone at all."

The fireplace made another crackling sound, loud as a bullet in the cozy room. There must be a lot of tar on the wood, Max thought. He rose again to adjust the logs.

"Why was she there?" Cotton, watching him, mused aloud. "Dressing down a volunteer? Surely it was too late or too early for that, and she would be needed elsewhere — or she would believe her presence essential elsewhere."

Max could only shrug. There was no telling what went on in the windmills of Wanda's mind. Again seated, he said, "I gather you've been talking with people about her. You've certainly summed up the essence of the woman."

"Yes. Rather a self-important type, they tell me. She headed up the Women's Institute, is that right? That's a relict of a bygone era, I would have thought . . . rather dying out."

"Not really," answered Max. "In fact, it's experienced a nationwide revival in recent years, vamping up its image quite a bit. That movie with Helen Mirren only helped, one would have thought. *Calendar Girls*. Here in Nether Monkslip certainly the WI has grown in influence, and in value given."

Cotton mused, "A remote village like this . . . It's unusual, isn't it, that a village this size would have a Women's Institute?"

"Not at all," said Max. "The WI has an enthusiastic membership here for that very reason — Nether Monkslip has little night-life or other entertainment to recommend it. You could say the lack of other options ensures its continued success. They do much good work for charity. And as a whole, the national federation has gone to great lengths to modernize its image."

"Not all 'jam and Jerusalem,' as the saying goes."

"Correct. Also, things like the Poppy Day collections and the children's party at Christmas, which might in the past have fallen to the Royal British Legion Women's Section, now tend to come under the sway of the Nether Monkslip WI. Everything does, now that I come to think of it. Even many things that would have been in the church's domain at one time. We simply don't have the resources we once had. And Nether Monkslip may be unusual — and blessed — in having so many businesslike, astute women in the population."

"And men, presumably."

"And men. But the power, behind-the-scenes and otherwise — my impression has always been that it belongs to the women. That was certainly my impression in Wanda's case."

"A lot of money involved, is there, in all this charitable work?"

Max looked at him with sharp appreciation. "Yes. Not in the millions of pounds, but enough to be tempting. It's one motive that occurred to me, too. Money changing hands; Wanda in an oversight position."

Cotton went on to tell him that the police had had little luck in pinning down exactly when Wanda had disappeared (it was more like an *absence* of noise and strife, noted Cotton, and thus hard to pinpoint), although when she was found was not open to question.

"A priest backed up by a witness," Cotton said. "You couldn't ask for more unless the witness was a judge."

"Not everyone would agree with that assessment these days, but thanks for the vote of confidence," Max replied.

"However, the Fayre volunteers all seemed to agree they were too busy to notice — and in some cases, it was said, just happy Wanda was leaving them alone," Cotton went on.

"No one exactly sought out her company, I gather. Some kid claims to have heard a commotion around noon, coming from the Village Hall. We'll put out a general appeal to the public, asking for witnesses to come forward, but I'm not counting on much to come from that effort. The usual crackpots will waste police time claiming to have seen Wanda, looking either wild-eyed, despondent, or deliriously happy — or all three at once — in her last moments on earth."

"No doubt," said Max, who had his own experiences of a too-helpful public in his past.

"Just for the record," Cotton asked, "who had keys to the place? Was it normally kept locked?"

Max made a seesawing motion with one hand: *sort of.*

"Things tended to operate on a basis of either trust or carelessness, I'm afraid."

But who had the keys? Max thought: Wanda; her second-in-command, Suzanna Winship; and the maintenance man/cleanup crew/gardener in the person of Maurice, an amiable and rather slow-witted man who did odd jobs around the village. Aloud Max listed them, adding, "These people for a start. Of course, as there was little in the building worth stealing, unless you count that ancient, erratically functioning slide projector, custody of the keys over the years was a haphazard venture at best. She could have been killed by anyone, in fact, if it were a question of someone getting in and waiting there for her — I gather that is the drift of your questions?"

Cotton countered with a question of his own: "Killed? We are talking about murder then, Father?"

"Call me Max, please. 'Father' never sat right with me. Yes, to answer you, almost certainly we are, I'm afraid. Unless she snuck off with a peanut biscuit to do away with herself in private in the middle of the Fayre, which is not at all likely, given her personality, for a start. Not at all. No one, in my estimation, was less given to suicidal thought or action than Wanda."

Cotton said, "An accidental poisoning, while possible, does not explain her excited demeanor when talking with Suzanna Winship at the Fayre."

Max leaned forward. "Really? Suzanna said that?"

"What Ms. Winship said was that if she didn't know better, she'd say Wanda looked and acted like a woman headed to an assignation."

Wanda? Max could not get his mind

142

around the concept. Beneath all the bombast, the corgi-walking ensembles, the scarves, he supposed there did beat the heart of a red-blooded female. Still . . .

"Accidents do happen," Cotton was saying.

"So does 'malice aforethought,' " said Max. "And that's what I think you're dealing with here."

Cotton gave him a thoughtful look. "That's what the local doctor thinks, too — Suzanna's brother, as it happens. Serious reservations, he has. He won't issue a death certificate and has kicked it over to our man in Monkslip-super-Mare."

Max thought solemnly of the marks on Wanda's wrists. There really hadn't been an alternate explanation for those that made sense.

DCI Cotton had rested as long as it seemed he was capable. Now he jumped up and began surveying the contents of Max's bookshelves. He didn't pick any up for a closer perusal, for which Max could hardly blame him. *The Collected Sermons of Josiah Pentworthy, D.D, 1630–1689* hardly made for riveting reading, even in its heyday.

"Did *no one* see her, notice her movements?" asked Max of Cotton's back. "Not see her walking toward the Village Hall? It

143

seems impossible . . ."

Cotton spun round, in nearly a Fred Astaire movement.

"We'll be asking everyone that, of course. I'll be sending my uniforms round house to house with pro formas to catalog everyone's whereabouts. It all takes time."

"Door-to-door inquiries. The village will never be the same." Max sighed at the thought of it. There would be those villagers who were horrified, and those who were titillated by the attention and excitement. But no matter what the individual reaction, the smooth, placid surface of the village had been ruffled and might never again be *un*-ruffled.

"Everyone was at the Fayre, or so it seemed," said Max, drawing out the words as he pictured in his mind the colorful, Bruegel-like scene. "I don't think you can see the Village Hall from the grounds of the Abbey Ruins, or from Abbot's Lodge."

"That's not going to help much when it comes to eyewitnesses."

"I know."

"And there were so many of them in attendance."

"I know."

"Including people from outside the village — whoever they were."

Ordinarily, especially at that time of day, shop owners and other people with jobs and obligations would easily be accounted for, Max reflected. Although, unless they went out for a pub lunch, that wasn't strictly true. They could be up to almost anything — especially, in the case of shop owners, if they put a discreet little sign on the front door of their shop: BACK IN 1 HOUR.

Bother.

He suddenly realized that in his thinking he'd placed himself squarely on DCI Cotton's team. Well, that was fine; this matter needed to be cleared up, and quickly. Festering suspicion could only harm the village, the longer the uncertainty went on. *His* village, as he thought of it.

Both men gazed at the fireplace in mutual frustration, as if the answers would somehow leap out of the crackling flames. Rain had begun to make a faint thudding sound as it struck the roof, echoing hollowly through the chimney into the room below.

"Do you know," Max said aloud, himself echoing the observation of most of the villagers, "I don't think we've ever had a murder in Nether Monkslip. Not to my knowledge."

"I can imagine," said Cotton. "It looks the sort of place where only officially sanctioned killing might have happened, and that, centuries ago. The odd hanging for sheep theft and so on."

He paused, flipping through his notebook, and Max suddenly thought of Nunswood, of the murder said to have taken place up on Hawk Crest centuries before. He hadn't thought of that in years. It was probably just a baseless legend anyway, retrieved and embellished by Frank for his book.

"There's nothing you can tell us?" Cotton was asking him. "The slightest memory of the smallest thing can sometimes be important."

"I can only tell you," Max said, as he combed slowly through his memory, visualizing the scene as he'd been trained for so many years to do, "that the last people I saw before setting out to retrieve the tea from the Village Hall were Awena Owen — the woman who owns Goddessspell — and her assistant, Tara Raine. But that means nothing, of course, because I can't say where they were all morning. Where anyone was all the morning. Musteile was by the marquee, and Guy Nicholls emerging from it. Again, that means nothing."

Cotton nodded in agreement.

"You say someone heard a commotion. I wonder if she yelled, 'Unhand me, you villain,' or something like that," said Max, after a pause. "I must say, Wanda strikes me as the kind of woman who would say something old-fashioned like 'Unhand me.' Perhaps someone heard her say a name — or say *something* that would help us."

Cotton said, "Far too much noise, and far too far away. Taking everyone at their word, they were at the Fayre and the village proper was a ghost town."

"Except for Wanda and whoever was with her. And taking everyone at their word."

Cotton said, "There's a dustbin in a little alley behind the Village Hall. Nothing found there that shouldn't be there, as far as we know now. Nothing found in the alley, at least, so far. But we don't know what to look for — if anything."

He was bouncing now on the balls of his feet. It was not unlike having a puppy in the room. Thea, perhaps sensing this, was nowhere to be seen, Max suddenly realized.

Cotton was in fact so animated Max thought he could see the thrumming of the man's heart beating in his chest. Then he realized it was his mobile phone.

"Excuse me," said Cotton, as he fumbled the instrument out of his pocket. He saw who it was from and briefly turned his back, muttering something curt and official-sounding into the receiver.

He rang off, and told Max, "There will be a postmortem. No surprise. I'm expected to be there."

Max felt a small frisson of revulsion course through his body. He'd always been loath to know too much about the necessary machinery of investigating a suspicious death. Custom did not stale its power to repel even as he applauded the advances in forensics that could help the police unmask the guilty, and exculpate the innocent.

Cotton went on, "I have some routine matters to clear up. Wanda's my priority, but I have to hand off everything else I was working on. If you need anything in the next few days, I'll be at the pod, or someone there will know how to reach me. Or you can try the Horseshoe."

Cotton, patting the mobile back into his pocket, then carefully straightening his pocket handkerchief, added, "Since the circumstances are unexplained, there will be an inquest as well."

Max nodded. *I know.* There would always be an inquest under these conditions.

"Did you notice her particularly today?" Cotton asked.

Max shrugged.

"Yes. And no. She was here and there;

everywhere and nowhere. She would grind to a halt periodically to admonish or chastise someone, then spin off again in new, seemingly random directions."

"Have you yourself noticed anything unusual — say in recent days leading up to the Fayre? Strangers in the village, anything like that?"

"Just the villagers themselves, being no stranger than usual. They're a close-knit bunch, in some ways. One would almost say inbred, but that was centuries ago — if it happened — and of course not true in the case of the new arrivals, which many of them are. In other ways they're . . . competitive."

"Like family, given to differences."

"You could say so. But . . . petty differences, grudges held over trifles — grudges quickly relinquished in the event of a real crisis, a neighbor in real need. Nothing on this scale. Nothing approaching murder. It's unfathomable. If you knew them as I do, you'd see how incredible this all is."

Cotton regarded him thoughtfully, the solemn, good-looking man with the dark gray eyes. "Perhaps you wouldn't be the one to notice someone plotting evil in the village — would you?" he said. "You are trained to see only the good in people."

A part of Max's mind immediately rose up in revolt at this Pollyannaish view of himself and his nature, as if he were some good-natured, feeble-minded rube, easily gulled. He may have been stung even more by the fact that he suspected the Pollyanna side of himself was true and, worse, ineradicable. He did tend to want to see the good in people, despite all the evidence at his command that men and women — all of them — were capable of the worst cruelties.

But he said, rather sharply, "I was with MI5 for nearly fifteen years, and trained, if you like, to see the evil in those around me." Despite himself, he felt better after this somewhat childish outburst, particularly when he saw the gleam of new respect in the other man's eyes.

"No shit," Cotton said slowly, wonderingly. Then: "Erm, I mean, gosh. Wow."

"But," Max went on, "I have to admit: whatever is going on here, I do not understand it at all."

Cotton had actually stopped jiggling about for a moment, Max noticed. The shifting firelight, playing tricks, carved deep hollows beneath Cotton's brows and cheekbones; his eyes glittered the color of pale rum. Cat's eyes. The two men might have been swapping ghost stories.

In this shifting light Cotton again brought to mind Paul, someone Max had tried very hard to forget.

In their young days together at university, he and Paul had cut a wide swath through the female population of London. There had been wine and women, a certain amount of never-missed opportunity for both. He didn't remember any singing, but he wouldn't have been surprised if someone told him there had been. They had been good days. But on the particular day that was etched in his memory forever, the two of them were nearly fifteen years older. Paul had recently married. They were into day three of a detail that involved tracking the movements of a Russian multimillionaire with suspicious ties to his homeland.

Under ordinary circumstances, they would have been elsewhere. But there had been in the preceding months an increase in terrorist chatter picked up by those whose job it was to listen, to visit Web sites, to intercept mail, to pretend to be what they were not so they could gather information. A covert listening agency, one of many dozens worldwide, had picked up what sounded like a plot to hijack an Air India plane flying out of Mumbai (using shards of broken pottery souvenirs as weapons) and had shared that information with MI5 and others. That was all that was known, a suspicion of a plot, but it was the impetus for an immediate reorganizing of personnel and priorities, and eventually a raising of the UK threat level from "substantial" to "severe." Normally, Max and Paul would not have been assigned to the Russian detail, for it was a gumshoe type of task below their usual level. The Russian knew he was being watched; they knew he knew he was being watched, and it was more a matter of letting the man know this would be a bad time to pull anything while the camera lens was metaphorically pointing right at him. If it had been a proper surveillance job, there would have been two teams of four officers just to follow the guy on foot: two ahead, two behind, four additional for backup. Not just him and Paul.

But the people who had originally been assigned to the Russian job had some prior, unique experience with the branch of al-Qaeda that wanted to take down the Air India plane, and everything was reshuffled.

The whole setup was outside the norm.

Backup, Max told himself repeatedly, would have made no difference.

Cotton was still looking at him in that assessing, thoughtful way. "Your help could be invaluable," Cotton said at last. "If only in gaining the cooperation of the members of your parish."

"Baptizing the teddy bear," said Max, nodding.

"I beg your pardon?"

"It's what I call baptizing the teddy bear. When a child being baptized is old enough to be afraid of or nervous about the baptism, I have been known to baptize the child's teddy bear first. Show them it doesn't hurt."

"I see," said Cotton, smiling. "Yes, then, something like that is needed. Perhaps it would be wisest to wait until after the preliminary inquest for you to do more than simply keep one ear to the ground. Probably Monday, if we put a rush on it. Despite the clerical collar, or maybe because of it, people may confide in you in the meantime. But no need to stir up the populace until we're quite sure what we have here. If you have time, that is," Cotton added.

In point of fact, Max didn't have time. Although he resided in Nether Monkslip, he was shared with two other villages in the surrounding area — Chipping Monkslip and Middle Monkslip. This spreading thin of resources was an all-too-frequent occurrence in the modern-day church of dwindling vocations.

There were countless calls on his time, and he said no to no one if he could help it. In a village, despite the social services that in theory met every possible human need, the village clergyman was often considered the better, more tactful, answer to complications related to illness, death, marriage, or simply an unspecifiable crisis of the soul. The only way to be effective was by the time-consuming business of home visits. Max was stretched thin on that score, in fact functioning as a one-man Citizens Advice Bureau.

But looking at Cotton, he felt that old, familiar pull, and immediately began reassessing his calendar. He needed to see Mr. Whippet, he who was almost certainly dying this time, but that was the only appointment that could not be delayed. There was his routine visit to Mrs. Dorman, a very old lady who admitted to ninety-something and kept what she called her anti-Taliban kit at the ready in a basket by her front door — batteries, distilled water, and the like. That the elderly — and others — had been reduced to this sort of mindless fear was the sorrow of life in the twenty-first century, but Max knew his presence alleviated her concerns, at least until the next news broadcast. He was often tempted to unplug her telly while he was there.

He also in the coming week had to take assembly at the primary school in Monkslip-super-Mare, filling in for an absent rector who was minus a curate for the task at the moment. There were matters of budget to attend to, the upkeep of ancient St. Edwold's being in effect an expensive and eternal DIY project.

But certainly he could put off his impending meeting with the future Cudwells, the very tall, middle-aged couple who were coming to him for premarital counseling. They would be holding hands when they entered the room, and holding hands when they left. They would sit before him the whole time holding hands like two very large children in a fairy tale. Presumably they uncoupled for meals or to get dressed, but he wouldn't have taken bets on it.

So the ideally suited Cudwells could wait; their coming to him was a formality only. Here was a new case, a wrong to be righted. A problem to be solved. A villain to be outwitted. A blight on the village to be eradicated.

He'd admit it to no one but himself, but the pull of his former life remained strong, and he suspected it would never leave him entirely. The qualities his superiors had praised, in words that now sat encrypted somewhere on an MI5 server — words praising his dogged temperament, his fierce curiosity, his almost atavistic need to pursue justice — these qualities sprang, with a surge that was palpable, to the fore. He was the proverbial hound who had scented the fox.

"Plenty of time," he told the policeman.

CHAPTER 12
LEGEND

Max's life revolved around Sundays, as did the lives of all parish priests. A person could name a date of any month — the nineteenth, for example — and Max would instantly think, *That will be two days after the Sunday.* An occupational hazard, he imagined, like an accountant totting up figures without really having to think about it.

This Sunday was unlike any other in his experience, of course. He preached a sermon of healing, of blanket forgiveness, injecting a reminder that we are always in the midst of death, to record-breaking attendance. But he knew this surge in his popularity had nothing to do with an expected uptick in the quality of his sermon — in fact, he hardly knew what to say to the villagers. They had learned — somehow — that there would be a preliminary inquest, and that no funeral would be held until that and other bits of officialdom were taken care of. So the Sunday service was the next best thing — a placeholder until the main event. A trailer, as it were. Lydia, his usually competent young acolyte, seemed in particular to be nearly beside herself, lighting the altar candles with an air of distraction that risked setting her robe on fire.

Looking out over the congregation, he saw that Tildy Ann Hooser was wearing a rhinestone tiara, dark sunglasses too large for her face, and a big-buttoned red coat with stand-up collar. It was disconcerting, like having a tiny Audrey Hepburn in the audience. Her mother, as usual, sat oblivious to the fact that her other child, Tom, was systematically building an unsteady fortress of hymnals and prayer books that was close to collapse. It was Tildy Ann/Audrey who made him stop, lowering the sunglasses only long enough to aim at her brother a lethal, basilisk gaze.

Despite the noise of the large crowd scuffling about in their seats, noticeably missing was Wanda's booming contralto voice during the singing, as the congregation bleated its way uncertainly through the hymns. Say what you might, Wanda was a leader in many ways, even if her voice tended to drown out everyone else. Max noticed all this as he struggled to focus on the service. People were here for comfort, he knew, as well as from curiosity. He prayed for the grace to allow the tone of his own voice to calm their fears.

After the service would be the usual mingling in the churchyard, the weak sun struggling to warm the gathered faithful. He would normally have stood chatting amiably with the members of his congregation as they filed out of the church, stopping to greet him and comment on the sermon, the weather, the economy, the crops. *More people here than last week,* Max might think, with the part of his mind not engaged in swapping platitudes.

This day, of course, was different. Max, braced as he was for the flood of curiosity on the day following Wanda's death, was almost amused by the varying attempts to hide (or not even bother to hide) avid interest, almost cruelly thwarted by his stern refusal to be drawn into conversation with the villagers about the only thing on their minds — the murder of Wanda Batton-Smythe. Since it was well known that Max had discovered the body, there were many eager attempts to glean facts that could be examined, polished up, and passed along to the next purveyor. Nether Monkslip was too small to sustain a newspaper of its own — in most weeks, there was not enough news or even gossip to bother printing, and what there was could more efficiently be shared by word-of-mouth. The days following Wanda's demise would of course prove to be the exception. The *Monkslip-super-Mare Globe and Bugle* — aka *UK Yesterday* (as a visiting American wag had dubbed it) — would have to print extra copies daily to keep up with demand.

"Great sermon. By the way, I hear the police are paying you late-night visits," said Frank Cuthbert, Author. Max smiled wanly. Was that meant as an accusation? Probably not. Cheated of their chance to speculate (Max dodged all attempts at sounding him out, subtle or otherwise, by saying the police had forbidden him to speak of the discovery of her body), they did the next best thing, and lingered for close to an hour swapping theories with one another. Max quickly left them and went to change in the vestry. Then, sneaking with furtive steps out a side door, he went for a walk in the village.

But it was hopeless. Whoever had not been in church waylaid him now. He noticed several strangers walking about, knocking on doors — plainclothes policemen all, as well as a handful of uniforms. There must be a barber in Monkslip-super-Mare that all the policemen went to, so similar did the men look.

There were other strangers in the village, as well — some going door-to-door, others buttonholing people in the streets, lanes, and alleyways. Judging by their generally scruffy-looking demeanor they were not police, unless they were police gone so far undercover as to be irretrievably lost to humanity. Going native, it was called. But no — Max recognized them, from long experience, as newspaper reporters. He saw that one of them was talking with Constable Musteile. *Oh, my: too late to warn Cotton. Damage done.* As he watched, a van made its way down the High, a BBC logo painted on its sides, with giant receiving equipment affixed to the top. The telly news had arrived.

No . . .

Max quickly set his feet in the direction of the path that led up to Hawk Crest, not wishing to be pinned down in the vicarage if he returned there, as he almost certainly would be. Thea would never forgive him if she knew he was headed for their special walking-and-exploring place, but he'd give her a good long outing later. He needed to be completely on his own.

And the BBC van couldn't make it up the path.

He had successfully avoided thoughts of Paul for so long that their return hurled him straight back into the past, to the days when he could hardly look in the mirror — which, if he'd thought about it, was probably just as well. It had been obvious from the fit of his clothes that he was rapidly losing weight, and, despite all the sleep, he had felt more like something very old that had been excavated than someone who was well rested and ready to rejoin the human race. Officially, the working theory was that Paul had been killed by underlings wanting to impress the Russian — hoping for promotion if they caught his eye. Max knew there was little hope of catching such small, nameless, unimportant fish.

On the seventeenth day, bored, mind blank and unable to focus even on a television show, let alone a book or crossword puzzle, he had gone for a walk in the park near his flat. His steps led him past a Thomas Cook shop, with its span of glossy posters in the window, and its notices of cheap flights to Spain and Portugal: HURRY, ONLY A FEW SEATS LEFT AT THIS PRICE! He found himself walking in, fishing for the credit card in his wallet as he went, and signing up for the first poster that had actually caught his eye: EGYPT, the letters written in some jagged typeface undoubtedly meant to suggest hieroglyphics, scrawled against a scene rendered in an Art Deco style, surely as if Hercule Poirot would be joining the party.

Max was a seasoned traveler, or so he thought of himself, his father a career diplomat. Another civil servant like himself. From a young age he had roamed the world with his parents, his mother being unwilling to deposit him in boarding schools except when it was completely unavoidable. He'd be left behind for safety's sake, while she followed his father to some remote posting or other, most often in Africa and later in the Far East. He thought later that his touristy trip to Egypt was perhaps an attempt to re-create that sense of adventure cushioned by the security, false or real, of Her Majesty's government having their backs at all times.

His father's diplomacy seemed to him now a matter of repressing his deepest-held beliefs and feelings. He would hold it in all day, but some days, when he came home, would stop on the mat outside the front door and say, quite clearly, "That asshole," never realizing Max could hear him from his room window above. Then his father would turn the handle and walk in, all smiles, to kiss Max's mother and inquire what was for dinner. It wasn't until much later, after his father's first stroke, that Max realized the stress this "double life" had been causing. It wasn't a lesson he had thought applicable to his own life.

Adventuring as a young man, Max had gone on an ill-advised solo trip through Western Africa. The object had not been to frighten his parents, but of course it had done. At one of the worst points in the journey, in Equatorial Guinea, he had traveled from the island of Malabo to Bata on the mainland on a Ukrainian boat called Djiblho. There, overnight, among thieves and strangers, as he lay awake to ward off the pickpockets, one woman had died as another was giving birth. He was dehydrated and disoriented himself at that point, but he later was sure he had felt fingertips of ice brush his cheekbone as the old woman died.

He gradually had become aware that many of those he came across on his journey were slaves, damaged and undocumented people from nowhere, some mentally ill or deficient, probably sold by their poverty-wracked families. In the remotest regions, children would come up to him and rub his arm, thinking his skin color was painted on. Poverty and isolation, wherever he looked, walking hand in hand.

He often wondered about the child born on that ship.

This time, he signed up for a glossy tour of Egypt. Just another old fogey being led around the sights. Fine with him. But on this tour, looking only for escape and luxury, rest and good food and forgetfulness and the need never (ever) to do or think for himself again, he found his compass. He found his God, as some would have it. The decision — rather, the clear view of the road ahead — was instantaneous and unquestioned. At the moment, he never stopped to wonder what Egypt had to do with a calling to the modern Anglican priesthood, or why faith had come to him in a reverse of the usual process: people generally *lost* their faith when faced with a tragedy that made them question what kind of deity would allow such things to happen.

The group had been in the second week of the Egyptian trip and the processes of getting to know one another had advanced apace. There were those whose company one might seek out for a drink at the end of the day. There were those to avoid — talkative, intrusive, loud, or boastful. Old couples, one family. Divorcées and merry widows galore. Again, he didn't want to have to *think* and he reveled at first in this mindless freedom. He had wanted someone else to decide what he should have for breakfast, and when, and where.

So he was simply drifting through days that were much of a sameness, despite the changes of scenery, and doing as he was told when it was time to get on the next bus. But his presence caused such a commentary among the single women and the older couples — why hadn't he realized how intrusive this would become? — that he was already planning to leave the tour and strike out on his own when they came to Luxor.

The land of the pyramids was a place as tawdry and mysterious as the glossy posters had promised, but somehow both at once — a Mae West of a country. They had stopped for the day at the vast, badly ruined temple complex of Karnak, such a staple of Egyptian travel literature as to be required viewing, with only the Giza pyramids for real competition. The complex was the work of over thirty pharaohs, or so the tour guide told them. A purely mankind-engineered enterprise, then, like Canterbury Cathedral or the temples of Machu Picchu. Lofty, exalted, and the result of a wonderful hubris amounting to madness that impelled their creation. Immortality for both pharaoh and worker, set in stone.

There among the massive columns, dwarfed and insignificant, he felt what he could only describe as a lightening, as if someone had taken from his hands some enormous, heavy container he'd been holding forever — and holding onto for dear life. As if someone had tapped his shoulder and said, Here, let me take that.

And the thought came to him clearly, unbidden: *I can't do this anymore.*

He couldn't be a part of it anymore, and that was all. The men poisoned to impress a higher up — initiative from below. The people garroted on a nod, a lift of the eyebrow from some unknown thug in charge, perhaps several thousand miles away. The lies that were becoming second nature to him. He'd seen it all, witnessed too much.

Paul's death could have turned him toward a quest for justice or revenge, but at that point he was at a place past revenge — at the point of tiredness and exhaustion with vengeance. He wanted, simply, something easier and at the same time far, far more difficult than hatred.

Time shifted, collapsed. It was his road-to-Damascus experience, and it came not with a blinding light, or a parting of the clouds by an unseen hand, but with a calm certainty, in the most banal of circumstances. He thought: Life was running out like water cupped in his hands. What was he doing with his time?

It was as if he were following a directive as instinctive as the impulse to stand and fetch a drink when he was thirsty. He was literally called. He went.

He returned to the rest of the group that day and looked about him at his fellows, at the couple that had squabbled its way across Egypt, at the women, young and old, without partners, at the man who had complained about the food nonstop since their arrival, and he understood their commonality was that one day all of them would put down their worries and their concerns large and small, and they would be forced to make that final journey alone. They suddenly became to him what they were — fallible, ordinary people all carrying stories to tell that they dared not tell anyone. The compassion that had always been a part of his makeup rose to the surface and remained there, subtly and forever altering his landscape.

So began his surrender to feeling rather than to thought. It was not until he was well launched in his theological studies that he came across the famous quote from Pascal: "It is the heart which perceives God and not the reason."

He stayed with the group, then returned to England to train for the ministry, ending up back at Oxford. A more complete contrast to his raucous undergraduate days could hardly be imagined. He would, after his training, be ordained a deacon, then serve as a curate. God willing, he would be ordained a priest. And then . . . it was the "then" he didn't know. Just that this was what he had to do, now.

And so he came to join the dwindling ranks of men and women who saw the church as an avenue of peaceful change. The ranks these days included escapees from all walks of life — civil servants, teachers, farmers, scientists. MI5 agents. Max didn't see himself as a rarity.

Now here he was, watching from the top of Hawk Crest the almost comic scene below as villagers were chased by invaders from the police and the news corps. A few yards behind him, the stone menhirs lurched, disinterested witnesses, in their uneven circle.

He sat a long while, staring at nothing but the tips of his trainers, which were again giving out — he walked miles every day, for one reason and another. He had joined Five in an excess of dewy-eyed belief that he could save the world; he had joined the Anglican priesthood when that world had shifted. In coming to Nether Monkslip — in seeking out the ordinary, the predictable, the boring, even — he had thought he'd be getting right away from things. It was a place where he knew no one and could start fresh. He had found himself looking eagerly forward to a quiet life where local scandal might amount to strong feeling and umbrage taken over the choice of reading material for the Church Book Club, or perhaps a dispute, easily resolved (or so thought Max in his blissful, city-bred ignorance), over a stray sheep or two.

He'd lived a life of fear, of defense against terrors known and unknown. In Egypt, he had wondered what life would be like if he relinquished those defenses. If he simply handed over that heavy burden and *gave in.*

In Nether Monkslip, he felt, he'd been given his chance to find out.

And now this.
A snake in his Garden of Eden.

Chapter 13
Medicine Man

By Monday breakfast, Max's disquiet was full-blown, and the invasion of his village complete.

He began the day with a breakfast of muesli with blueberries, buttered wheat toast, and a pot of strong tea — a wholesome meal consumed over the appetite-destroying pages of the *Globe and Bugle*. The paper throbbed with the news of Wanda's demise, the bare facts of which were related in near-histrionic tones by a reporter apparently suffering from sleep deprivation and lack of adult supervision. Following in the great tradition of its big sisters in London, the paper managed to imply a great deal without actually saying a great deal at all. The reporter had turned DCI Cotton's "No comment at this time" into a veritable indictment of a corrupt police force and lax British penal system, the result of which was a populace at the mercy of every stray madman for hundreds of miles round.

Max rushed through his meal, anxious to get a start on the day. He had again had a hard time convincing Mrs. Hooser that the old-style sausages, bacon, eggs, mushrooms, kidneys, and tomatoes fry-up could not be consumed by mortal man every single day, not if he didn't want to demonstrate his mortality almost immediately. She considered that a strapping man such as himself would waste away on muesli, which she maintained was related to cat food. They had reached a détente of sorts on the subject but Max felt it would not long last. Mrs. Hooser aside, his arrival in Nether Monkslip had been an introduction of his taste buds to unprocessed, unirradiated food, much of it not more than a few minutes or hours from the field, nourished by the region's mild temperatures and deep, rich soils.

He quickly downed his honey-sweetened tea. He was scheduled to appear at a preliminary inquest that afternoon, once he'd attended to the religious and secular affairs of St. Edwold's. After that, he would begin his "officially unofficial" investigation of Wanda's death, as he thought of it, with a visit to Dr. Winship's.

So Max later that day found himself, for the first time in his life, giving evidence at an inquest. He provided only the sketchiest details surrounding the finding of the body, and his and Guy's efforts to resuscitate Wanda, reliving the moment when, for a brief fleeting second, there had been hope, however false and instantly quashed, that Wanda might be revived. Dr. Winship likewise gave testimony — a formality, merely, but what he had to say clearly made an impression on the coroner. The expected adjournment was announced.

Afterward, DCI Cotton held a media conference where he read out a statement of cryptic opacity, having first announced that he would be taking no questions at that time. Max, sliding uncontested into the back of the room (the clerical collar opened doors it really should not have, although it also sometimes closed them), had the chance to marvel again at Cotton's ability to appear perfectly open and forthcoming while revealing nothing whatsoever. When the jostling mass of reporters began yelling out questions, he turned heel and left the room.

Max timed his visit to Dr. Winship's for late afternoon, when he thought it likely Bruce's sister Suzanna would be gone, and for when normal surgery hours and times for rounds might allow for a little break — even though the National Health Service didn't allow for much in the way of respite. Max told himself he wanted a free and uninterrupted conversation about the pathology of the case: he knew from previous experience of Dr. Winship that murder was a bit of a hobbyhorse for him. But dodging the delectable Suzanna was, Max quietly acknowledged, part of his motivation for the timing.

"I thought I might see you again today," the doctor greeted him at the front door. Leading him into the sitting room, he carried in one hand what looked like a medical journal, published in lines of microscopic type. Like many surgeries in small villages, Dr. Winship's offices were a part of his house, and tucked behind the main dwelling. The path to that door was worn almost into a rut: as sole GP for the village, Dr. Winship was kept busy.

"The mind of the murderer," he now said ruminatively, and with barely concealed glee, settling into an overstuffed chair by the warm hearth, tossing aside his reading, and waving Max into the seat opposite. It was a slightly smaller chair that Max imagined might, in the evening, be occupied by

Suzanna.

"Let's come straight to the point," said Dr. Winship, rubbing his hands together in a down-to-business manner, having first offered the contents of a well-stocked drinks tray. He might have been counting the hours until Max showed up to discuss the case. Likely he had. "Death was due to anaphylaxis — a severe allergic reaction," he said, now wagging a forefinger (Bruce had a pedantic streak). "But we know that Wanda would not have committed suicide. Well, not unless she took half the village out with her. Sorry, Vicar, but you knew the woman as well as I did. This was not her style at all. I told that Cotton chap on the day that there could be no death certificate issued for this kind of sudden death without her being looked at by a specialist. Of course he agreed. Had no choice — the police would be mad to ignore the indications that gave me pause. Nothing too obvious, but enough to make me wonder, you understand. Told him that in my opinion he needed to get a Home Office pathologist onto it right away."

Max nodded, taking in the lecture but following his own train of thought. Many sins might be laid at Wanda's door, most having to do with pride, as most sins were, but suicide he would certainly agree wasn't among them.

"You treated her?" he asked. Dr. Winship had not been many years in the village, and it was always possible Wanda was one of those who made the trek into Monkslip-super-Mare for medical treatment. "You were her physician?"

"Yes. I saw her for routine care, although strong as two oxen, she was. No diagnosis of the sudden onset of an existing illness would be possible here. Nothing like that. She also saw a specialist in Monkslip-super-Mare, but that was nothing serious. Not a thing wrong with her except sometimes she liked extra attention."

Sometimes? Max, looking at him squarely, said, "You're not satisfied with what you saw on Saturday. Can you tell me why?"

Dr. Winship paused, allowing a silence to hang in the air between them as he took a sip of his drink. He had the face of a cherub — an exceedingly worried cherub — with a receding hairline and round glasses.

"No, I can't say I can," he said at last, "because I'm not entirely sure myself. If the choices we're given are accident, suicide, or even murder, well . . . All I can repeat is a less suicidal woman than Wanda Batton-Smythe never was born. Nor one less prone to accident. Everything with Wanda, if you know anything of the woman . . ."

Here Max toggled a hand equivocally. *Not so much.*

"Well, everything," Dr. Winship continued, "would refute the possibility of her making a careless mistake. You saw the plate of biscuits in the kitchen there at the Village Hall?" Max nodded. "The peanuts were whole or roughly chopped and quite visible. It's not as if they had been ground into a fine powder, like glass, and mixed into her tea or something. She hadn't suddenly gone blind — she'd have seen the peanuts. Smelled them, even. So . . ."

"So . . ."

"So someone fed her the peanuts deliberately, knowing she was allergic."

"How?"

Somewhat testily: "How do you mean, how?"

"There were no signs anything was forced down her throat, I mean," said Max. "That her mouth was forced open. No bruises on her face. Whatever she ingested, she ingested deliberately."

"Yes, you're right, of course," said Dr. Winship. "That's what makes it so difficult. Someone must have ground up the peanuts, and introduced them to her disguised in some other food — those biscuits we saw in

178

the Village Hall had nothing to do with it. But what is certain is she didn't eat a biscuit with some big honking peanuts in it. That plate of biscuits was staged, I think — left there deliberately to mislead. That tells you something right there.

"And I'll tell you something else." Here the doctor paused for dramatic effect. He might have been taking lessons from Wanda.

"Ye-s-s?"

"The fact that her auto-injector was not in her handbag is the major clue. I had the police look for it, as I testified at the inquest. Not there. It was *always* with her. She would have used it to inject epinephrine into her outer thigh the moment she realized her mistake, if she ingested peanuts by accident."

"Unbelievable," Max breathed. "And definitely suspicious. So . . . suicide is absurd even to contemplate, but an accident is nearly as hard to believe," said Max. "Could she possibly be so distracted she didn't notice what she was eating? Let's say that is just possible. If so, where was the ever-present auto-injector . . ." he trailed off, then repeated, "Unbelievable."

Dr. Winship was nodding so enthusiastically his glasses nearly slid off his nose. He settled them back around his eyes and, leaning forward, told him, "She had a supply of three injectors — two at the house, one in her handbag. Always. She was terrified of ever being caught without óne. Have you ever seen one?" Max shook his head. "It is about the size of a permanent marker pen. Anyone who has ever experienced a severe allergic reaction can tell you that you *never* want to experience that kind of fright again."

Max puffed out his cheeks, thinking.

"But it comes down to why," the doctor went on. "Why would anyone want to kill Wanda?"

"You mean apart from the fact she exhibited all the diplomatic skills of a Latin American dictator?" asked Max.

"Well, yes. She must have trampled on someone's feet, and hard."

Max nodded. His thoughts had trodden, so to speak, down much the same path.

"The psychology of crime," Dr. Winship murmured, now openly astride his hobbyhorse. "Most fascinating. Do you know I toyed at one time with the idea of becoming a psychiatrist? But I opted instead to address diseases with a higher cure rate than psychosis and all the rest. So much of what we see nowadays is drug-fueled, after all, rather than being a good old mother fixation or something amenable to Freudian analysis."

"You're not allowing for plain, old-fashioned evil as the culprit in crime, then?"

" 'The Devil made me do it'? I wouldn't discount anything, Max. I try to keep an open mind. But more often than not the motivation for crime can be traced back to all the usual, boring suspects. Greed and lust, for example."

"Plain, old-fashioned evil, in other words."

Dr. Winship smiled. "If you like."

Max looked at him speculatively. He'd never in his career with MI5, which employed a lot of shrinks in one capacity or another, run across one who wasn't a teensy bit barking in one direction or another. He liked Bruce Winship, and overall was glad, for his own sake, that he'd made the career choice he had.

The doctor was offering him tea, which he waved away politely, and more whiskey, which he did not. He was thinking: people lie, cheat, and steal — Max felt he was rather a pragmatist about this. People were, without exception and by definition, far from perfect. But murder . . . Committing murder did such damage to the soul, it put the whole business into a category unto itself. The one crime to make one an outcast from the human race. Who would have done such a thing, and over Wanda? A silly woman, a nuisance, a disruptive force, certainly. But what could she have done to put herself in the way of such depravity?

As if answering his unspoken questions, Bruce Winship said, "When you come to think of it, murder is prompted by two things. Mainly: desperation and hatred. Desperation can stem from a lack of food, fear of exposure — any number of things. A lack of love, too, I suppose. Hatred, though . . . A murder prompted by hatred is the crime that may be unforgivable. Also, to my mind, that is a crime committed by the type of killer who, having once killed, would find it easier to kill, again and again. Although I suppose all that's more in your line, Padre." Like the Major, Bruce Winship had a military background but always used the colloquial phrase more lightheartedly. "More whiskey? I barely gave you enough to wet your whistle."

Max distractedly held out his glass. He thought, I wonder if the taking of a human life is ever justifiable. All those years of theology and I still don't know the answer. In man's eyes, yes (and he thought here of people like Paul, blown to small pieces for the latest political cause, the most recent cut in religious fashion, or simply to impress the boss), but did God not ultimately regard each fragile life, having been created, as worth saving? Was murder ever justified in God's eyes?

"We're not going to agree on the causes," said Max. "Since the causes aren't known."

"Genes or environment?" said Dr. Winship musingly. "We're as far from getting this right as we've ever been — you are correct about that. If there's a gene marker for genius or ambition, believe me, we'd be busy manipulating it. If there's one for cold-blooded killers, we'd be busy suppressing it."

"I still wouldn't discount the Devil . . ." said Max.

"Back to 'the Devil made me do it?' "The doctor finished his own whiskey and stood to fetch more from the drinks tray. He lifted the bottle in invitation.

"It can't be ruled out," said Max mildly, shaking his head.

"I prefer the scientific method." Dr. Winship poured another inch of the liquid into his glass and lifted it in a toast. The whiskey shone like liquid amber in the firelight. "Each to his own."

"I'll say a big amen to that," said a sultry feminine voice. Suzanna Winship stood in the doorway.

CHAPTER 14
TEMPTATION

Suzanna gazed at Max with frank interest, a gaze he returned with what bug-eyed equanimity he could muster. "I'll just go put the groceries away and join you," she said, indicating the shopping bags she held in each hand. Her brother having no objections, Max felt he could hardly protest. Returning minutes later, she sat down, shedding her cardigan in the somewhat overheated room to reveal a matching blue sweater.

"What do you think of all this, Vicar?" she asked him, smiling through her lip gloss.

"I can't begin to know how to think of it," he replied. "It's impossible for this to have happened, here in Nether Monkslip. And yet it did."

"Of course, it's nonsense to think this is connected with the Fayre nonsense," she said, adding (Max thought somewhat guiltily), "Isn't it?"

184

"What exactly was that particular nonsense about?" asked Max. Although he thought he knew in general terms, it would be interesting to hear the specifics from someone who'd been in the forefront.

"There was a screwup over the order for the chairs — oh, sorry. Is it all right to say screwup?" Max, having no idea, shrugged.

Suzanna crossed her legs, the firm, fleshy thighs encased in black tights. She was unquestionably an attractive woman. Feline features, eyes tilted, mouth with a curl at the corners, jaw coming nearly to a point on a triangular face. Thick, wavy hair the color of Devon cream. She looked at Max, taking in his gray eyes and black hair, and all but purred.

"Wanda, who had the heart and soul of a Head Girl, went on and on about it. I heard someone call her a cow during the last meeting, under her breath, of course," (here she adopted a self-deprecating grin, which showed her dimples to full effect) "but whoever did it would never own up to it now, in light of subsequent events."

A *married* attractive woman, he reminded himself. Max's first thoughts on hearing Suzanna was separated from her husband, however, had been an unclerical blurt of Anglo-Saxon derivation, for which he immediately sent an apology heavenward. Suzanna was a complication he felt he didn't need.

Separated, but married. Irretrievably married for all he knew. And as unsuitable as a consort for a small village priest as could be imagined. Vicar's wives (and in his position, a lawfully wedded wife it would have to be) seemed to him rather standard issue, with drab hair and clothing and an earnest demeanor. Even if Suzanna were available for the role, the very idea that she could be persuaded to tamp it down to suit the villagers was preposterous. And wrong to ask her to hide her light under a bushel, so to speak, of gray worsted wool and sensible shoes.

For something to distract him from these unprofitable thoughts, Max gazed about him at his surroundings. The furniture in the doctor's sitting room was teak and Scandinavian in a style that had been popular in the middle of the last century. Max thought some of it was collectible now but imagined it had been inherited rather than collected, Dr. Winship not striking him as a man to pay overmuch attention to his environs. But Suzanna looked like a sultry fifties siren against the backdrop; she might have been on a stage set.

"Anyway," Suzanna was saying now, smoothing her skirt over her knees, a modest gesture that somehow only drew further attention to the magnificent legs, "Wanda had no business making it into such a cause, embarrassing . . . people . . . that way."

"People?"

"Well, Joyce Carol Goats mainly," said Suzanna. Off his look, she added, "Sorry, it's rather an affectionate nickname around here for Lily. But I suppose Elka, as well, became a target. And Awena. Wanda on a mission meant sooner or later everyone was stuffed."

Max sighed inwardly. It was too true.

"Also," Suzanna continued, "you mustn't overlook the various tradesmen and farmers involved with the Fayre in one way or another, if you're combing our bucolic countryside looking for suspects. Most had been told off by Wanda — completely given the rounds of the kitchen — in the lead-up to 'her' big day. Notice I say 'her' — she did act as if she owned the whole parade. You should have seen her when she waylaid poor Guy Nicholls in the High. He would have agreed to anything to get away from her, and he did. It was her usual technique."

"Sounds as if the Fayre brought out the worst in her," put in Dr. Winship.

"You know as well as I do, there was a lot

of worst to bring out," said Suzanna. "Wanda — now, *nil nisi bonum,* but . . . Wanda was the sort of woman who exemplifies what is wrong today with the Women's Institute. There's a WI in North Yorkshire offering its members pole dancing lessons. Now, that's more like it — bringing the light of the twenty-first century into the stodgy WI."

"Is this the same WI as did the nude calendar?" Bruce asked.

"No, this is actually a different one."

"Makes one wonder what is going on in Yorkshire."

Max, feeling the conversation could be brought back into more productive lines, merely said, "It is hard to see how Wanda's . . . bossiness could have led to her death."

"You find it hard to see, do you? Well, you are a dear man. Wanda had a gift for the wounding remark. I was the recipient of more than one, before you ask."

"Really? Such as . . . ?"

"Such as what was I *really* doing in Nether Monkslip? Was I fleeing some scandal in London? Conjecture such as that." Her chocolate-brown eyes snapped dismissively. "Well, let me tell you, if I were the walking scandal of London, I'd like nothing better

188

than to hang about and see how it all played out. Oh, and was Bruce really my brother? Wanda would wonder aloud, eyes wide and aglow with malice."

"You're joking," said Max, looking over at the doctor, who shrugged resignedly.

"Not at all," said Suzanna. "Is that outrageous, or what? I suppose we should have threatened her with a solicitor or two. But I simply didn't care what Wanda thought, and if anyone believed her nonsense — well, so what? I told her more than once to go wax her you-know-what and leave me alone."

Max, genuinely puzzled, asked, "Her floors?"

Suzanna smiled. "No. Not her floors."

Bruce, horrified, said, "Suzanna!"

She looked at her brother. "What? Anyway," she continued, "others were unable to develop the rhinoceros hide required for dealing with Wanda."

"Lily, for example."

"For example. But there were others. Our Lily is simply less able to hide it when the arrows hit home. Very highly strung, she is. Of course, her uncle was barking — the one who left her the farm. People like Lily never learn to guard their expressions. Botox has taken care of that for so many nowadays."

"Still," put in the doctor, "still, there was

no reason to think Wanda might not have gone on forever, mixing her clichés and metaphors with reckless abandon."

Suzanna nodded. "So true. God moves in a mysterious way."

Didn't God just, thought Max. But in this case, he thought not. Man moved in a mysterious way, and often a terrible way. There was a lot of rivalry in a small village, Max had learned. Some cases of mutual loathing went on for years — rather like the typical feuds between MI5 and MI6. Something of the sort must be behind this, as incredible as it seemed.

Suzanna was saying, "I suppose we'll be blessed by a visit from the son now."

"Yes," said Bruce Winship. "I wonder if he'll bring the girlfriend? Wanda was telling us about her — or was it the Major? We had them over for bridge one night."

"Yes," said Suzanna. "And what was her name, the girlfriend? Something unusual. Clementia? — something like that. I remember thinking at the time it sounded like some kind of feminine complaint. Still, if one is burdened with an unusual name like Jasper, I don't suppose one can complain."

Max regarded her. She was observing the play of light on her whiskey glass. As he watched, she threw back her head and drank the dregs, displaying the long white stem of her lovely throat. Now she looked at him; her catlike gaze suddenly made him think of DCI Cotton. She struck Max as completely city bred, and as out of place here as . . . well, as people had thought him once. He then wondered aloud why Suzanna had joined the Women's Institute in the first place. "It doesn't seem your style, if you don't mind my saying so."

The doctor laughed and said, "I told her the same thing. It's a slippery slope; the thin edge of the wedge. Join the WI one day, join in the gossip at the Cavalier the next."

Suzanna, not offended, said, "There's bugger all to do in Nether Monkslip. And frankly, if you are not in the WI around here, you are totally out of the loop on all things. And what precisely is wrong with the occasional tea and bun at the Cavalier, anyway?"

The night was drawing in. Suzanna rose to close the heavy lined drapes against the night, stretching as she pulled the fabric ends together across the top. Max averted his eyes and trained them steadily on the mantel clock, as if he'd never seen such a mechanical marvel in all his days.

"You were a reporter once, weren't you?" asked Max when she was again seated.

"Must be a bit of a sea change."

"Oh, yes. Glamorous, right? Actually, it was a job I likened to going to work in a rice paddy every day. Although I knew that was an unfair comparison. The rice paddy didn't have my boss, the overpaid fuckup, in charge. It was basically a job rewriting press releases, so in theory it was easy. This guy spent most of his time walking over to see what I was doing, which was annoying in the extreme, since he himself never did anything. This seemed to be his full-time job, when he wasn't busy trying to look down the intern's dress, or mine, which explained (only partly — the content-free condition into which the paper had fallen may have had something to do with it) why the paper was in a constant state of financial crisis. Until it folded, which was a mercy for its readers, if not the staff."

Really, thought Max. With Suzanna one had to master the art of the bland expression that registered nothing.

"But then I moved here to our Brigadoon," she continued. "The rest you know."

Her look implied he could know so much more. So much.

"Well," he said, slapping his knees, as if preparing to leave. "Interesting. That's just so, erm . . . interesting."

"Isn't it?" she said. Again, the slow smile, the white teeth and the lip gloss gleaming. "Have you ever noticed how many of the villagers are transplants? Some of them have similar stories to tell — redundancies, retirements. Few people are from here. Which is going to make the police's job jolly difficult, I would think. Bad enough no one honestly seems to recall where anyone was during the Fayre, themselves included."

"And during the Fayre, you yourself were . . . ?"

Suzanna laughed, a tinkly sound that ran up and down the feminine scale.

"Oh, you don't seriously think I slunk off to do in poor old Wanda, do you? I think I find it almost flattering that you think me capable of such skullduggery."

Seeing that her flirtatious manner was not being all that well received at the moment, she reined it in. "I did see Wanda here and there that morning, and mark my words: she was up to something. Practically hugging herself with excitement at times. But mostly I was trapped behind a stall helping to sell children's clothing. Someone would have seen me," said Suzanna, with the confidence of a woman people did tend to remember seeing.

No alibi at all to speak of then, thought

Max. People, even men, couldn't have positively stared at her every second of the day.

"And you?" he said to Bruce, more out of a sense of inclusive thoroughness than anything else.

"Where was I? Well, you've got me dead to rights. Sorry, no pun intended. I was generally dogsbody — here, there, and everywhere. I did see Wanda steaming around earlier, being officious with the hoi polloi yet condescendingly gracious to any well-dressed visitors. Oh — and earlier, I saw her running around shouting 'Action stations, everyone!' — she might have been rallying some paramilitary force instead of our wretched band of volunteers — but that was early in the day."

"What sort of time was this?"

The doctor waggled one hand, a bird uncertain in flight.

"Rallying the troops was early on — say nine. You yourself were there being drafted for various tasks, as I recall. Then the lady-of-the-manor act came later. Noonish? Say, before noon and once things were well under way."

Well, that nails it down, thought Max.

Reading his expression, Bruce said, "It was a mash of people and even if I'd had one eye out for Wanda, I might not have spotted her. Anyway, no alibi for me. Sorry."

But he didn't look sorry. He looked like a man who didn't care one whit what anyone thought. A good quality to have, really, thought Max, to keep one from being at the mercy of the world.

Or was it a dangerous one, for a doctor?

CHAPTER 15
THE BAKER

It was Monday night, following his visit with Bruce and Suzanna Winship and the inquest of earlier in the day. Max, trying to relax, had been watching a BBC show on the Great Wall of China, back-to-back with a reprise of the Medici reign, a comparison which served to highlight both man's inhumanity to man as well as his endless inventiveness when it came to headgear.

When the Medici show was over, the news came on. He had for years been unable to watch the world news without wondering what untold story lay behind it. The further he got from MI5, the more he was falling out of that loop. The adjourned inquest into Wanda's demise was given a brief summary which highlighted the role of the WI and tried inanely to draw a cause-and-effect along the lines of "jam and scandal." Finally, the broadcasters wound up with a scolding little cautionary tale featuring Prince Harry, doing his best to fill the royal party-animal role vacated by Edward VII, Princess Margaret, and the Duchess of York.

Another knock at the door. This time, somewhat to his surprise, it was Elka Garth who stood there. She was looking over her shoulder in a way that suggested she was worried about being observed. Nearly as soon as he opened the door, she barreled in.

Max, following her into the study, did not have to guess at the cause for her visit.

She declined anything stronger, so they talked for the next half hour over a strong coffee that he prepared in the French press. Max took the occasion of fussing over cups and spoons to look at her: gray-threaded hair that cried out for a rinse or whatever it was women did to liven the color. Makeup haphazardly applied, but not thickly enough to mask the dark circles under her puffy eyes, just enough to settle into the surrounding creases. Her thick glasses magnified the sad effort at concealment, turning the creases into hills and gullies. The aging skin of her neck was starting to sag in origami folds.

Strange how worry and guilt produced the same corrosive effect on people's faces. He of course knew the trouble she had with her son — that he was a constant worry, and of little help or comfort. He also knew she was one of the hardest working women in the village, juggling, in effect, two shops where one would have been a full-time job, as well as operating her online store, which he supposed counted as a third shop. (The village was becoming so hi-tech even St. Edwold's had a Web site, but so far Max had firmly resisted all attempts to give the church a Twitter feed or a fan page on Facebook. Max had recruited a computer genius, aged twelve, to build the site and put the parish magazine online, and thereafter had induced him to remove the somewhat risqué avatars he had created for the churchwardens.)

Elka observed Max now out of those weary eyes — eyes that, though tired, held a spark of shrewdness. Seeing him sit back, still looking at her appraisingly, she launched right into the topic uppermost on her mind: "I couldn't be at the inquest today; I've business to attend to, as you know, and I wasn't summoned. But folk are saying it must be murder or the police wouldn't be so interested. I want you to know and I need you to understand: whatever happened to Wanda, it had nothing to do with me."

"All right," he said, thinking he'd take that

as a given, for now, since if Elka had wanted Wanda gone, it would be a huge risk to use a method that so clearly could be brought back to herself. "Has someone accused you?" he asked gently.

"No. But Guy was in the Cavalier telling people how she looked when she was found. You know him? Owns the French Revolution in Monkslip-super-Mare. Always reminds me of someone — some movie star or other. Anyway, it was allergic reaction, plain as day. My aunt had allergies like that and we knew the symptoms. Swollen face and lips, choking. Everyone knew Wanda was that allergic to peanuts. I did, too, which is why I was ever so careful to label things properly."

Max raised his eyebrows and held his peace. Wanda had come into possession of a biscuit or other food that to her was purest poison. How had it happened? Finally he asked, "This was your usual role for Harvest Fayre, wasn't it? The baked goods."

She nodded. "Me and a few others, mind. Baked goods, homemade-like, being popular on the day. Especially with the kiddies, but with everyone, really. An excuse to go off the slimming regime for a bit."

"So you brought along your goods on the day and displayed them for sale on a predesignated table, is that right?"

"That's right."

"There were extras held in reserve?"

"That's right."

"And those were in . . . ?"

She sighed. "They were in the Village Hall. In the kitchen. Along," she hastened to add, "with a lot of other cakes and scones and biscuits and things. There wasn't room to display it all, and we didn't want it all sitting in the sun for hours, anyway. So . . ."

"Was there anything that identified your contributions from anyone else's?"

"The biscuits came in boxes that I use in my shop, for bulk orders. But some I had put on paper plates covered in cling film."

"No way to differentiate them, then?"

"Not really, no. I would say that my goods were better than the average contribution, but I would say that, wouldn't I?" For the first time since she'd entered the room, a trace of a smile appeared on the usually friendly face.

Max regarded her, trying to frame the next question. Finally, he said, "Were you surprised by her death?"

She caught him off guard by saying, "No. Not really. You were expecting me to say I've never been so shocked, weren't you? But somehow with Wanda, the wonder

200

always was that she'd managed to live as long as she had."

"Does that mean you have ideas about who did this?"

"No, and that's the other side of the same coin. Who would actually do this? Want to do it, yes. Think about or plan to do it even, sure. But actually kill her? Impossible to imagine."

"You had your own issues with her . . ." Max let the unspoken part of the sentence hang in the air.

"You can't be serious." Elka twisted her features into an expression of distaste. "Everyone had issues with Wanda. But no one would kill her." It was clearly a subject on which her mind was made up and no mere facts were going to shift her.

"What exactly was the issue you had?" Max asked. He indicated the coffee pot for a refill. She shook her head.

"I'll be up half the night as it is," she said. "Not that that's anything unusual."

Max took a stab at what he guessed was the issue.

"Something to do with your son, was it? With Clayton." It was not really a question. Clayton was the dearest thing to her heart, and the cause for much of its heartache. She pursed her lips, reliving the grievance.

"It was just . . . Father, it was simply the attitude of superiority. Her son, such a high flyer. Clayton — well, he's a success in his own lights. He's reliable — well, mostly. I'm training him up to maybe take over the business one day . . ." Her voice drifted a bit on this last. The chances of Clayton maturing in time to take on such huge responsibilities must have struck even Elka as remote in the extreme. If not, her self-delusion was complete.

"Why did this have to happen?" she asked, the note of hysteria in her scratchy voice becoming more pronounced.

For the first time, Max wondered: Could Clayton have finally gotten his act together long enough to commit murder? Perhaps in some misguided attempt to become the protector his mother so clearly needed, at last?

The look in Elka's eyes suddenly made him realize: this thought had occurred to her as well.

CHAPTER 16
THE MAJOR

The following day, at nearly the end of September, was Michaelmas — the feast of St. Michael the Archangel. It was three days since the death of Wanda Batton-Smythe. Max felt it was time to pay his formal respects to her spouse, the Major. Max had telephoned soon after the tragedy to offer his assistance, but as was usual in these cases, the Major didn't even know yet what kind of help he would be needing. Max knew a follow-up call, in person, was in order.

His visit had an official investigatory tinge to it as well. He'd run into DCI Cotton on the High Street quite early that morning — almost literally run into, he on his morning run with Thea, and Cotton clearly engaged on his own keep-fit scheme. Knowing their conversation would be closely observed by anyone awake at that hour, they'd only taken time for a hushed consultation regarding Wanda's death, looking airily about them the while, as if commenting on the weather.

"I've kept one ear to the ground as promised but there's nothing I can tell you as yet," Max said. That was literally true: he decided, for reasons of his own, to say nothing of Elka's visit last night. Why point the police in the direction of Clayton, when there was nothing but his mother's worry as an indicator of his guilt?

"No new developments this end," Cotton had told him in his turn. "There's an undisputed lack of grief, except in the case of the husband. And his grief seems to be genuine. I'd say he's lost without her."

"That's a typical reaction," Max had replied. "Men don't realize how much their wives fill a void in their lives until they're left on their own. Many come near starving to death, for one thing. I'll be stopping in to check on him."

"I was hoping you'd say that. Try to see if he's remembered anything that could help our investigation — something he might more easily recall for you than when talking with me. I seem to make some people nervous." He smiled a devilish smile that made Max understand how people might clam up around him.

So a few hours later, having taken service and otherwise fulfilled his morning parish duties, Max stood at the door of Morning Glory Cottage and gave a tug on the old-fashioned bell pull. After quite a long wait, during which he had time to fully appreciate the tribute to Gothic architecture in the plate tracery windows overhead — windows perhaps more suited to a cathedral — the heavy door of the opulent bungalow was opened, and Max was admitted into a varnished hall worthy of a small stately home.

The Major (as he was always called — few could remember his real name, which was Montague) gave the clear impression of a man pottering around in the absence of his wife, quite lost, like a child handed a grocery shopping list and sent off alone to Sainsbury's. He hadn't a clue where to start and was looking for oranges, metaphorically speaking, in the bread aisle.

The man looked desperately tired. He had shaved, missing patches of white stubble and leaving a nick on his left cheekbone. The trickle of dried blood threatened to bleed anew as he attempted a welcoming smile. Now he pointed in the direction of a sofa in the sitting room and said tentatively, "Seat?" He looked troubled, however, as though wondering how such an object had found its way into his home.

From the sitting room, Max could see into the dining room and from there, the door being ajar, into the kitchen. The remains of a serving of what he imagined was tuna casserole, probably the well-intended gift of a neighbor, sat pungently congealing on a plate on the dining room table. The solitary table setting of placemat, fork, and glass struck Max as inexpressibly sad. The Major had many such lonely meals ahead of him.

"Would you like . . . something?" asked the Major hesitantly, waving a hand in the direction of the kitchen. "To drink, perhaps?" He paused, as if trying to remember the universe of beverages deemed fit for human consumption. "Tea?" he finally hazarded, a game show contestant desperate to beat the odds of a wrong answer.

"No, thank you," Max started to say, then suddenly realized what the Major needed might be exactly that British panacea. "Only if you'll let me make it. Actually, I'd love a cup. I'll just put the kettle on, shall I?"

The Major buying into this fabrication (Max had already had three cups that day during home visits), the next few minutes were spent in trying to sort out the location of the tea caddy, the kettle, the water, and the various other essential ingredients and implements, all of which seemed to mystify the Major. It was as if he'd never been in his own kitchen before. Indeed, Max thought it likely Wanda was one of those women who forbad men entrée into their exclusive domain, on the grounds of man's innate, clodhopping destructiveness in the presence of glassware and china.

Kettle on the boil, Max began the washing up, first depositing the casserole remains in the bin. The Major didn't extend even a token offer of help, not out of sloth, so far as Max could tell, but because he seemed hardly aware Max was still in the room. Wanda's imprint could be felt everywhere: every dishtowel looked to have been lightly starched and ironed, and every jar hand-labeled in black ink in a neat, precise hand.

The Major began absentmindedly eating a scone he'd lathered in peanut butter. Noticing Max's regard, he said somewhat guiltily, "Wanda wouldn't have it in the house, of course."

As he rinsed a few glasses, Max could see from the window to his left a small garden with flagged paths and nary a fallen leaf in sight. The Major must be one of those who found gardening therapeutic. He would feel the same way, Max imagined, if he had the time for it. The garden at the vicarage would soon wear a carpet of wet and dangerously slippy leaves if someone didn't see to it soon. Max had let it slide, and Maurice, who usually saw to such things for him, had not been much in evidence during the past week.

The teakettle screeched to announce that the water was boiling. Max found some cake in a tin and, putting one slice on a plate for the Major, arranged all the tea paraphernalia on a tray to take into the sitting room. He had the feeling the Major would infinitely have preferred they have their drink in the kitchen, but Wanda would not have stood for the informality with such an important guest as the Vicar in the house. Similarly, there are those who only allow visitors (but never tradesmen) in through the front door. So into the sitting room he and the Major must go. It was as if Wanda had never left the scene.

Handing out the tea things, Max took in the sitting room, consciously seeking out the photos that were often the most revelatory thing in any home. Everywhere were further signs of Wanda's absence: several days' worth of newspapers allowed to fall where they may, and several cups and saucers that needed to be cleared.

He spotted the photos on a sideboard tucked toward the back of the room. Max interrupted his task to walk over for a closer look. There was one recognizably of Wanda standing with the Major, she holding a small baby as her husband looked on, an expression of proud astonishment on his face. Max was himself astonished to see how lovely Wanda had been, before lines of dissatisfaction had etched themselves into her face. There was a more recent photo of two more elderly people — grandparents on one side or the other, more than likely. A picture taken at the seaside, with the Major looking fit and youthful and holding a small boy by the hand. A photo of what must be the son in his teenage years revealed him to be the spit of his father, albeit two stone lighter, and with an extra inch of dark rather than white at the hairline. The same dark eyes with perhaps a whit more of resolve in them gazed out of the photo, and presumably the boy's complexion was pale rather than gray (it was a black-and-white photo). Any resemblance to Wanda was not in evidence.

"I've forgotten the sugar," Max told the Major. This wasn't true, he had forgotten it on purpose, but he wanted a chance to inspect the room unobserved. Dutifully, the Major trotted out on this specious errand.

Max looked at some of the photos more closely, then looked about him, taking in the dull and utterly respectable décor. The only touches of reckless gaiety were a hammered-brass table and a matching pair of Japanese courtesan vases that had been converted into lamps. Both had no doubt been picked up during Wanda's travels as an officer's wife. The rest of the room was of a Laura-Ashleyish theme of prints and patterns of coordinating colors and contrasting patterns, a style so irredeemably British as to be impossible to eradicate from the Jungian collective design unconscious. Stretched across the width of the room was a blowsy, chintzy sofa for which it looked a thousand rosebushes might have been sacrificed. A surprising touch were several original oil paintings, accomplished and abstract in execution, and drawn from a bold palette. The colors clashed badly, however, with the already overheated color scheme.

Little upholstered stools and varnished tables were scattered about, cruel traps for the unwary, and Max had threaded his way carefully through them with the tray to reach the florid haven of the sofa. Becalmed before this sofa was a reddish brown, kidney-shaped table of fifties vintage and stupendous awfulness. Everything was scrupulously clean and neat, however, or had clearly been so in the time of Wanda's reign. But it was a cleanliness that was dispiriting rather than comforting or peaceful. It smacked of rules and rigidity, and, for all the Major's military background, it must have been rather a trial to live with. Or perhaps, Max reflected, he was merely extrapolating from what he knew of Wanda's character.

Near the sideboard were vintage stereo equipment and a collection of records. Max noticed the musical choices, which consisted, in part, of romantic hits of the halcyon days of the Batton-Smythes: "Turn the radio up for that sweet sound. Hold me close, never let me go . . ."

Not what he would have expected. What he would have expected he could not have said. John Philip Sousa marching music, or opera hits of the uber-bombastic type, perhaps.

The curtains were a focal point, and were of a fulsome wine red velveteen looped and draped and tied back with gilt-edged rope, a fitting frame for a production of *Figaro* more than for the normally mundane comings and going of the Nether Monkslip villagers. Max noted, however, how well situated was the window for anyone with more than a glancing interest in her neighbors' doings, and somewhat revised his opinion as to the appropriateness of the curtains. All the world was indeed a stage and Wanda had had a front-row seat.

The Major returned. He'd put some sugar in a coffee mug with a large tablespoon to ladle it out. Finding the sugar bowl was apparently beyond his capacity. Holding the mug, he gestured vaguely toward the window. "I haven't ventured out much. No one out there seems to understand."

Max nodded, sure that was true. The room was uncomfortably warm — heat from a gas fire mingled with the sun streaming in from the window. African violets would have thrived here. The Major didn't seem to notice. Perhaps he was at the age where too much heat was welcome for aching joints. What was he? — over sixty, surely. Maybe sixty-five. Forever "the Major," a higher rank having escaped him due to a stunning ineptitude not quite amounting to treason, although it had been a very close thing. At least, so Max had been given to understand. The people in charge had put him in administrative positions of increasingly lessening responsibility where, it was hoped, he could do only quiet harm. To Max, the Major seemed an innocuous man, to be found contentedly puttering in his garden, deferential to his wife (but then, like so many villagers, it seemed, having no choice in the matter).

He had served on the parish council, which is how Max had met him, but without distinction other than having the punctuality of Big Ben and near-perfect attendance. His fellows on the council treated his contributions with a mild contempt at which he seemed to take no offense. Max wondered if this was because he received worse at home, and so was used to worse. An unimaginative man, requiring orders to get through the day. And hadn't he married the perfect woman for that?

Because of a temporary defection of the Batton-Smythes to the church in Monkslip-super-Mare (Wanda preferred her church high), Max didn't feel he knew the Major all that well, however. There had been a certain awkwardness — on their side — following their defection and return. Not shamefacedness (Wanda was too brazen for that) but a sense that they'd been caught out in foolishness. Max, for his part, didn't care, except that it now left him feeling ill-equipped to cope with the Major in his grief.

He looked at the Major closely, guiltily, having spent much of his pastoral time until this point trying to avoid him.

Apart from the red nose that could light London, which was perhaps his most prominent feature, everything about the Major otherwise suggested a man bleached of character into a bland uniformity, whether because of his military duty or marriage to Wanda, Max could not have said. His other distinctive characteristic was a walrus mustache designed for twirling, each hair neatly marshaled into line. It was an embellishment of such luxuriant, glossy precision one could not help but be reminded of the famed little Belgian detective. His bushy white eyebrows normally were shellacked to within an inch of their lives into a roguish updo. As a result he perpetually looked happy and smiling, as if someone had just handed him a prize. Today, however, the mustache drooped and the eyebrows, freed of their usual constraint, veered wildly off in all directions.

Max spooned a mountain of sugar into his tea and said quietly, "What can you tell me, Major, about your wife, and what she was doing that day? Do you have any views on what led her to the Village Hall?"

Here the Major thought, and thought hard.

"That inspector chap asked me the same

thing, more or less. Well, she was president of the Women's Institute, of course."

Yes, yes, we know that. Max smiled encouragingly as the Major engaged the gears.

"She was of course a presence in the village, an important one, and thus expected to lead in the area of charity work and so on, so forth."

"And in her personal life? Would you say she was happy?"

The Major looked perplexed, as if Max had asked him to estimate the square footage of Istanbul.

"Yes. I would say so. Yes, definitely. Wanda's mother died last year, as you know. It was only to be expected. The poor old thing was ninety and had been fading for some time. But Wanda took it hard for a while. Quite naturally — they were close."

"Yes. Quite." In fact, Max had forgotten. Given the average age of his parishioners, and the nature of his calling, he heard quite often of a parishioner's losing one parent or another. It was difficult to keep so many passings straight in his memory.

Max saw that a beautiful Persian cat had entered the room as they talked and sat on a deeply cushioned chair in the corner — clearly it was Her Chair. She gazed with regal, cross-eyed contempt on the conversation, no doubt wondering how far the death of her mistress would go toward interrupting prompt mealtimes at Casa Batton-Smythe.

"She had no . . . enemies?" Max asked the Major. Softly, softly here. Max had little solid reason for his question, still less reason to upset the man unnecessarily.

"Enemies?" repeated Major Batton-Smythe bleakly. "Enemies! Why, Wanda was one of the most beloved of women. The very milk of human kindness flowed —"

Catching Max's mild and unintentional look of skepticism, quickly suppressed as it was, the Major said, "Oh, Wanda had *standards*. And people who won't or can't toe the mark may have resented having that brought up to them."

I'll just bet.

"But anything like a *real* enemy? Impossible."

Warming to his theme, the Major added, "She was a woman of great passions, Padre. Firm in her beliefs. Unstoppable." His voice broke on the last word.

Max, who felt there were many in the village who could testify to that — except that someone *had* finally stopped her — merely said, "A woman in a million, Major."

The Major nodded.

216

"Stood by her principles — that was Wanda's way. When she felt the hairdresser here in the village was overcharging for her hair treatments, she began going into Monkslip-super-Mare instead."

Thank heaven, thought Max, that we still have people willing to take a firm stand on the important issues. But he gave the Major a wan, approving smile.

The Major suddenly burst out, banging one fist on the arm of his chair, making the cat jump: "How in Hades did this happen? *How in Hades?* Oh, beg pardon for the language, Padre."

Max, whose everyday vocabulary and that of his colleagues in his former MI5 life could have scorched the earth, waved his hands munificently.

"Full of life, she was. Here we were, in the middle of planning a catered dinner party . . . She so loved to entertain in style . . . She loved people so. And who will there be to entertain the carol singers at Christmas? Think of the loss to the village."

Max imagined this was the biggest benefit of matrimony — to have someone who admired you without qualification, who made your slightest charitable impulse into a sacrifice of Mother Teresan proportions. Wanda was a subject which the Major would never be able to see in an undistorted way, that much was clear. Max asked a different sort of question now: "When did you first meet your wife?"

"We were both in the army, didn't you know? She was quite a different person in those days," the Major told Max. "Softer, perhaps. Always . . . rather straightforward in her thinking, of course. But Jasper's growing up and leaving — it changed her. It was a normal process, of course, but . . . it changed her completely. Empty nest, what? It was from that point, as I saw it, that the need for . . . control crept in."

Max waited quietly. He judged it not the time for further questions. The man would come to it in his own time and in his own way.

"We were happy here. Sometimes we *forgot* we were happy. All married couples do. But we were happy here."

It was a near-poetic sentiment for the Major, and Max felt the man's loss intensely, his attitude belying Max's earlier impression of there being no there, as it were, *there* when it came to the Major. Even he, who did not live in Morning Glory Cottage, could sense the emptiness of a house suddenly deprived of Wanda's spirit. How the Major was going to fill that vacuum Max

could not imagine. The usual diversions —
drink, women, birdwatching — seemed
outside Max's prior experience of the
Major. He was a man of no known hobbies
or interests, apart from a little golf, gardening, and local history. Would that prove to
be solace enough?

"Your son?" he asked, tentatively, returning the Major to the subject he'd only
skirted the edges of before.

"Yes, the one good thing to come of this.
I'll get to see him. Perhaps I can talk him
into staying for more than a few days."

"He was your only child, is that right?"

"Yes," the Major said briefly, leaving Max
to wonder if that were by medical chance or
by design, and if the latter, by design on
Wanda's part or his. Quite right for him to
be brief on the subject, thought Max, it's
really none of my business. And how it
could be connected to the murder anyway
he could not begin to fathom.

But the Major surprised him with an un-
customary breaking down of the barriers,
allowing Max a peek at the man behind the
bluster and the "Dress right, dress" habits
of thought.

"He was a single child and the only one
we were likely to have," he said. "The
thought of his loss terrified me sometimes.

Would it be better if I had had two children — the heir and the spare — or would that just make me worry twice as much?"

"I have the idea it can't be quantified, that kind of love," said Max.

"Yes," came the distracted reply. The moments passed, with only the soft *tick-tick-tick* of the ormolu clock on the mantel to disturb the deep quiet of the room. The clock featured Napoleon astride his horse, a nice accompaniment to the basic militaristic theme of the Batton-Smythe's existence. Just then it chimed the hour, and the Major, coming momentarily out of his stupor, noticed Max's regard.

"He'll be coming for the funeral, whenever they release the . . . the . . . *her.* Wanda," the Major said. "That's one thing good come of this sorry mess," he repeated, bitterly this time. "I haven't seen Jasper since his grandmother died." He indicated the mantelpiece with a vague toss of his head. "Left us that clock, she did."

Max avowed that the item was beautiful, then once again gently changed this subject back to the Major's son. There might be solace coming from that department, if he could keep the Major focused.

"He's done a bit of this and that," said the Major in reply to Max's gentle probing.

"He's exhibiting some paintings in Argentina at the moment, but I know he was in Italy several weeks ago. He's moved around Europe a bit, and further afield. Africa. The Far East. He found a girl at some point and that settled him. It comes to us all in the end." Apparently forgetting his grief for the moment, he gave a har-har, man-of-the-world laugh. "Before that, footloose and fancy free," he continued.

"You've never met her?"

"No. Perhaps she'll come with him to the . . . the . . ."

"Yes," Max said. "Perhaps she will."

The Major picked up a letter lying on one of the little tables in the room.

"This is from him. About a month old. Before . . ."

Max took the letter and envelope, which bore an Italian stamp and postmark. The letter was conventional in its phrasing, thanking his father for some money he'd apparently wired to his son.

Unsure how to act, scriptless for this kind of personal loss, the impulses flitted across the Major's face now like images on a faltering television screen. Finally, as something of the finality of the situation seemed to penetrate his understanding, he suddenly gave way to wracking sobs. This display

221

came to Max, who had been expecting a militarized version of the British stiff upper lip, as a relief. Grief was normal. Energy expended in buttoning it up was not. His face folded into an expression of compassion, Max comforted the man as best he could, giving him several resounding thumps between his shoulder blades, the standard macho expression of heartfelt sympathy. "There, there," he said. "I'm so frightfully sorry this has happened to you." Max knew instinctively that his human impulse to take the Major into his arms like a child would have been a gesture too much for the man to bear. When the Major's sobs began to subside, Max said, "We'll figure this out. Don't you worry."

He wasn't himself entirely sure what he meant by that. Figure out this grief? Figure out who killed her? Or wasn't it all part of the same process — of putting the horror of loss to rest?

Max didn't feel this was an act, unless the Major was far more cunning and duplicitous — not to say intelligent — than he had ever credited him with being before. It was clear to Max that the man had adored his wife — the contrast with her general loathedness in the village was a conundrum.

Grief was a curious thing that had no

rules. Sometimes, as Max knew, it sent you into a tailspin. When you awoke, you might find yourself halfway around the world.

Coming out of Morning Glory Cottage some time later, Max ran into Awena walking along St. Edwold's Road. She told him she'd just come from giving a statement at the Bobby Pod, and as if reading his mind, informed him, "I told them it was bollocks to suspect the Major. He'd never have done away with her in such a sneaky way. Doesn't have the brains for it. A cosh to the head in anger, maybe. But the fact is, he adored her. Thousands didn't, but he really did, the poor old bugger. Oh, sorry, Vicar. Pardon my French, if you will."

She bustled off in a swirl of opulently embroidered fabric. Watching her departing back, he realized the sturdy set of her shoulders reminded him of no one so much as Wanda herself. Another woman, albeit of a much different type, who would brook no interference.

He was recalled to his current mission, to find out what he could about the events surrounding the demise of the woman who would brook no interference. The woman, he thought, who liked to stir hornets' nests. Until someone stopped her.

Where to start? It seemed to Max that a return to the setting of the Harvest Fayre would be in order. Surely whatever had prompted someone to kill Wanda, the site of the Abbey Ruins was where it had all started — sadly, at the scene of what was meant to be one of her greatest triumphs.

CHAPTER 17
AT HOME

The death of Wanda Batton-Smythe affected everyone in the village, some more than others. Lily Iverson, expecting to feel something like relief, found her life surprisingly unchanged. There was always *something* to worry about, after all. Wanda was just one less thing.

Lily lived just outside the village proper in a farmhouse she'd inherited from her uncle — an old farmhouse fallen into disrepair that she had proceeded, in nearly miraculous fashion, to rescue from ruin. The ground floor, where she sat watching the news, was really one large room, with a kitchen occupying one end; at the other end she'd marked out a large living area with a colorful rug, a sectional sofa, a large square coffee table, and a refectory table she used as both dining table and desk.

A typical man of his generation, Lily's uncle had taken one look at her knobby-kneed, wiry-haired self, aged twelve, and privately predicted she would never marry unless a female-targeting plague killed off every other woman on the planet. Untypically for a man of his generation, he felt no contempt for a woman of single status, and set out to ensure she would at least have a roof over her head for her lifetime. That the roof in question leaked sporadically did not detract from the kind intent behind the bequest.

Lily gradually had turned the ramshackle farmhouse into something resembling a cozy and welcoming home — in the hours not filled to capacity by her burgeoning business. She had paved the narrow dirt track leading to the building, replaced mean little windows with larger ones to allow the sun to spill onto the old wooden floorboards, and generally applied a coat of paint to everything until the whole place shone like a showcase.

Upstairs were two bedrooms, one holding Lily's double but virginal bed, headed by a brass Victorian bedstead purchased from Noah's Ark; the other held a double walnut bed for guests that never arrived. (Lily's uncle, long a widower, had been her last living relative, and she had few ties to her old life in London.) Both beds were covered in knitted bedclothes of colorful and wondrous design, and appliquéd with flowers and animals, starbursts and sunbursts. Between the rooms, down a narrow hallway, Lily had had installed a bathroom gleaming with modern fittings. When she had arrived, the only convenience had been an outhouse, the only source of water an old hand pump at the kitchen's stone sink.

Between the kitchen and living area on the ground floor, where Lily spent much of her days, were an old spinning wheel and a loom she had found in the attic — objects that had once belonged to her aunt. Necessity being the mother of discovery (for Lily had been underemployed most of her life, and even living rent-free she needed spending money), in playing around with the equipment, Lily had come to realize that her real talent was to take wool and make from it uniquely beautiful creations in a riot of design and frill and color. Originally she had begun by purchasing wool from a neighbor's farm, spinning and dying the wool herself. Then she became particular about which sheep the wool came from, ascribing to the lambs as they grew different personalities and traits, and from there it had been a short step to buying the sheep themselves — complete artistic control.

She began labeling every new sweater design with a sheep's name. The Dolly model was so popular, especially in lavender, she could barely keep it in stock.

A boutique in Nether Monkslip had begun carrying her work; now Lily's creations and the licenses to reproduce them were much in demand: clothing and home furnishing boutiques in London, Paris, and Milan carried her designs. She also sold a great many to select customers over the Internet. More than enough to have moved into one of the fine Georgian houses in the village, for on occasion Lily felt her isolation keenly, but then where would she keep the sheep? And she was already looking into raising goats, too.

It was her isolation behind a gnarl of hedgerows that made her membership in the Women's Institute so important to her. Dolly and Co. were her friends but sometimes one needed human contact. And the threat that Wanda posed, all unawares, by her sheer awfulness was a threat that the timid, such as Lily, felt keenly.

But apart from that isolation, Lily was happy — for Lily. The care and feeding of the sheep was ridiculously satisfying, probably because they made so few demands and were unconditionally glad to see her.

She even liked the smell of the well-ventilated barn, which she kept so spotless, and filled with sweet-smelling hay and straw bedding, that it was hard to believe farm animals were anywhere nearby. She had the outlet for creativity in her design work, the work itself, and the reward of running a successful business — these things, most days, were enough. She tried not to remember or dwell on the other days.

For Lily had always been an anxious, highly strung personality, her mind like a channel tuned permanently to the emergency frequency. For many years she had been nearly anorexic, not because she feared gaining weight, but because she feared food. Everything was potentially contaminating, everything a potential health threat. If she couldn't boil it herself, she didn't eat it. Since her inheritance of the farmhouse, with its promise of fundamental security, however, many of these symptoms — as her uncle had hoped — had gone into remission.

But she remained the type of precise, neatly hemmed woman who would run her recyclable tins and bottles through the dishwasher before throwing them away. Turning off the telly and taking her empty plate and glass into the kitchen, she started to do this now, having emptied a container of mushy peas in preparing her meal. Then, catching herself (for she had sworn to try to loosen up, just a bit), she decided, just this once, to go wild. In a what-the-fuck gesture, she merely rinsed the tin in hot water for several minutes before tossing it into the recycle bin.

Half an hour later, she came back, retrieved the tin, and put it in the dishwasher.

Suzanna Winship was in her bedroom at her brother's house, touching up her French manicure while planning what to cook for their dinner. She and her brother had quickly fallen into stereotypical, sexually assigned household roles, but Suzanna didn't mind. Bruce was providing her a refuge — rent-free — while she sorted through the worst financial debris of going through a divorce. (There didn't seem to be a lot of emotional debris: her ex had been a faithless jerk and that was that as far as Suzanna was concerned.) If her presence in Nether Monkslip meant her brother got three square meals a day and unobtrusive, mildly entertaining company, she considered it a fair trade. She had begun helping him keep the books of his practice balanced, as well: being a doctor was 90 percent paperwork these days, it seemed.

What she was going to do in the future wasn't certain, but for now, this life suited her perfectly well — except for occasional tiny glimmers of boredom in the late afternoons. What a pity the Vicar didn't seem to be taking the bait.

It really was too bad, she thought, how Wanda had taken over the show at the Women's Institute. Of course, all that had changed now. And not a moment too soon, in Suzanna's estimation.

Suzanna had a wide competitive streak that had served her well in the thrust and parry of London life. While overall she was finding Nether Monkslip a blessed relief, she also had a vague sense of something missing, of mental muscles gone too long unused. The WI was chicken feed, of course, but it was what was available. Suzanna had enough self-awareness to realize that she didn't care much of a toss about the WI; the real fun would be in seizing the reins now that Wanda had been sent to her reward. In a way, she was sorry to have been cheated of seeing the look of outrage as Wanda was toppled from her throne at last.

It was petty.

It was small of her.

It was the reality of life in town and village, Suzanna reminded herself. Hard cheese if you don't like it, as her mother might have said. Suzanna stood, straightening her long, lithesome figure and throwing back her stretched-and-aerobicized shoulders. She had the carriage of someone trained to the stage, and she tended to make an entrance rather than simply walk into a room like a normal human being. It was a training that came more from knowing that every male eye followed her every move than from time spent trodding the boards, although she had done a fair amount of that in her college days.

Today she wore a short black wool skirt with a crisp white shirt. Around her neck was a frilly gray scarf of gossamer-like wool — one of Lily's creations. It was decorated at the ends with clusters of tiny cockle shells that rattled gently as they shifted across the vast expanse of Suzanna's chest. Silver ballet slippers that she wore at home were on her feet, replacing the spike heels on which she normally — some would say miraculously — teetered down Nether Monkslips's cobblestone streets.

Some hours later, after a gourmet dinner of chicken and wild rice, Suzanna sat quietly with Bruce by the fire, but she tossed aside her book (a racier-than-usual biography of the libidinous Catherine the Great and her horse) after reading a few chapters.

Like Catherine, she was a woman of many and diverse talents, and they were going to waste here in the village.

She wondered if it were too soon to put the cat among the pigeons.

Noah Caraway lived in a house that was a romantic's dream of what a house should be. Abbot's Lodge began as part of a Benedictine monastery before the buildings and the land they stood on, which included a lake and parkland, were appropriated by Henry VIII. Following the Dissolution of the Monasteries, only the Abbot's Lodge remained intact. Promptly forgetting the noble purpose supposedly behind these seizures, Henry handed the property over as payment to his courtiers, who themselves cashed in by selling it on. Neglect finished what greed and vandalism could not accomplish, and, apart from the Lodge, only the skeletons of these remarkable architectural achievements remained. Noah had been heard to say it was not unlike the job the Taliban had done on the ancient Buddhas in Afghanistan.

Max, walking across the fields toward Abbot's Lodge, reflected that the complex of medieval and sixteenth-century buildings had almost certainly been built on the site of an even older religious tradition, as were most abbeys and monasteries throughout England — a fact of which Awena Owen of Goddessspell never tired of reminding him. It was true: the sixth-century St. Augustine and his monks had had an immeasurable and lasting impact on the beliefs and the very appearance of the country. Abbot's Lodge reflected their success, with the Lodge now restored to much of its original glory.

It helped, as was always the case when indulging romantic architectural fantasies, that Noah seemed to have endless supplies of money. Noah's Ark Antiques of Nether Monkslip was viewed by many as a front, a rich man's hobby, and Noah himself merely a dilettante, for the shop was closed more often than it was open. The "Open by Appointment" sign on the door was felt by many to be disingenuous, at best, as the telephone number to which the visitor was referred generally went unanswered. It was widely regarded also as a tax fiddle, although no one could quite say how the fiddle benefited Noah — other than the fact that he could indulge his love of beautiful things, unrestricted, with room to store the overflow from his own house.

But Noah's Ark, unlike many of its kind in the trade, sold (when it was open) real antiques, not secondhand rubbish. In his more candid moments, Noah admitted he found it difficult to part with any of the acquisitions he made for his shop.

Max, who had called ahead, now went around to the back of Abbot's Lodge, as he knew was customary: Noah could more often than not be found "whipping up a little something" for tea or some future snack or meal — although the word "snack" demeaned the whole enterprise. The "little something" would earn five stars in any gourmand's universe.

Max detoured before he reached the terrace at the back, however, turning his steps toward the Abbey Ruins. He looked up, and then about him. The hubbub that had reigned during the Fayre was gone; it was completely still. A blurry sun sat atop a clump of gray clouds like a portent of the world's end.

Part of the reason for his visit was to spy out the lay of the land and confirm his belief that the view toward the Village Hall from anywhere in the Fayre grounds was obstructed. He found he was right: the spinney of Raven's Wood blocked the view wherever he stood in or near the ruins, and the only possible clear view not blocked by Morning Glory Cottage was obstructed by the mound beneath the Plague Tree and the huge old tree itself. His impressions confirmed, he turned back toward Abbot's Lodge.

Noah, seeing him as he approached the flagged terrace, greeted Max with his customary effusive warmth and then led the way through the kitchen past the enormous refectory table — a table that somehow always made Max think of homemade soup and thick slices of bread lashed with yellow butter. Noah, himself a bit doughy in build, was a dapper and well-groomed man, today wearing trousers and a tailored shirt of the finest wool, with an elegant belt and shoes of matching leather. Balding, he wore glasses in trendy black-and-green rectangular frames. He had a face formed for humor — round, puckish, and often alight with mischief.

The two men headed toward the drawing room ("Too cold now for sitting in the garden — more's the pity"), Noah carrying an enormous polished silver tray of tea things and homemade sandwiches and biscuits. Max noted that some of these were peanut biscuits, and wondered if they were Noah's own or if they came from Elka's bakery. Life went on, he supposed, but he did wonder how often the sight of a peanut biscuit would evoke disagreeable memories in the village. Hungry (Mrs. Hooser would have blamed this on an inadequate breakfast), Max followed Noah and his tray down a long carpeted corridor, the strains of "Le roi s'amuse" in the background. Max was not a connoisseur but this gentle, lively music he recognized.

Both walls of the corridor were lined with oil paintings of inestimable value, and the corridor itself led in shotgun fashion to double-reinforced glass doors through which could be glimpsed the starkly haunting Abbey Ruins. Noah had positioned floodlights throughout the grounds; when he held a dinner party, the beauty of this scene at night took one's breath away. They passed the door to the dining room with its vast fireplace, prompting Max to recall many a convivial meal in the company of Noah and his numerous gifted acquaintances.

They reached the end of the corridor, and Noah indicated that Max should open the door on the right. Noah carried the tray into the drawing room, which was another inviting room of dark-timbered walls and polished wooden floors with rich rugs scattered everywhere. Here a fireplace large enough for a man to stand in dominated one wall.

Against another wall was a large, built-in cabinet where porcelain Dresden figures, hard at work gathering flowers, and Staffordshire shepherds and shepherdesses were lined up with martial precision, like the vanguard of a Roman army. A painting of one of Noah's ancestors looked down upon the shepherds from across the room — a man in royal blue wearing the frills and feathers of his day, his rosy face gleaming with smug self-satisfaction. Antique furniture dotted the room; Noah's collection of teapots filled another matching cabinet.

Max had to hand it to Noah. While extensive repair and renovation had been necessary at Abbot's Lodge, not to mention modernization to make it all habitable in the twenty-first century, nothing looked glued on or out of place. The house always seemed to shimmer, glowing with the patina of centuries — partly the result of the cunning spacing of windows, it was true, plus the fact everything Noah served was poured into sparkling cut glass and presented on bone china of near-transparent fineness. But Max chose to believe the pervasive glow held remnants of the sanctity of the place itself: close your eyes, and you could almost hear the strains of the monks' chanting.

Noah indicated a little gilt chair for Max to sit in — a chair whose sale might have helped repair half the church's roof. These were always the worst moments at Noah's — everything looked to be of a venerable age and of matchless value; everything looked so fragile and ancient that one felt the slamming of a door might cause it all to disintegrate. Max lowered himself carefully and perched on the edge of the seat, thighs tensed and ready to spring at the first creak of imminent collapse. As often before (for Noah was an inveterate entertainer, and the Vicar was frequently on the guest list), Max felt as if he'd blundered into an exquisite dollhouse and grown extra arms and legs with which to knock things over.

Max had come to know Noah Caraway the previous year, when his mother had died and Noah had come to the vicarage to discuss the arrangements. Max had been struck by the man's humor, and by his forbearance in the face of what was clearly a primal loss.

Noah sorted out the tea and then, in response to some gentle questioning on Max's part, began talking of the events of the day of the Fayre. He told Max what he had seen, and had reported to the police, which was Wanda disappearing at the halfway point in the day.

"Nether Monkslip's own warrior queen," said Noah, with a grin. "Boadicea had nothing on our Wanda. Anyway, I was taking a little tea break or I might not have noticed."

"Unusual, wasn't it? Her disappearing like that?"

"Like a comet giving up the spotlight, so to speak. Yes. Wanda was always one to think her presence essential to the success of any event, if not the very survival of the human race. No meeting on any topic was complete without her ringing input, did you ever notice?" He sighed. "Not since the time of the enclosure riots has there been so much kerfuffle as over this Fayre."

"Do you have any idea where she got to?"

"Well, apparently, she got to the Village Hall, where she was found dead."

"Yes, presumably. But did you see her headed that way?"

Noah shook his balding head decisively. His mouth was one long squiggle, like a child's drawing. "Neither saw nor heard. And with Wanda, it was more likely to be the latter, for miles 'round. No, it would seem she positively *snuck* off. I'll tell you what else was odd . . ."

"What was odd?"

"She was excited, hepped up," Noah replied.

"Well, she usually was hepped up about something."

"Yes. I guess what was odd was that she looked, well, *happy*. Even rapturously so. You didn't often see Wanda looking happy. Busy, self-important, yes. Happy, no."

That struck a chord. What was it Cotton had said? That someone would come forward to say they'd seen Wanda, looking either wild-eyed, despondent, or deliriously happy — or all three at once.

"I do see what you mean. That *is* a bit odd," said Max.

"Generally she stood, stolid, immutable as Hadrian's Wall — a talisman against sloth, against the beauty of the wasted, idle hour — when she wasn't rushing about, haranguing everyone to pieces. Biscuit?" Here he offered one of the plates; Max took a wedge-shaped confection that looked like it might be lemon flavored. Noah made his own chocolate selection and chewed contentedly for a moment. "But, overall, Wanda was at a dangerous time of life, looking down the diminishing horizon as she hurtled toward death, assessing the detritus. Perhaps the passage of time could change even her. In the immortal words of the crooner, 'Is that all there is?' It passes through all our minds, does it not?"

"You're asking a vicar that question?"

Noah smiled. "Of course. It's practically a job requirement."

"What was she, about fifty?" asked Max. "It's a dangerous time for men, too, although hardly an ancient age for anyone in these days."

"She was always dangerous, if you ask me." Noah's expression was one that Max recognized and was willing to exploit in the name of getting at the truth: joy in discussing the doings of the village and the villagers. Noah was an inveterate gossip, and Max was relying on this proclivity.

"You know about the cocktail fiasco?" Noah asked now, wiping his fingers with pretended disinterest on a napkin of starched white linen. He seemed to be near hugging himself with suppressed excitement.

"Only the broad outlines."

"*Well.*" Noah settled himself more deeply in his chair. "Suzanna got it into her head that the Women's Institute needed a break from the stodgy, from the mundane, from the tips on how to pickle this and stuff that.

243

So Suzanna suggested they all get pickled with a course on how to mix cocktails. Not really, of course, but that was the result. They had a 'mixologist' come in to demonstrate. Wanda never let her or anyone else within earshot forget it."

"They sampled the mixologist's wares, I gather."

"For hours. Drunk as lords, they were. In some cases search parties were sent out. Mrs. Bandy was found asleep hours later on Hawk Crest, much the worse for wear."

"And Wanda blamed Suzanna."

"Didn't she just."

"How well did you know Wanda?" Max asked. "For example, where was she from originally?"

"Why, do you know, that I couldn't say, really. Almost no one here is *from* here — I've been here yonks but the oldest villagers consider me one of the 'young' upstarts who've invaded their tranquil village." Noah, in his forties, waggled his fingers in quotation marks on the word "young." "But as for the rest of us, the newcomers, we've all just come to respect your right to have come from wherever you want, or at least we don't question that right. Odd, when you come to think of it. I want to say she began life in Yorkshire but I can't think why

244

— she had a trace of an accent, perhaps, but carefully ironed out. She'd catch herself just in time, saying 'nowt' for 'nothing' and dropping an h — saying 'er' instead of 'her' — that kind of thing."

Carefully husbanding his expression to have his question received as neutral, Max said, "You got along well with her, did you?"

The look of surprised outrage on Noah's face was almost comical.

"Do you know *anyone* who got along with her?" he demanded.

"Apart from the Major, no."

"Do you think that's genuine?" Noah asked, then answered his own question: "I suppose when two people have been in harness together that long, it's a shock to lose the familiarity, if nothing else."

"Did you?" Max repeated. "Get along with her?"

"Well . . ."

Max waited, giving every sign of being willing to wait forever. Noah capitulated with a shrug.

"Well, she once got the better of me in a business deal. It doesn't happen often, I can tell you, and I wasn't best pleased."

"Really?"

"Yes. I know." Wounded professional pride struggled with personal dignity. "Hard to

245

imagine, isn't it?"

"What happened?"

"She had two chairs she'd inherited from her mother. You know the old battle— the old woman died last year. Wanda wanted to sell them and extorted a ridiculous price. She knew how I was about mahogany Chippendale — mad for it — and she had two chairs she swore had been made by Chippendale himself. I doubted that part of the story very much, but at least I was sure the chairs were authentically from his shop, as it were."

"And they weren't."

"Well, yes and no. Parts of each were real."

"I don't follow."

"Someone had got hold of a real Chippendale and cannibalized it for parts. They'd also got hold of a Victorian copy and taken what they needed from that and cobbled the whole thing together."

Max's face reflected his puzzlement. Noah, seeing this, asked the unspoken question: "Why would they do that? Because a set of chairs is much more desirable than a single chair. Victorian reproductions are antiques in themselves, but not to the level of a real Chippendale."

Warming to his subject, he said, "Now, it is one thing to replace parts of an authentic antique, up to ten percent of the whole, and be honest about the repairs. This was a wholesale mishmash of chair parts — two Frankenstein's monsters made from one real thing. A tragic, criminal waste by someone unscrupulous enough not to care. This kind of thing goes on all the time, more than ever before, since the number of real antiques left in the world is rapidly diminishing."

He added, his voice thick with remembered resentment, "It's the oldest artful dodge in the trade, and I fell for it. It ticked all the right boxes . . . Maybe I just didn't want to know."

"Surely Wanda was unaware . . ."

"That the chairs were fake? You know, I will never know that for certain. I know only that she didn't have the skill or tools to perpetrate such a fraud herself. She — or to be precise, her mother — may have been taken in by a dealer with ties to a skilled cabinetmaker."

Noah stood restlessly — a genial, dapper man of middle years, with a crustless watercress sandwich now gripped forgotten in one hand. Max counted him as a friend, as he had been both generous with his hospitality and staunchly welcoming when lines were being drawn over Max's selection as vicar. Max pushed these favorable thoughts aside, setting apart his liking for the man, and reverting to old and entrenched MI5 methods: everyone was a suspect, and there could be no favoritism shown. Noah now walked over to the mantel, made a minute adjustment to the position of the ormolu clock which sat there, and turned back to face him.

Max asked him, "Why are you telling me this?" For had Wanda not been murdered, he doubted he would have come to hear of the affair of the chair, which by any standard hardly rose to the level of tragedy. More a tawdry little village episode among, undoubtedly, dozens over the years. Funny how murder pulled back the curtain to expose events — events that might or might not have a bearing.

Noah gave him a wry grin. "I'm not sure why. Perhaps I'm just going on the principle that you'd find out anyway. It made the 11:00 a.m. news at the Cavalier some time ago."

"Or perhaps you are a naturally honest individual."

Noah smiled modestly and, with a wave of the sandwich, acknowledged the compliment. "Perhaps."

"How did you find out that something was

suspect about the chairs?"

Noah grimaced at the memory. "I had a friend visiting — a man also in the antiques trade. He looked it over and saw the fraud."

"When was this?"

"Last week."

"At the Fayre?"

Noah nodded. "Just before."

"And you confronted Wanda."

"Well, no, you put it like that. I, well, I . . ."

"You confronted her."

"Yes. All right, yes. I 'confronted' the old horse trader. She told me she'd sold me what she thought were two genuine chairs, and she still thought they were genuine. But I didn't really believe her, you know. First she swore the chairs were genuine, then in the next breath she did a big song and dance disclaiming all responsibility if they weren't genuine."

"So, 'Let the buyer beware' was her attitude."

"Yes, that's it exactly," said Noah, the expression on his face now positively sour. "No apology, no hint of putting things right with me, or attempting to verify what my friend said was true. 'I'll go to my grave believing the chairs my mother left me were real' — she actually said that." He gave Max a look of horrified understanding of the import of those words.

"And that's what she did, not long afterwards," Noah said bleakly. "Wanda went to her grave."

CHAPTER 19
WHAT'S COOKING

The wind had kicked up and Max, on leaving Abbot's Lodge, found himself in a changed world of scudding clouds and overcast skies. Leaving the safety of Noah's house, a home surely graced by long centuries of prayer, he seemed to have stepped into an enchanted but sinister parallel world that Awena might have recognized.

He pondered what next to do. Noah's revelations certainly cast new light on Wanda's character, but didn't they similarly cast a light on Noah's motivations? Still — would a guilty man have admitted what transpired over those antique chairs? While the Major might have mentioned it to Max or to any of the other villagers, in actuality the chances of Max's ever hearing of the dodgy transaction were slim. Maybe it was in the nature of a double-blind — a "full" confession on Noah's part to mask his deeper involvement in Wanda's death.

251

Max hadn't told Noah he was talking to him partly at the instigation of DCI Cotton — of course he hadn't. How Max chafed now at the subterfuge, even knowing it was in the cause of truth, of finding Wanda's killer. But something in him jibbed, even at that sound and logical excuse. Wasn't that the reason always given him for the lies and deceits of his MI5 days? But then, he'd had to go on whatever was told him about the justice of a given cause. This, he knew for himself: the worm that had insinuated itself into the goodness that was Nether Monkslip had to be destroyed.

As he walked in the waning hours of daylight, head down into the wind, his steps took him toward the High Street, and he found himself standing in front of the Cavalier Tea Room. He had half intended to go in, but at the sight of the avid faces peering at him from the window, he had a sudden change of heart. After pretending fascination for a few moments with what the nearby newsagent's window had to offer, he set off in the direction of his old Land Rover. He would go into Monkslip-super-Mare for an evening meal near the harbor, first stopping for a word with the priest at St. Alban's on some minor but long-neglected church business.

And he knew exactly who else he wanted to see while he was in town. Perhaps just an appetizer course wouldn't break the budget.

At French Revolution, Guy Nicholls popped his head out the swinging kitchen door long enough to say, "Just a sec and I'll be with you" before popping back in again. Max had only time to note that his hair stood out in its usual artless tufts — the kind of coiffure that sold for seventy pounds sterling in London, but might today simply be the result of harried preparations for the evening trade. The door, as it swung closed behind Guy, pushed out the heavenly scent of just-baked bread mixed with the slow sizzle of garlic in olive oil.

Max picked up a menu he'd taken from the reception stand and perused it idly as he waited. The descriptions of the offerings just escaped the sanctimony of most trendy new restaurants: even the humble coley had a place on the menu. His eye caught on the lobster risotto starter flavored with basil and orange, the main-course turbot with tartar sauce and peas, and the honey-and-whiskey parfait to finish — although the chocolate mousse with black cherries ran a close second. He heaved a wistful sigh, even though tea at Noah's amounted to a full meal of Edwardian proportions. Everything sounded delicious, even the standard warnings about allergies and consuming raw food at the bottom of the page. If the food was as good as it sounded, French Revolution was in for a good run. Perhaps he'd find a special occasion to dine here one day.

Guy eventually emerged from the kitchen, wearing black-and-white checkered chef's pants and a white cotton chef's jacket, meticulously starched and ironed. Well-muscled and athletic, he moved with a lithe, nimble grace, weaving his way in and out between the closely spaced tables while managing to balance a heavy tray over his head. If he sampled too much of his own wares, as chefs were said to do, Guy was evidently at pains also to work off the calories.

"I thought you might want something while you waited. I'll be right with you." With that, Guy placed a glass of white wine before him, and a small plate of the lobster risotto described on that night's menu. Max could hardly believe his luck — how did the man know?

Max watched as Guy served a lone middle-aged couple in the far corner. Apparently being the chef/owner also involved pitching in to help wherever needed. Max reflected that he had come across many men like Guy in his career — in tight situations, they were often the most useful of men, because of their intelligence. They were natural leaders, as those around them sensed that all risks taken would be carefully calibrated to enhance everyone's chances of survival. Liking had nothing to do with it, really, although Guy struck him as a highly personable and attractive man, with his choppy hair, his craggy mien, and his earrings lending him the touch of a Renaissance man. He returned carrying two cups of coffee as Max was polishing off the risotto, which was perfection. He set the cups on the table and, pulling out a chair, said, "I'm afraid I may have to run out on you if we get busy. Midweek is usually slow, though." He signaled to a passing waiter: "*Crème et le sucre* — cream and sugar, please."

Settling in and turning to face Max, he said, "What a rum business, this thing with Wanda. I assume that's why you're here — word is getting around that you've been talking with people about it, sort of officially-slash-unofficially on behalf of the police — or so the villagers think. You know how they gossip. The world really is going to hell, isn't it?"

While it wasn't clear if Guy were saying the police must be desperate to call on a priest for investigative services, Max assumed he meant that Wanda's murder, taken in the context of a depressingly high national crime rate, was generally deplorable.

He merely said, "I certainly hope not. That would make my job a lost cause before it started."

Guy looked puzzled for a moment, then laughed.

"Right. We're *not* going to hell with men like you at the wheel."

They were interrupted by the waiter bringing the coffee accoutrements. Max looked around. The restaurant, while pub-like in appearance, seemed to be a conversion of a large private dwelling. Max placed its origins somewhere in the seventeenth century. It now was spartanly modern in decor, but with whitewashed walls beneath beamed ceilings, crisp white tablecloths, and late summer flowers on each table, it exuded a low-lighted coziness that would encourage customers to dwell over several courses with wine. A gray cat slumbered on the hearth, so unmoving that Max at first thought it was merely ornamental until it turned, stretching out one unsheathed paw.

"Things are going well with the restaurant, you say?"

Guy nodded. "Better than I could have hoped. I'm trying something different here — a return to basics, really. I wasn't sure it would fly. But I knew in this economy, fancy restaurants were failing left and right."

"It must make a change from Paris."

"Hmm." A nearby waiter, apparently unused to juggling heavy trays, had caught his eye; Guy watched until he was safely inside the swinging door into the kitchen. "I bought the place from old man Gardner, who was retiring," he said, returning his attention to Max. "He'd done the work, long ago, of converting the kitchen area and installing the equipment. That's usually the worst part of a conversion, anyway. It was the menu and the seating areas that I had to build from scratch. I was a pâtissier in my former life, but I got fed up with the whole Michelin-starred restaurant scene. Far too much pressure there, to keep chasing after the brass ring that is always *that* much out of reach." He held up thumb and finger, an inch apart, to demonstrate. Another burnout case like me, thought Max. But in a different way from me. At least, he didn't imagine people were killed when a soufflé fell, although he had heard of people taking their own lives over a Michelin star.

"I saved up enough to travel around, and regain my sanity," Guy was saying. He offered the cream and sugar to Max, who refused, then he flavored his own coffee with minute servings of each. "I spent some time in Mumbai and a few other places, but then I returned to Europe. This time I worked at a *cave à manger* — a wine bar. The new generation wants something more casual — basic wholesome food, less expensive. The recession changed everything, but this trend started even before." Guy warmed to his theme. "Before we had God-knows-what style. I mean, fuck fusion cooking. Oh, excuse me, Father . . . um, Reverend. I meant no disrespect. Anyway, food has all these fads, you see, and once everyone is through running around experimenting and being arty-farty — sorry — what you are left with is a populace desperate for a nicely cooked rare steak with two veg. That's what I aim to provide, only better than anything anyone in Monkslip-super-Mare has ever tasted. You'll see if we haven't driven Jeanne d'Arc out of business by the end of next year."

Max noted for the first time the rings of exhaustion under the other man's eyes.

"It's hard work, I know, the restaurant life.

That's why I always overtip," Max told him. It was true. He always emptied his wallet over waiters, especially young people, because he was so thrilled to see them employed, regardless of the service, so long as it wasn't rude service.

Guy smiled. "That plate was on the house, no worries. Tell your friends, though. Actually, a mention from the pulpit wouldn't hurt."

That earned him a small chuckle. Max, turning the conversation, asked, "Did you notice Wanda in particular during the Fayre that morning?"

Guy laughed, and Max was struck anew by his youthful handsomeness. He had to be over forty, but the force of life was strong in him, taking years away, even with the fine etching of wrinkles and those dark circles beginning to appear under his eyes. Here was a man fully engaged in his world.

"Notice her? Well, no more than you did, I dare say. Doing the 'Dance of the Sugar Plum Fairy' she was not. I don't think Wanda had quiet days, like most folk. I hid in the marquee all morning, surrounded by a wall of people, and didn't emerge until I ran into you on your way to the Village Hall."

"Did she look happy to you?"

"I guess so. Happy, for her."

Max considered this slowly.

Just then an attractive blond waitress walked by. Not too subtly, Guy gave her a wink, then followed her surging, hip-swaying progress with his eyes. The incident seemed to prompt his next remark.

"Damned attractive woman, that Suzanna Winship. She's got her sights set on you, my good man — or didn't you notice?"

Max shot him a warning grimace and changed the subject.

"I wanted to ask if you remembered anything that struck you as unusual, that day we found Wanda — now that you've had some time to think about it."

Guy laughed at Max's expression. "If you are really not interested, would you mind . . . ?"

"If you asked Suzanna out? Of course not."

"Brilliant. Now, about Wanda that day. I've thought about it quite a lot, and I've come up with nothing that seemed — I don't know, that suggested she was headed for disaster. Do you have any theories?"

"None," said Max flatly.

"I was knocked for six when we found her," said Guy. "Just unbelievable, isn't it?"

"That seems to be the general reaction.

But we'll have to start believing it if the killer is going to be caught."

Guy shook his head. "One minute she's after me to do a presentation for the Women's Institute — 'One Hundred Ways with Zucchini,' you know the kind of thing. Or to cater a meal for her — of course, she wanted my services practically for free. And then, the next minute it seems, she's gone. It really makes you think, doesn't it?"

"That was your only extended contact with her?"

"Just about. Of course, I got dragged into donating to the Fayre. No one was immune. But it was for charity, so no one really complained. Not really."

Max said, "Wanda came into Monkslip-super-Mare periodically — for one thing, she used the hairdresser here in town rather than the one in the village, according to her husband. Did she ever stop in here, perhaps for lunch?"

"Never. Not that I'm aware, and I'm here most days. I live above the shop, as it were. For now, until I have time to buy my own place. Then I'll expand the restaurant into the upstairs rooms, when the timing's right. Anyway, I'll ask the staff to be sure — they'd remember her if she'd ever come here."

"Wanda did have that effect."

Max sipped his coffee, which was excellent and carried a slight sweet scent of chicory. Putting down his cup, he said, "She doesn't appear to have had many friends, people she confided in."

"Odd you should say that. I was just going to tell you: not she but the Major did confide in me. I was taken aback. You know how he is — the original stiff upper lip. Not a confiding sort at all. Anyway, I used to see him in the village, you know, pottering about, looking important, or trying to. I'd go in there for supplies — the fresh produce from the farms around Nether Monkslip is often better than what I can get here. Anyway, one day I stopped in the Cavalier and there he was. He invited me to sit with him. Well, I didn't want to really, but I could hardly refuse. He started talking about the son, Casper."

"Jasper," corrected Max.

"Jasper. That's right. Well, I gathered Jasper was trying to find himself and the Major was worried about the length of time it was taking."

"Many of that generation are," said Max. "Trying to find themselves, I mean. More so than at any other time in history, is my impression."

Guy laughed. "Well, if what the Major said

262

was true, he wasn't trying to find himself through any sort of paid job. The whole time he lived in Nether Monkslip, after he finished school, he wasn't looking for work, which I gather was the problem for Wanda. Well, all the evidence suggested he wasn't looking — drawing and painting all day instead. I guess she didn't see that as work. So Wanda chucked him out one night. And who can blame her?"

"I didn't realize you knew the family so well."

"I don't," said Guy smiling. "This bit about the chucking out — the Major didn't tell me that. It was picked up in a mere half hour when I stopped at the Cavalier for tea on a different afternoon. Information has to be pieced together in Nether Monkslip to make the whole sometimes."

"The village grapevine."

"God, yes. Isn't it something? Everybody knows everybody and everything. I'm glad I'm living over here. I miss a lot and that's fine by me. But there were other occasions. For example, the Major also let some things slip in talking one evening at the Hidden Fox. So I don't imagine he confided in me especially — I think half the village may have heard him whinging on. He and Wanda were not exactly love's young dream, you

263

know, and disagreements about Cas — I mean, Jasper — were part of that."

So, thought Max. The chance to put the Major in the frame as the most likely suspect was known to many, if what Guy said was true. Max imagined it was. "He had, as they say, 'issues' with his son's vocation as well?" he asked.

Guy spread out his hands in a "Who can say?" gesture. " 'Every unhappy family is unhappy in its own way' — isn't that the saying?"

"Tolstoy would certainly have known something about that in his own life. Anyway, when was this, when you spoke with the Major at the Fox?"

Guy sighed. "Now you're asking, it must have been a night when the WI was meeting. I don't think the old boy would have been off his lead otherwise. Maybe two weeks ago? Three? I had gone into the village and stopped in for a quick half pint. The regular delivery man had failed to show so I was reprising my jack-of-all-trades role. I could look the date up if it's important."

Max shook his head.

"I doubt it." He blew out his cheeks. Apart from the risotto, it hadn't been time well spent.

■ ■ ■ ■

An hour later, well after dark, he returned to Nether Monkslip. He was just parking the Land Rover as DCI Cotton was coming out of the police pod. The detective waved him over.

"Just the man I wanted to see," said Cotton. "Any news?"

"Nothing that gets us any forwarder, I'm afraid. I've just come from Guy Nicholls's restaurant. Apparently, there was some friction between Wanda and the Major."

"So says half the village."

"Sorry, I did realize that probably wasn't news to you. However, I also learned that Wanda and Noah, our local antiquarian, had come to a disagreement." He briefly explained what Noah had told him earlier that day.

Cotton said, "Noah's not the only one who had 'issues' with her, usually over something of that nature. Something trivial, but maddening if you were on the receiving end. She seems to have been a bit money mad."

"If that's another way of saying 'cheap,' I'd have to agree."

"I'm afraid it's really not much in the way

of motive, though, is it? Not something a jury might buy. We've talked with everyone about the Fayre — their whereabouts and so on. Their stories are so identical as to be interchangeable. For example, Lily Iverson was selling her knitted goods all day, she says. Dozens of people saw her doing it. That sort of thing. Anyway, I'd like you to look over the Village Hall with me, now forensics have done with it and it's been restored to order. We've had a bit of a break in one direction. We just don't know what it means."

There was a constable guarding the entrance to the Village Hall, a young man not too many years away from doing his homework and playing video games.

He stepped aside as DCI Cotton turned the lock on the outer door, and he and Max went into the building.

Cotton turned to him and said, "We've interviewed Maurice — he's some sort of village all-around handyman, I gather?"

"That's right. And he often deals with repairs and so on around the Village Hall, and the vicarage."

Max pictured Maurice: a gentle, somewhat backward man who nearly had to be dissuaded from tugging on his forelock, and whose thick, expressive eyebrows gave him an unfortunate resemblance to the crazed author in *The Shining*. He was always to be seen with a toothpick tucked behind his ear. Whether it was the same toothpick or not, Max was never sure.

"Was he able to help you?" Max asked.

Cotton indicated the old-fashioned door lock. "You need a key to get in from the outside, but inside you could simply slide a bolt home. See?"

Max nodded. "Yes, I seem to remember that."

"Well. Maurice came along about midday during the Fayre and — Get this: he found that the door had been bolted from the inside. There was no way for him to get in, without breaking a window."

"He's sure of that?"

"Quite definite. He was annoyed, he says, and shouted for someone to open up. Because, you see —"

"Someone had to be inside. Locked inside."

Cotton nodded. "Do you notice anything missing from in here?"

Max looked around — the little stage, the windows with curtains undrawn and giving onto the night. He could clearly see the churchyard with its brooding plague tree. "You're thinking in terms of a break-in.

Something stolen . . ."

"It's one possibility. She may have interrupted someone committing a crime of some sort."

"I'm perhaps not the best person to ask," said Max. "One of the women from the WI might see more than I do. They're all over the place most days, arranging flowers, rehearsing for a play, and whatnot. Suzanna Winship may be a good choice — I'd say she's . . . observant."

"We're on it now, asking various people. One other thing: do you know an elderly woman named Miss Pitchford?"

"Everyone knows Miss Pitchford. She taught school. I gather she taught half the village. She's been retired for years. Knows everyone — and everything about everyone."

"Well, Miss Pitchford told one of my men she actually saw Wanda just before noon, walking — so Miss Pitchford thinks now; who knows if it's hindsight — but walking, she says, toward the Village Hall. She was rummaging in her handbag, says Miss Pitchford, and muttering something like 'Key?' Or, as she thinks, 'Oh, key?' "

Max wondered, would anyone say, "Oh, key"? As in "Hello, key"? Possible, but odd.

"Could she have been saying, 'Okay'?" he

asked aloud. He frowned in frustration. The information got them no further.

"We thought of that possibility, too," Cotton told him. "Of course, her hearing . . . at that age it might not be at its sharpest."

"But it's more likely Wanda had found the door locked herself and was looking for the key in her handbag," said Max. "Isn't it? And muttering aloud as she looked? Or, did she *expect* to find the door locked and was looking to make sure she had the key?"

Cotton might have been reading his mind. "I feel we're making bricks without straw here," he said. "It's quite a puzzle either way."

"I'm to have tea with Miss Pitchford tomorrow," Max told him. "I'll see if I can get anything from her that makes more sense than that."

CHAPTER 20
MISS PITCHFORD DISPOSES

The next day, as he had told Cotton, Max was scheduled for tea with Miss Agnes Pitchford, an engagement that had been arranged far in advance — part of Miss Pitchford's rather diabolical appointment-arranging technique. Max reflected that while one could claim pressing engagements in the coming week or two, it was harder, unless one were planning to be out of the country or on another planet entirely, to find excuses in June for an October meeting. October, one felt, might after all never arrive.

He made slow progress on his way, for he was as usual frequently stopped by people wanting to chat, although Awena, carrying a basket from which obtruded wild flowers, a loaf of French bread, and a newspaper, simply waved and said hello as she glided by. Members of the press who tried to waylay him got the cold shoulder. Among those who stopped him was the Major. The man seemed to have shrunk, his still-large girth hanging on a somehow smaller frame.

"I just got a letter from my son, from Argentina," the Major told him. "Of course, the postal service being what it is, it was written several days ago. He's been on the telly, it seems."

The Major, clearly proud of his son's achievement, or perhaps just his neat handwriting, handed Max the letter. It was a simple, short note, again thanking the Major for wiring money and helping subsidize his career. It mentioned that he was waiting in a greenroom to be interviewed in the next half hour on live television. He had included a clipping from the local paper about an art show held the day before, complete with a photo showing the young artist standing in front of one of his vigorous, abstract creations. Max, looking at the envelope, noticed that by a terrible coincidence it was postmarked the day Wanda died. "You always understood my art, Dad!" That struck Max as unlikely in the extreme, but it was a nice bread-and-butter note just the same. The letter was signed "Jasper," and finished with xox, symbols for hugs and kisses. The letter put Max in mind of the long-suffering Theo, brother of Vincent van Gogh, who had kept the genius alive for so many years. Max had often thought van Gogh's suicide had much to do with Theo's increasingly turning away from Vincent toward his new young family and adult concerns. That the Major, however, continued to support and care about his son was evident from his pleasure as he reread the letter, then tucked it carefully in his jacket pocket. But his face fell into somber folds as he said: "Needed to talk with you, Padre."

Max had been told by Mrs. Hooser that the Major had called in at the vicarage while Max had been out on an early walk with Thea. Now the Major said, his voice lowered and his eyes looking left and right to see who might overhear, "It's all so awkward. They — the police — still won't release . . . her. Until. Well, until, you know. Difficult to know what to do."

Closure, thought Max. What one of his American colleagues at Oxford, a big blond rower from California, would call "closure" was precisely what the Major needed, and could not have. All the bureaucratic niceties had first to be observed, all the forms filled out.

Max nodded understandingly. As always, Max found the Major both affable and difficult to grasp, intellectually speaking. There seemed little to hold on to, and even though the Major and Max shared backgrounds with some similarities, Max always felt himself floundering, trying to find commonality. It wasn't as if the man left one with a sense of depths left unplumbed. It was more as if the placid surface of the man was all that there was to him. A near impossibility, in Max's experience. Wasn't it?

But now, of course, the situation was complicated by the fact that Max had seen the man at his most vulnerable: now there would be that extra English layer of reserve to chip through. Someone of the Major's background and breeding might feel that some position had been lost and would need to be reasserted.

Max was not disappointed in his guess. The Major now put on a show of hearty bluffness that wouldn't have fooled a child, and said, eyes stark with loss, "What can't be cured must be endured."

Just then Lily Iverson crossed the street to greet them. She wore a heavy fawn woolen coat wrapped tightly against the chill of the day. Her small face peered up at them in turn, beautifully framed by another of her scarves, this one in a fluffy yarn the color of apricots.

Max had noticed several other people

avoiding them in the way people will avoid the recently bereaved, and he wondered at her temerity. The normally retiring Lily placed a hand briefly on the Major's arm, and said, "I am so sorry for your loss. I saw her at the dentist's all the time, it seemed. It's so hard to take in what's happened." She gave him a small, sad smile; sunlight glinted briefly off her braces. Max knew she was self-conscious about the bands on her teeth, purchased when she started to come into money from her business. He thought they lent a charm to her vulnerability that had been somewhat lacking before. With a parting glance at them both from under her lashes, she quietly went about her business. The Major seemed nearly undone by this kindness, devoid of mawkish curiosity as it was.

The Major then spent several more minutes swapping comments of zero substance with Max, as Max struggled to get down to the question uppermost in his mind. Finally he was given a chance to ask, "Were there any changes in your wife's habits in recent days? Or concerns over her health, perhaps? Were the allergies worsening?"

"Funny you should ask," replied the Major. "She'd started seeing a new GP in Monkslip-super-Mare. She'd decided she didn't trust the local man."

"Winship?" Max was surprised. It was not the done thing to switch doctors in a small place like this, especially if one weren't in urgent need of a specialist. It would be bound to cause comment and speculation. He supposed Wanda might not have thought of that, or cared. But Winship himself had painted a somewhat different picture. Why? Professional pride, or something more?

"Why didn't she have her auto-injector? That's what I don't understand." This burst out of the Major like gunfire, a sign of the tenuousness of his grip on himself.

"Why, indeed," Max said flatly.

"It was always with her. It comes in a spring-loaded syringe — easy to use. They prescribe them for people like Wanda, who are at risk for severe allergic reactions. She was *never* without it. It would have been in her handbag. So, why?"

Max thought perhaps if it *had* been in her handbag, she didn't have time — the reaction was too strong. Or perhaps the auto-injector wasn't in her handbag when she went to look for it. Or she was prevented from getting to it. But he said nothing, just shrugged and shook his head in helpless sympathy. *Don't know.*

Parting with the Major after a few anodyne

words of comfort, Max carried on toward Miss Pitchford's, his steps slowing as he thought over what he'd learned.

Miss Agnes Pitchford was of an age where making and returning calls was a way of life, and text messaging was no substitute for face-to-face socializing over bridge and heavily stewed tea. Max had to agree about the texting.

He ambled over to the tiny cottage on River Lane, feeling as always, as he gently pushed open the gate into the immaculate front garden, like a giant who had stumbled upon a miniature land where fairies might be found living under toadstools, and a cat might wander by and wish him a good day. The river churned softly nearby, foaming its way to the sea. Autumn was clearly re-establishing its stronghold in the South West region, the landscape blurred by a gentle mist in the mornings, but the haze later dissolving to reveal a sky of Constable blue. The lilac-colored Michaelmas daisies had arrived on cue, along with the autumn crocuses.

Miss Pitchford was a pink-and-white, elderly lady of deceptively fluffy aspect and all-seeing china blue eyes, her cheeks as soft and unwrinkled as a child's. Her former pupils maintained that she had an extra pair of those china blues in the back of her head. She wore the white hair on that all-seeing head in a style Max thought might be called marcelled, without quite knowing how on earth he knew the word or what he meant by it. But he had seen similar elaborate waves and curly swooshes on the heads of film stars of the twenties or thirties. Her clothes were immaculate but old and old-fashioned, her dress frilly at the neck and with a long skirt nearly covering her calves, which were encased in thick orthopedic stockings the color of poached salmon. On her feet she wore lace-up brogues, polished, but of ancient vintage. He saw that she had missed a button on her cardigan, or perhaps a button was missing altogether. In anyone else, this would be a sign of mild forgetfulness. In the fastidious Miss Pitchford, it was a clear measure of her distress, bordering on incipient madness. Although excitement would have been the better-chosen word.

Together they scooched past the hallstand and into the sitting room, where they were subsumed into the type of decorating scheme designed to defy winter by blooming all year long. There was a certain bold dreadfulness to the scheme that was, as with the décor at Wanda Batton-Smythe's, a stir-

277

ring reminder that, come what may, there would always be an England. Wallpaper fought with cretonne for floral dominance (Laura Ashley v. William Morris in a duel to the death); gimcracks and gewgaws adorned every available surface, many of them probably gifts from a grateful (or not) student populace. Most items had the look of having been chosen to please a somewhat elderly lady of presumably sentimental inclination. With all the newspapers and periodicals scattered about, Max felt as if he'd stumbled into an Edwardian reading room, or a stage set for an instructive Victorian entertainment.

A cat jumped onto the back of Miss Pitchford's overstuffed chair, then peered over her mistress's shoulder to appraise the visitor with that look of distant yet apoplectic contempt only cats manage to achieve. Max found himself engaged in a brief staring contest, which of course he could never win, the cat's baleful glitter never faltering, its hard heart never softening. Max, uneasy (what *was* it about these creatures that made them so self-possessed?), dragged his gaze over to Miss Pitchford's more benign but no less all-encompassing gaze.

Max knew what the topic of their discussion eventually would be. There was no other current topic in Nether Monkslip. Without leaving her house, Miss Pitchford seemed to know most of what went on in the village, what had gone on, and what was likely to go on after she had passed to her snoopy reward. So over tea, a complicated business that would put a Japanese tea ceremony in a geisha house to shame, he got Miss Pitchford to tell him what she knew of the Batton-Smythe family. Since Miss Pitchford's goal was to pry information from the Vicar, their goals were not, at first, in sync. First forcing upon him little plates of sandwiches and cakes and peering at him over the rim of a Crown Derby cup before taking a delicate sip of Earl Grey, she said, with a beguiling smile that would have fooled no one, "Always such a pleasure to talk with a real man of the world."

Oh, Lord, wondered Max. What does she want now? Something to do with the flower rota, no doubt. He smiled at her expectantly. But instead she said, "Detective Chief Inspector Cotton reminds me so much of you. He was here on Monday. I insisted on speaking to the man in charge, and I was *not* going to be seen going into that horrible little pod thing."

Max decided an ambush might be best. Otherwise, Miss Pitchford and the point might never meet. "DCI Cotton tells me you saw Wanda," he said. "And that she was muttering something."

"Lovely to know you have his confidence. Yes, that is correct. She was looking through her handbag for her key."

"You're quite certain she said 'key'?"

Her teaspoon clattered slightly against the bone china saucer.

"There is nothing wrong with my hearing, Vicar," she said firmly.

True or not, that ended that for now. Max decided to try angling in from another direction.

"Did you know Wanda and the Major's son?"

Rather sharply: "Of course I did. I was his teacher, wasn't I?" Max felt almost as if she might rap his knuckles if a ruler were to hand. "A wild, dreamy child he was, too. *Quite* talented."

"The Major did mention Jasper's girl-friend the other day. I gather he felt she might be a stabilizing influence."

Miss Pitchford raised one pale eyebrow with schoolmistressy skepticism, a look that said, "You might very well think that," but instead she said, "How very interesting." Her cheeks flushed a slightly darker shade of rosy pink at the extremely vague sexual reference, and her cup clinked faintly as she set it back on its saucer. Miss Pitchford, for all her hardened campaigner experience with the young and their hormones, was rather like that, thought Max.

"More tea, Vicar?"

There was a pause while Miss Pitchford fussed about some more with the tea and the sugar bowl. Then she sat back in her chair and went on, "Jasper — the thing about Jasper was that he was like a foundling child. So creative and artistic — so *driven* to create. Does that sound to you like either of his parents?"

Max had to admit it did not.

"Mind you, I'm not suggesting anything in the way of . . . improper carryings on. No, indeed! Jasper was the natural child of the Batton-Smythes, I'm certain of that. I simply mean that it is so interesting to see a child grow up to be so different from its parents. One wonders, you know."

"Shakespeare was a glover's son, they say."

"There you are," she replied, clapping the flat of her hand against the chair arm, as if that settled the matter conclusively. Absurdly pleased, Max felt as if he'd been given a gold star for the correct answer. "Jasper was more inclined to oil and watercolor painting than to poetry, but the principle's

281

the same, you see."

Max, recalling the paintings on the walls of the Batton-Smythe sitting room, felt certain now that they were Jasper's. He'd have to ask, or go in for a closer look at the signature next time he was at the house.

"You say he was wild . . ." Max spoke quietly, and yet Agnes Pitchford seemed to sense something forbidding about the man who sat before her. Her next words were spoken tentatively, as if examined with great care before being released into the room.

"Ye-s-s. The wanderlust showed up early. He loved picture books, you know. Travel books. France, Italy, Peking, Sophia. Bombay was a favorite. Of course, he had the usual problems of a youth living in a small village or on a remote farmstead. It is isolating for youngsters, and for those who have some difficulty making friends . . . well, for them there can be special problems to overcome. I think the other children found Jasper a bit of a wet fish — is that expression still used?" Max nodded. "That is why programs like the Young Farmers' Clubs are such a blessing," she added brightly. "Brings them all together, so they can mix. I remember he made friends with young Larry Hawker — his parents kept the Sumner farm outside the village until they sold up and moved away. Couldn't make a go of it." There was a pointed emphasis to her words; Max wondered if she was indicating that a farmer's son was slumming it for Jasper. "So, Vicar, what exactly have you learned from the police?"

Max dodged the bullet as best he could. "It is difficult to know," he said. "Most people are accounted for, if only somewhat accounted for. They were manning the stalls or browsing around the stalls, or trying the tests of strength, or simply sampling the food."

This was greeted with a puzzled stare. "The what, dear?"

"The food."

"I thought you said 'the mood.' Well, not *quite* all," said Miss Pitchford demurely.

"What do you mean?"

"Well. It's just that I . . ."

"Go on," Max said flatly, keeping the eagerness from his voice and hoping it didn't show on his face.

"It's just that I wanted to buy a knitted tea cozy — one of those designed to look like a head of lettuce, so clever — but no one was at Lily's stall. There was a handwritten sign propped up there that read BACK IN TEN MINUTES. However, that's just one example of someone who was not where she was expected to be the whole time," she added. "I'm sure there were a few others."

Max sighed. He was sure there were.

"You yourself were at the Fayre all day?"

"Most of it," she replied, not apparently offended by the hidden question as to her own whereabouts. "Even though Saturday is normally my baking day. One has to make allowances for a special event like Harvest Fayre. I did my baking the day before. On cleaning day," she added, to clarify this difficult point for him.

Indeed, DCI Cotton had told Max he had been most persistent, slogging through the details of Miss Pitchford's activities, all, according to her, of a nature not only innocent but irreproachably civic-minded. Looking about him at her clearly seldom-used front room (there had been much internal debate, he was certain, as to whether the discussion of Wanda's passing merited such formality), Max's eye fell on her collection of seaside souvenirs as internally he marveled at their sheer volume and dreadfulness.

"I don't suppose . . ." he began. How to ask this? "I don't suppose any of your baking involved peanuts?"

She surprised him with a girlish, trilling giggle. For a moment he could see the young woman she had once been. "You *are*

284

a devil, Vicar. Yes, as a matter of fact, I did make some biscuits with peanuts. Is it being said I tricked Wanda into eating one? Perhaps got her to look the other way and then stuck one in her mouth?"

He grinned somewhat sheepishly. "I suppose it is absurd of me to ask." Although this he didn't suppose for a moment. The deadly biscuit had come from somewhere, from someone's kitchen.

"Of course, I did see her, and few other people did. Or, will admit that they did."

That was precisely true. How many might be out there unwilling to come forward, for whatever reasons? He looked about him, at the cherished accumulations of a lifetime, at the bookshelves stuffed with her favorite reading, so indicative of personality: Austen, Dickens, and the Brontë sisters, of course, along with what looked to be the complete works of several French authors — Flaubert, Maupassant, Proust.

Not everyone was like Miss Pitchford, who would see it as a moral obligation to report all she knew to the police.

"Can you tell me how it was you came to see her?" he asked now.

"I had to answer," and here she blushed prettily again, "a call of nature. I wasn't going to use one of those horrible portable

285

things they'd set up for the Fayre. No indeed. The spread of germs — well, it doesn't bear thinking about. So I was headed toward home and who should I see but Wanda?"

"Really? What time was this?"

"Just before noon. She was headed toward the Village Hall — must have been. I was just starting to walk down St. Edwold's Road, from the fields."

"Did she speak to you?"

"That nice detective asked me the same. So dashing! No, she didn't. She was completely preoccupied. Rummaging in her handbag for her key."

"So she said nothing to you?"

"No, she was just muttering about her key."

"How did she look?"

"The same as always — but rather flushed and flustered. She didn't even see me, I'm certain of it, and I didn't want to see her, if you know what I mean. She'd try to corral me into doing something or other. So I picked up my pace and made my escape."

Max sat, very still, suddenly alert. The onset of a vague unease caught him by surprise, but it was tinged with a familiar harking back to his old training. Something she had said . . . a disconnect somewhere . . .

The cat, sensing a kindred spirit, opened her eyes wide, and cocked her head for a better view of a fellow natural-born hunter.

"What?" said Max.

"Wanda always reminded me of women in wartime," Miss Pitchford was saying. "One just had to get on with it. People's feelings didn't matter — there was no time for that."

"Surely, though, Harvest Fayre . . . It's hard to see that in a national context."

"Oh, certainly you're right. Wanda always was one to overdo. No harm in her, really, although . . ."

"Although?"

"Well, she generally ended up *doing* a lot of harm. There are people like that, you know."

"Thousands, actually."

"Quite."

"Most of them in politics, or government." She nodded.

"Won't you have another slice of cake, Vicar?"

The conversation moved on to matters ecclesiastical (Miss Pitchford was against most of the encroaching inroads of secularism, as she called them) and it was half an hour before Max could say his final goodbyes on the doorstep.

He had eaten far more than he'd intended.

Miss Pitchford had a mean way with a Dundee cake, one that included a large splash of brandy in the ingredients. Apparently she felt no need to warn anyone of this beforehand, and Max suspected it was part of her arsenal for extracting information from her visitors. She also had in her repertoire a dandelion wine that tasted like water used to boil cabbage but that had brought grown men to their knees. It had been, he recalled, in great demand at Harvest Fayre.

He said his farewells in an effusion of tipsy goodwill, forgetting his umbrella in the process (which item she would hold hostage until he agreed to another visit) but only later realizing the reason for his cheery bonhomie.

He had the niggling sense that one or two interesting points had emerged from the conversation, but for the moment, what they could be, and whether they got him any further, he couldn't have said. But something the redoubtable Miss Pitchford had told him didn't match what he felt he knew to be true.

Miss Pitchford stood and fondly watched Max make his moseying way in the general direction of the vicarage. She was essentially an observer, a village spy whose coin of exchange was information. She would have been most at home in Elizabethan England, employed, like Chris Marlowe, in skullduggerous affairs of state. Nether Monkslip, she had often thought regretfully (in an unconscious echo of the thoughts of Wanda Batton-Smythe), offered too small a canvas for the full display of her talents.

The woman who ran the newsagent's fondly believed she was the hub at the spoke of village information. Miss Pitchford was magnanimous in letting her think so.

Usually Miss Pitchford was content to wait like a hatchling for tidbits of data and gossip to be delivered to her chintzy, slip-covered nest, but this was too much excitement to be contained. Feet on the ground — that's what was called for.

Setting her felt hat atop her head and throwing on her cape, grabbing her shopping basket to disguise her true intent, she set out for the village at the brisk pace of a woman half her age. Not knowing, she often thought, was the worst, and this was far beyond the usual parish-pump type of event. She'd pick up both word of mouth and a few papers at the newsagent's — and some milk, while she was at it. Nether Monkslip being in the national news didn't happen every day, after all.

It was one for the scrapbooks, she thought.
It certainly was.

Chapter 21
Goddessspell

Another Sunday had arrived, passing without incident, unless one counted the religious revival that had gripped Nether Monkslip: attendance at St. Edwold's continued to break records. Now, tired from a long week in the village spotlight, Max was nearly late for drinks at seven, dinner at eight. This time it was an invitation of short standing, from Awena Owen.

When she had telephoned him earlier at the vicarage, she was clearly in search of information. Max was happy to oblige, since he hoped for information from Awena in exchange, much as he had done with Miss Pitchford. An added inducement, however, was that Awena was an excellent, adventurous cook, and Max was always grateful for a reprieve from Mrs. Hooser's cholesterol-laden idea of what constituted a proper British meal. It helped that he'd dined at Awena's on several occasions in the past, without its giving rise to scandal: her solid reputation in the village was such that even the villagers saw no reason for pointed comment on these unchaperoned meetings.

But in the early days of his arrival in the village, he'd been a hard sell, rejecting her invitations less because of concerns about his reputation or hers, but from a fear the menu would consist of something made only of beans. Perhaps legumes ground into a fine paste, molded, and artfully painted to resemble a rack of lamb.

"No, no," he'd murmured, hoping he did not sound as deeply wary as he felt. "I have . . . things . . . at the vicarage. Things to eat."

"Like what?" Awena demanded.

Like what? That was quite a good question, actually, he'd realized. Normally, Mrs. Hooser would leave him some mystery odds and ends wrapped in foil to reheat in the oven. He had even been known to whip up some beans on toast for himself. But his larder had been unusually empty at the time, the housekeeper distracted by an outbreak of measles in the Hooser household. Moldy bread loomed large in his gastronomic future.

Awena had said, "Come on. I'm quite a good cook, if I say it myself. And you look like you could use a good meal." With her usual uncanny ability to intuit the truth of a situation, she said, "I doubt Mrs. Hooser, for all her good intentions, and in the best of circumstances, is much of a chef."

And so she had surprised him, seduced him, even, into a rustic way of eating that would have astounded his friends from his gluttonous-gourmet life in London. He was a carnivore, as Awena was not, but she had demonstrated to his admiring satisfaction that she gave up nothing in the way of flavor by her diet. That night, long ago, seeing his look as she brought out the main course, a pasta dish made with spinach, goat cheese, and pine nuts, she had said, "I know what you were thinking. It would be a meal of roots and shrubs or, at best, berries and stinging nettles, all gathered at the full of the moon. Which it happens to be tonight. A full moon. No nettles, however."

He smiled self-consciously.

"Something like that. Sorry."

"No need to be sorry. People don't half think the most absurd kind of rot about people of my persuasion. I'm quite used to it, actually."

Tonight he walked the few minutes to her house under gray clouds as a cool breeze played at his back. The moon was again full, appearing intermittently as the clouds shredded and regrouped.

Leaded-glass windows lined either side of Awena's door, where she had hung an intricately woven wreath of grasses, leaves, and ribbons to celebrate the season of harvest. The wreath surrounded a brass door knocker, representing the face of a Celtic warrior-goddess. Awena's own face appeared in one of the door windows as she checked to see who it was before opening. This was new behavior, and undoubtedly a reaction to the recent murder. His heart sank to realize how much Wanda's death had changed things.

Awena herself could only be described as an earthy type of woman, and past experience of her had shown Max that for all her otherworldly preoccupations, she had a healthy skeptical streak. He imagined that running a business as successful as Goddessspell required ballast to stabilize her clearly genuine preoccupation with the well-being of her soul. Today she was looking particularly priestessy in a robe of a deep saffron color, gathered at the waist by a belt of red beads — the usual high-waisted style she wore to accentuate her buxom figure. Her dark hair was held back by a matching band that caught the light as she moved.

She had a slow walk, as if perpetually on pilgrimage; she might have been starring in a singularly campy revival of *The Phoenician Women*. Her face was, as usual, devoid of makeup — not that she needed to enhance the creamy English rose complexion: her plump rosy cheeks, red lips, and blue eyes were striking left as they were.

He handed her the wine he'd brought as a gift, and she showed him into the sitting room, a space she'd filled with good-quality furniture with clean, modern lines and upholstered in cheerful patterns and colors. The art was Art Deco by way of China and India, the walls hung with bright woven tapestries and the floors thick with beautiful rugs. Max had the idea that Noah might have given his eyeteeth for just one of the rugs. All in all, the place was an unusual but pleasing mixture of Spartan ethos and homey charm.

She left him to fetch the before-dinner drinks, soon returning from the kitchen with a lacquered tray, her voluminous dress billowing out behind her. The tray held bottles of homemade hawthorn wine, a specialty of hers, and a wine from Montepulciano — not from Mme Cuthbert's shop, then, for Madame recognized no other wine than French. Max had thought he'd never see the day, but he found himself choosing the hawthorn wine.

"Dinner will be ready in a few minutes," she told him.

He knew from previous visits there was an atrium at the back of the house that she had turned into a sort of prayer space, filled with luxuriant green plants, a small tinkly fountain, and an altar of sorts on which candles, flowers, seashells, and polished stones were arranged. The room smelled of incense and the oils that she used in whatever rituals she performed as part of her prayer and meditation. She had explained to him that the objects in the room — the incense, candles, the fountain, and the plants — were there to represent air, fire, water, and earth.

The Anglican Church stretched wide to embrace all points of view, but Max had wondered if it would reach to encompass Awena's gently wacky worldview, a view that included all manner of things that went bump in the night. Taking in the beautiful and peaceful atrium, he had expressed his skepticism, but politely — a skepticism both inbred and reinforced by the orthodoxy of his theological training. Awena had merely turned to him and quoted, " 'It is the heart which perceives God and not the reason.' That's Pascal, if you didn't know."

He had been struck by her calm assurance as she went on that night to talk of something she called rhamanta, a method of finding omens by surrendering the self to nature — a listening to the heart in stillness until a sign was revealed.

"I suppose much like the monks that used to live on Noah's property," he had said.

"What do you mean, *used to?*" she asked him. She had been smiling . . . but a seriousness underlay her words. "Just wait until Halloween. If ever a place was haunted, it's the Abbey Ruins. I don't know how Noah gets any sleep."

Despite this kind of thing, or because of it, of all the people in the village, he had come closest to unguarded friendship with Awena. He recognized the attractiveness of her person and her personality, while acknowledging their differences in outlooks, in approaches to this world (and the next). These differences seemed to him insurmountable, particularly for someone in his position. Knowing this, he did not dare risk — realized he was afraid to risk — the friendship in an attempt to replace it with something more. Awena was too important to him.

But even given his trust of her, he found it impossible to pierce the veil he had drawn across his former life. How to tell her why he'd left his old life behind, or even to tell her a fraction of what he'd witnessed and helped perpetuate? In polite conversation, it just didn't fit anywhere. Awena hardly came from a background of protected privilege — her father, he knew, had been a Welsh fisherman, and she had told Max something of the man's struggle to raise a large family on his own. Presumably she knew something of the occasional brutality of real life — of strife and hard times. But there was a level at which it seemed impossible to expect anyone to understand what he himself had once been paid to do.

The sitting room overlooked a walled garden in the back, its boundaries marked by a hawthorn hedge, probably the source of their current drink.

"We'll have rain later," she said to him now, looking out the picture window.

He followed her gaze to where peace reigned in the moonlight. The silence of Nether Monkslip was one of its qualities he had slowly come to embrace. They were miles from any flight path, and the train stuttered in so infrequently as to cause very little noise. The stillness was total, suggesting a purity of place and people unlike anywhere else on earth. Max, who had been used to uncontained traffic noise in London, had taken some time to grow accustomed to the few night sounds of the village, which struck him as a riotous cacophony of alarming and unwarranted outbursts, each more life-threatening than the last. The snap of a twig was surely a wild animal approaching, of a type long thought to be extinct. The rustle of the trees in the wind, a portent of doom, of the King's men coming to string up some hapless serf for some unknown, minor offense. His mind had run riot as he tossed uneasily in his bed, uncertain what dangers the countryside might hold.

But certain he was now, with Wanda's death, that the dangers were not of his imagining.

He took a deep swallow of his wine. The chances were good that someone in his bran-muffin-eating, antioxidant guzzling, holistic congregation was guilty of murder. Impossible. But true.

He raised his glass. "Here's to rain to make a beauty spot more beautiful," he said, adding, "It's easy to believe in God, isn't it, when we live in such an idyllic village, in such a pretty part of the world. It's in places like Darfur that belief must be nigh impossible."

Awena's fine blue eyes met his in a graceful, upward movement of her head. A necklace of azure stones set in gold gleamed against her neck. She was one of the most physically attuned people he thought he'd ever met, with the deliberate movements of a ballet dancer or an accomplished actress. "I'd have to agree," she said. "On the surface, at least, we have it made — living in our own little Eden, untouched by the world's pain." She again looked out the window that gave on to the back garden.

Eden, thought Max. Funny she should mention . . .

"You would almost expect to see Wanda out there now, walking across the lawn, wouldn't you? Coming to collect for something, or to ask for something, or to simply 'borrow' something from the potting shed without asking." She turned to look directly at him. "I'm sure you're the person to find him — or her. The killer. She would want that."

"I suppose she would. Certainly in life, she would let no score go unsettled — that was my impression."

"If a death is unavenged, the dead can linger," Awena said, without emphasis. "You must believe that as well."

"Many believe that," Max said with studied neutrality.

She gave him a long stare. Suddenly she straightened and said sharply, pointing at the wall behind him, "What's that?"

Max, startled, turned to look over his shoulder.

"Just kidding," she said.

Max grinned at her. "Point taken. Very funny."

"Look," she went on. "I know what people think. You have to have a screw loose if you're not following the 'traditional' religious path. But who is to say I'm not doing just that? The worship of God in nature — supplier of everything we need — was around long before today's established religions. When you look at the healing power of plants, just for instance, medical science is not far behind me and 'my kind' in catching up. There is nothing weird or otherworldly about this: it's common sense. Every seed that produces this miraculous bounty has the code that will heal all ills — and a sprout travels from the darkness toward the light, just as we all must do. We simply aren't evolved enough yet to understand how it all fits together."

"That I grant you," said Max.

"Belief in a dimension beyond this one goes hand in hand with these daily miracles," she went on, refilling his glass.

"On the most basic level, a case could certainly be made that my beliefs are the cause of fewer wars than what I would call 'man's religion.' Mine is hardly a radical, or a new, concept. Like you, I concern myself with the great imponderables that possess us all — at least, once we stop long enough to think of them."

"Or are forced to stop and think." He thought fleetingly of Paul.

She continued, "More people than not are pushed into taking stock. And a vicar tends to be the person they turn to when that day comes. Or someone like me. The scientists — all the sources we've come to trust for all the answers, especially in recent decades — in the end they can still fail us. We're forced to look elsewhere for answers."

"Any enterprise that involves humans is going to invoke failure. Vicars, scientists . . ."

"All I'm saying is there are Christian successors to all the gods, goddesses, and feasts that came before. Who is to say who is right? All we know for certain is that prayer is powerful. It can heal the sick — you have seen that for yourself. People rebounding despite all the odds.

"And prayer heals every believer — not just the Anglicans."

Later they moved into the candlelit dining room, where mirrors in frames of semiprecious stone reflected the gentle light, and where she served him a harvest meal of pumpkin soup, acorn squash spiced with garlic and sweetened with honey, mushrooms sautéed in butter with garlic and cream, salad with lemon and olive oil, and sprouted-wheat bread still warm from the oven. He suspected tofu was involved in the salad — a food item he always thought rather pointless, like marshmallow — but if so, its presence was innocuous. These courses were followed by an ambrosial apple pie with brandy and a three-cheese plate sprinkled with nuts, the whole rounded out by more hawthorn in the form of tea. Meals were often accompanied by a talk on what Awena self-deprecatingly called The Owen Food Laws.

"The nightshade vegetables have to be eaten in moderation," she said. Her hands, beautiful and white and plump as doves, fluttered gracefully in the candlelight. She had been approached repeatedly by the WI Cookery School at Denman College to teach a course in cooking with herbs, and the medicinal uses for herbs. "A Pomona Sprout role, if you like," she had told him. But it would mean leaving Nether Monkslip for weeks on end, which she wasn't sure she would ever be free to do.

"Tomatoes were thought to be poison for a long time," she said now. "There's a reason for that. Potatoes and eggplant, too. Especially if you have arthritis, you should avoid them. Speaking of your scientists: they often confirm what the 'folklorists' have known for centuries."

"They are hardly my scientists — I agree with you, in fact. There is a basis for many so-called folk cures, as there is in most religious dietary restrictions and prescriptions."

This led him to think of the natural poisons like monkshood (found in abundance in Nether Monkslip), and of allergies, and from there inexorably to think of Wanda.

"Wanda," Awena said aloud, in the eerie way she had of tracking his thoughts. "There might have been hope for her in new therapies that introduce the allergy food in very small, very carefully controlled and supervised doses. Hard to believe she would be so careless, knowing her fatal weakness."

"She wasn't a careless woman."

That earned him a look of interest, but she said merely, "More tea? Hawthorn is good for the heart. It increases blood flow to the heart muscle itself, you see."

She used honey instead of refined sugar, which she claimed not to have in the house. Handing him the glass honey jar, which was shaped like a beehive, she said, "I suppose you don't believe either in the magic power of bees."

"I can't say I've thought much about it. Why, can they pull rabbits out of hats?"

She sighed, carefully replacing the honey dipper in the jar. "Think about it, Max. If I were as flippant about your religion as you are about mine, would you be happy with me?"

Abashed, Max looked at her. After a long moment, he said, "You're absolutely right. You are one hundred percent correct, in fact. I do apologize."

" 'A closed mind is like a closed book,' after all. I accept your apology — and I will try to be more accepting of your beliefs. We might both learn something."

Max, still confounded, merely nodded.

"Now, what makes *you* think Wanda wasn't careless?" he asked. "And I gather you agree she was not."

"Actually, in one way, I think she was. She

305

was unpopular with the villagers, in rather a foolhardy way. Careless with people's feelings, you could say."

"That's putting it mildly."

"Traditionally, someone in Wanda's position should advise and encourage, not run the show like the ruddy march on Leningrad," said Awena.

"Why did the women of the Women's Institute not break with Wanda?" Max asked. "Oust her?"

"Engineer a palace coup?" Thoughtfully, she poured brandy into her cup and stirred. Max imagined that would give the hawthorn a jumpstart. "I suppose because the WI provides nearly the whole social life of the village, as you know. No one wanted to fall away or to instigate the kind of rift that could fester for years. Private conversations on the subject — and there were many — often included proposing someone to replace Wanda. But the fact was, no one wanted to go head to head with her. There were several 'handbags at dawn' occasions but no one seriously wanted to take her out — out of her position, I mean."

"I suppose I can see that."

"Life is too short," was Awena's summing up. Max thought this typical of her — what he saw as being in the plus column of a life devoted to a smorgasbord of philosophies of dubious lineage. "Nor did anyone want to shoulder the responsibilities Wanda so eagerly shouldered. It's a pain in the you-know-what, volunteer work, and you have to have the kind of personality that thrives on it. Anyone who doesn't thrive on public speaking wouldn't want the job, for one thing. Wanda was good at that, but rather tended to thrill to the sound of her own voice."

"She must have had some good in her."

Awena arched an eyebrow at this, silently wondering at his limitless capacity to trust. Typical Max, to see the good in everyone, in that baffled, "Why can't we all be friends?" way of his. It was that religion of his, of course. The older religions were much more accepting of life as it is really lived, full of characters both devious and divine.

Max caught her reaction: there it was again. This fond belief that Max was some naïve babe in the woods. But he had come to accept that in fact it was this quality, tempered by later experience, that his bosses at MI5 had relied on for some of his under-cover roles — a fact he had come to under-stand rather late in the game. It was a qual-ity impossible to fake, Max's inclination to look for the good side of everyone he came across, even despite what he knew of the truth from reading their dossiers. It was, strangely enough, a quality that allowed him to excel at undercover work, befriending some of the most repellent people on the planet. By focusing on the good in them, Max could find the common ground, whatever it was — music, fine wines, cars — and play his target for all he was worth. Even a monster can love his dog, his mother, his family; crimes that had been committed in the name of "family values" were in fact too numerous to list. If Max had not been able to look past the negative, he'd probably be at the bottom of the Thames right now.

"I hear the son is coming back for the funeral," Awena was saying.

"You've met him?"

"Only years ago. He was young."

"What were your impressions then?"

She drummed her fingers on the tabletop a moment as she considered her response. "He was intelligent. More intelligent than anyone he'd ever met." She gave Max a sly wink. "He was, if you'll please excuse the expression — there is no other that fits — a jackass. He knew it all; he could be told nothing. He was the world's great unrecognized genius. Irritatingly enough, when it came to his self-assessment of his artistic talent, he was probably right."

Max raised his eyebrows; she replied to the implied skepticism.

"I'm afraid I'm spot on here. Others would tell you the same." Perhaps, thought Max, not Miss Pitchford, at least not in so many words. Certainly she had been hinting at something the other day, though. "Once he finished school, he hung around the village for a bit, perpetually on holiday, it seemed, in training to become a professional boulevardier, one supposes. He didn't want to go to university — besides, why bother? He already knew everything. In fairness, all he knew to do well was paint and draw, and instruction can spoil some talents. Then one day he announced he was going to travel the world to study the museums or whatever, and off he went. China, I think it was."

Max was not necessarily of the blame-the-parents school of psychological profiling but he felt Wanda and her progeny might be a special case — the exception that proves the rule.

"I gather there was bad blood between him and Wanda."

"Oh, that came later. They were extremely close at one time. Extremely. She was a 'smotherer,' I always thought. Well-intentioned mothering, much overdone — much too intense. Well, you can imagine: he was her project. Which is no doubt why he left. You have to escape that choke hold, and distance is the only way sometimes; I can see that."

"What happened to him eventually?" he asked.

"No one knows, but I gather he's had some success with his painting. The Cavalier grapevine has revealed that he'll be coming back for the funeral, from somewhere in the Americas. Or was it Europe?"

"The Major just heard from him. He was in Argentina."

She nodded. "The prodigal son, a bit late returning."

"Let me ask you what I've been asking other people," he said, in a cards-on-the-table manner. "Did you notice anything out of the ordinary going on with her at the Fayre?"

"Only that her clarion notes tended to drown out all else, including the choir. I saw her by the children's clothing stall at some point, looking regal but rather giddy and lighthearted with it. Like a queen amongst what she fondly supposes are her adoring subjects — you've seen that look on her?"

Max nodded.

"Anyway, I would say Wanda was enjoying life that day — absolutely in her element. Until it was all cut short, of course. Seems a shame, doesn't it, really? I got no sense of a premonition, and I picked up nothing amiss," she added.

"No aura about her?" he asked gently.

"You mock, but I will reply in all seriousness. No. There was nothing to tell me — or her — what was coming. It doesn't work that way always. You should know that, of all people."

"I suppose I should. But you would say there was no — I don't know . . . no sort of atmosphere?"

"With Wanda, you always got atmosphere you could cut with a knife. But nothing in particular that I noticed, no. She was basking at being the center of attention. In her element."

"All grievances forgotten, then, among her friends at the Women's Institute?"

"All in all, we're an amiable group," Awena told him. "The personalities — well, they're just that, and everyone recognizes that not every one can be the same."

"No bun fights at the meetings, then?"

She grinned. "No. But believe me when I

say it came close some evenings."

"How did Wanda come to head up the WI?" asked Max, chasing and successfully spearing a wayward slice of cheese. "Not by popular vote, surely?"

"She achieved prominence in the WI in the way curling became an Olympic sport, I would imagine — through dogged determination, sheer willpower, and that indefinable goofiness of character that is behind so much innovation and change. Quite frankly, no one else wanted it near so much as our Wanda. Meetings in the past had sometimes devolved into either frenzied spectacles or monuments to apathy, and I suppose Wanda, hyperorganized and energetic as she was, saved us from much of that. Plus, she knew how to squeeze a shilling until it begged for mercy, and that is a good quality to have for someone in that role. In particular, the people over at Totleigh Hall had expressed no interest in seizing the reins, as they would have done in the old days, so Wanda had assumed the leadership to fill a vacuum of indifference from that quarter. But she still had far too little to do with her time, which was probably the start of the trouble. It usually is. Bound to lead to mischief."

"Mischief?" echoed Max, caught on the

word. "Do you have anything in particular in mind?"

"I wish I could say exactly. But Wanda was operating on far too small a stage for her gifts, or so she felt, and so she often expressed. How a woman like Wanda might branch out — who can say? I daresay she was not sure herself, and was frustrated and vulnerable. Oh, yes," she added, off his look, "not a word that first comes to mind with Wanda, but believe me, she was at a dangerous age. With some women, it ends with all their savings going for Botox injections."

"Funny. I mean, you're not the first to mention it. Men have these stages too, of course. Generally involving a blonde and an expensive sports car."

Awena nodded appreciatively. "Of course. But I've met women like Wanda before, and I've often thought their ferocious energy is as much sexual as it is targeted to organizing everyone to within an inch of their lives. Misdirected energy, perhaps, but there."

Max thought, carefully setting down his knife and fork. Then he said, "Did you notice any particular conflicts at the Fayre — involving Wanda, or not? Odd moments? Someone there who seemed out of place?"

Awena said slowly, "We-e-ll. One thing, and I tell you this only because I know you'll take it with a grain of salt and not rush about making a lot of assumptions. It was this: Frank was guilty that day of lèse-majesté as far as Wanda was concerned. I was passing by on some errand or other and overheard her making fun of those pamphlets of his; the word 'tripe' was uttered. Well, his pamphlets are rather . . . unique. But he just lit into her — really, he was quite angry. You know how touchy writers can be."

Max nodded. He'd only known a few writers in his life — one a former MI5 agent who had made a vast fortune writing spy thrillers. The man was rumored to have sunk into a deep well of paranoia, making regular appearances on the various government-conspiracy, lunatic-fringe blogs and LISTSERVs. "Touchy" didn't even begin to describe it.

"She didn't like this response of Frank's, I take it."

Awena laughed — a dry, mirthless sound. "Wanda could give as good as she got. In fact, she was expanding on the theme of Frank's general lack of talent and virility as I scarpered out of harm's way. Wanda always liked putting the boot in."

Just then a candle on the table sputtered and went out. Picking up some matches to

314

relight it, Awena said, "One could so swiftly be banished to the outer darkness of Wanda's orbit. The aggravating thing was that one was supposed to care."

"Did you?"

"You must be joking. But I think, you know, that some people did." Her eyes now looked worried as they met his over the candle flame. "What madness," she said.

"Madness? Is that how you think of it? Or rather a cool calculation. This murder . . ." began Max, who for all his experience of the subject felt genuinely uneasy. He faltered, choosing his words with care. "The planning, the cunning. 'To smile, and smile, and be a villain' — isn't that how Shakespeare put it?"

She nodded. "Someone with the beatific smile of a madman, like bin Laden. I suppose we're looking for someone like that. Only there is no one like that here."

"How, well . . . *Shakespearian* it all is."

Awena nodded. " 'At least I am sure it may be so' — in Nether Monkslip."

"What complete wickedness."

"Yes."

CHAPTER 22
QUANDARY

He left Awena's around ten in a good humor induced by good wine and food, unaware that this reaction to her company was typical of him. He felt exhilarated, and at peace, and able to go on. Perhaps, he thought, it was all that hawthorn. Hadn't she said it was good for the heart?

His mind overflowed with their wide-ranging conversation that had put the world to rights, and with a few new items of interest. These had left him, alas, no nearer the solution to Wanda's death. And solution there was, he reminded himself, if somewhat blearily. It was a matter of excavation, merely. The truth always was there, as in archeology — belowground, just waiting to be exposed by the fall of the pickax.

A lunar halo, now fading, had formed earlier around the moon, by a trick of the atmosphere appearing in the form of a silvery cross of light. It was easy to see why most cultures had worshiped a moon goddess, he thought — elusive, but in reality ever present and watchful, and designed to make us feel insignificant as we hurtle through space in the darkness.

He tarried by the wrought-iron gate that led into his front garden, quietly looking up at the anointing sky. Passersby, had there been any that time of night, might have wished for a camera, seeing a tall man in clericals, bathed in light, standing outside a house of a barely contained eccentricity, for the vicarage was a twee, lopsided building of many windows and assorted chimneys; it looked like something drawn by a child, and it always looked to be near collapse. But Max had been assured it would stand many hundreds of years more. Come summer, the front garden would be shady, giving the visitor a respite from the heat even before reaching the vicarage's front door. In autumn, the shade cast a chill on the grass.

A puff of smoke from the chimney of Dr. Winship's nearby cottage briefly obscured the stars. Winter was not far away.

The snap of a twig set his heart racing, and he spun in the direction of the sound, reflexively poised to defend himself. DCI Cotton appeared out of the mist, walking along Vicarage Road, and carrying a briefcase, looking like a well-dressed commuter on the way to catch a train. It was apparent he'd been waiting for Max's return.

They exchanged greetings and Max ushered him inside, where Thea gave Cotton the once-over and then disappeared. The two men had not spoken except in passing for several days. Max offered the policeman a glass of wine, which had been a gift from a parishioner, and of such a rare vintage he had put off finishing the bottle himself — it was the kind of special treat that needed to be shared, not drunk in solitude. Now he doled out a glass for both of them with a flourish and a final, sommelier-like twist at the end of each pour. He turned his attention to the fire, for the night had turned chilly, then said, "You have news?"

Cotton tweaked the perfect crease of his trousers before sitting in one of the fireside chairs. He said, "Developments, big and small. My people have found the discarded auto-injector in the pond in Raven's Wood."

"You're not serious. Constable Musteile . . . ?"

"No. But I'm letting him take credit for now. He would anyway, and feeling that he's solved the case already may keep him out of harm's way for a bit. But that's all by the way. The real news is that even though it's waterlogged, it looks as if the auto-injector had been tampered with, and the antidote substituted with something innocuous. Tap water, at a guess. It was very subtly done — Wanda wouldn't have noticed the difference. Well, not unless she'd had to use it and found it . . . useless.

"But even better," he went on, "in going through her things at Morning Glory Cottage, we found this note." He showed Max a single page of foolscap, with writing in block letters. Max saw the words: I CAN WAIT NO LONGER. MEET ME. THE USUAL WAY. DESTROY THIS.

"No prints," Cotton informed him. "Nothing about the page to provide a lead — even with a handwriting sample for comparison, it will be hard to trace who wrote this. So what's it about? Blackmail? An anxious lover?"

"We are talking about Wanda, are we not? A lover is hard to imagine. Still harder, blackmail. Although, as a pillar of society in her own mind, I suppose she would be vulnerable to that threat."

"There's more," said Cotton. "Wanda kept a diary. Not a 'Dear Diary' type of thing, alas, but more a calendar of appointments. A bound book, wrapped around with an elastic band, with receipts and fabric swatches and so on stuffed into a pocket at the back. The pages are bound and numbered, so we know the volume is intact — no missing pages ripped out. In it she notes the usual kind of thing: dates for the dentist, the hairdresser, menu items to purchase. Some appointments had a star by them but there was no pattern to that. The doctor might get a star one time, and not the next."

"That is interesting. Not much help, but interesting."

"It is helpful, actually, but in a negative sort of way. We've spoken with the various receptionists involved at the various establishments, and the dates don't match up. Sometimes they do, but not always."

"So . . . what's the thinking? She was keeping a fake calendar because . . . ?"

"That, we don't know. We've looked at the hard drive of her computer, hoping she had a password-protected calendar, but no." Cotton jumped up. As usual, his default mode was one of combat readiness. The line of his jaw and the cords of his neck looked as taut as wire.

"I also have news of a negative, no-help sort," Max told him. "It seems there was no shortage of food contributions that day. Guy Nicholls was roped into donating. And Miss Pitchford. And Awena Owen."

"We know. Elka Garth, the woman who owns the bakery and runs the tearoom in the village, made similar donations — was perhaps the key contributor. People are being very up-front about that, but why wouldn't they be? They know how easily we can check up on who donated what, given time."

"There may not be time to spare."

"Believe me, I know. We've talked with Elka at length, of course," Cotton continued. "The baked goods that did for Wanda could have come from her shop — her being a baker by trade rather puts Elka in the spotlight. She is adamant that Wanda could not have taken one of her peanut biscuits by accident."

"Yes, she told me that, too."

"But Wanda had peanut — what shall we call it, peanut residue? — in her mouth and it came from somewhere."

"Peanuts are used in a lot of ways, as filler, sometimes finely ground, aren't they?" asked Max. "I think we also have to consider the supposition that Wanda got hold of the peanuts unawares, perhaps not through one of Elka's confections."

"Or at least not a confection so clearly containing peanuts," replied Cotton.

"You don't think . . ." Max began.

"I don't think what?"

"Elka might have been careless. Gotten some peanut residue mixed up in something else she provided to the Fayre. A moment's chaos in the kitchen . . . it would be easy enough to do."

"She swears not," said Cotton. "Says she was extra careful about that sort of thing because of Wanda — Wanda had made her aware of the danger."

"Yes. So she says."

"They — the forensics guys — think that maybe, with a lot of sifting and sorting of ingredients and a chemical analysis, they can determine whose batch of what was responsible for the death, but is it worth it, knowing that? Anyone could have made sure Wanda ate a fatal item — not necessarily a peanut biscuit, and not necessarily a food item that the killer had donated to the Fayre."

"That is part of what is so clever about this, don't you think? We could search forever and not find the 'murder weapon,' so to speak."

Cotton, now staring at the crown molding, surprised him by asking, "How does this crime strike you? Masculine, or feminine? Because no matter what anyone says, there are some crimes — poisonings, for example — that still tend to skew feminine."

Max said ruminatively, "Perhaps. Just as the reaction to crime can follow certain patterns, have you noticed? After 9/11, women tended to want to plant gardens of remembrance. Men wanted to build new towers, more towers, bigger, taller, better towers. 'Try knocking *this* down' — that kind of thing. But to answer you, I get no sense of there being a masculine or feminine sensibility behind this crime. It could have been committed by anyone who wanted a method that was hard to trace back to any one individual. It's rather a sneaky crime, rather than a forthright one, don't you agree?"

DCI Cotton nodded. "But this whole masculine/feminine question may speak to my ideas about Wanda's character," Max went on. "She doesn't seem the type to have aroused sexual jealousy, for example — would you say?"

"You knew the woman better than I, but no. I'm not getting that kind of picture at all. If I were looking for that kind of reaction, I'd look to someone like Suzanna Winship. Trouble of that nature must follow Ms. Winship wherever she goes."

Max sipped his drink. "Undoubtedly," he said.

"There's somewhat of a sticky wicket for

Noah, your antiques man, I'm afraid. He was seen hanging about the Village Hall that day, by Frank Cuthbert. He's some kind of writer, I gather."

"Yes. Frank is . . . some kind of writer. He has a vivid imagination, to say the least. Does Frank say that Noah went into the building?"

"No. But what makes Frank's statement notable is this: Noah never told us about being in the area. When I called him on it earlier today, he simply said he had forgotten — he'd been for a walk (he said he got someone to manage his booth in his absence), and his steps had taken him in no particular direction."

Max looked at the flames, seeming not to hear what Cotton had said.

"Did Wanda or the Major have financial problems?" Max asked at last.

"Quite the opposite. She came into a tidy sum — property, jewelry, cash — when her mother died."

"So . . . the Major is . . . ?"

"Sitting pretty. He inherits the lot. There's a sizable life insurance policy, also, for which he is the beneficiary."

"I see," said Max slowly. "And *his* whereabouts at the crucial time?"

"The Major's whereabouts are not well

accounted for. You told us you chatted with him at the Fayre, but after that, his 'position,' as I'm sure he would call it, was abandoned. He says he got tired of sitting and reading and went to stretch his legs and use the gents."

"Daring to leave the booth unattended? That is interesting. As if he knew Wanda wouldn't be there to check up on him."

"I thought of that, too. He says she stopped by, and perhaps he felt that having been recently checked up on, it was safe for him to leave for a few minutes, at least. Frankly, since the husband is always the first to be suspected, I'm surprised he doesn't offer a better accounting for his time. As you probably are aware, the husband is always top of the charts in these matters."

"A real alibi," said Max, "is so often unverifiable. Don't you find?"

Cotton nodded distractedly, his fair hair standing on end — surely a sign this polished and sophisticated man was at the end of his tether — and his face a scowl of frustration. He returned to his seat but Max knew the illusion of repose would be only temporary.

"I don't suppose," Max said slowly, "there's anything suspicious about the mother's passing? Wanda's mother?"

The look Cotton gave him was admiring. He all but whistled. "You are a suspicious one, aren't you? A regular Miss Marple in Holy Orders. We'll look into it, but the fact is, she was quite old, and unless questions were raised at the time, well — I'm not sure what could be done about it now. Without strong evidence to the contrary, we'd have to assume a natural death." He heaved rather a large sigh. "We certainly have a job of work to do in terms of checking alibis and general paperwork, in all directions. We looked at Wanda's bank records as a matter of course and noticed the uptick in the finances at the House of Batton-Smythe. She also had a private account, and that's where she stashed the serious money."

"Presumably she had a will?"

"Yes. She had a will leaving everything to her husband — as I say, he inherits the lot. A few charities mentioned, but mostly he inherits."

"A recent will?"

"Yes, in fact. Dated this past summer. What makes you ask?"

Max answered indirectly. "Can you get hold of the previous will?"

Cotton nodded. "Her solicitor is in Monkslip-super-Mare. She didn't use the local man."

"That's not uncommon. People assume, rightly or wrongly, that they'll enjoy more anonymity if they use someone not in the village."

"I'll get someone on it. Why do you think it's of interest, though?"

"Not to leave anything to her son is strange. Very strange indeed."

"Is it? Presumably she would feel her husband would simply leave everything to the son, when the time came. No need for a special, separate provision."

"Why change the existing will, though?" Max asked. "Let's see if there isn't a separate provision for the son in the old will — a provision that she had removed. I suspect there is."

"In a way," said Cotton, "we have gathered a lot of evidence. How it all fits together, we just don't yet know. But we will — I hope."

Max had earlier passed along what Miss Pitchford had told him of Lily Iverson's disappearance from her stall. "She wanted to buy a tea cozy from her, Miss Pitchford said. But it's not much in the way of evidence, is it? Lily's temporary disappearance was, I'm sure, being replicated by others, throughout the day. A call of nature, that kind of thing."

"Interesting, though," said Cotton. "When

I asked Ms. Iverson about it, she said she'd just forgotten to tell us earlier, but she looked scared to death. For all we know, she's another Madame Defarge, knitting coded names into her sweaters of all those who won't make it out alive come the Revolution."

"Lily always looks scared to death," said Max equably. "Perhaps she's telling the simple truth, though."

"There is no simple truth in a murder investigation. As you know." Musingly he added, "I still say poison is generally a woman's weapon. And of course, effectively Wanda was poisoned."

Max shook his head, trying to take in the idea of the timorous Lily as poisoner. Her timidity seemed endemic, but he supposed it was just possible. Anything was possible. But her motive? Hurt feelings over the Fayre Chairs? There had to have been more to it than that.

"Lily is another 'newcomer' to the village, like me," he said finally. "Like all of us who weren't born here."

Cotton flipped through his notes. "Yes. Born in Yorkshire. Moved about a bit. Pitched up in London at some point."

"Yorkshire?"

"Yes, why?"

"No reason, really. Lots of people are born in Yorkshire."

"What is it you know? Out with it."

"I don't know, really," said Max. "I just was talking with someone who thought Wanda might have been from Yorkshire."

Cotton nodded. "That person might have been right. It was years ago, but she did live there. It came up in the routine we ran on her."

"Doesn't even count as coincidence," said Max. "What's the population of Yorkshire? Chances would be well against the two of them ever meeting."

"Same as with all of the villagers — most are from somewhere else. Madame Cuthbert, of course, is French. She and her husband, Frank, lived in Paris for a time before settling here. Guy Nicholls was from Belgium, and —"

"Belgium?"

"Yes. What about it?"

"He indicated he was from Paris most recently. He didn't actually say that but I gained the impression . . ."

Cotton shook his head. "Belgium."

"But . . ." began Max. "Why would he mislead me?"

"He didn't want you to know he'd been in Belgium, obviously. But he didn't mind me — the police — knowing where he'd been, so it can't be for any reason he'd want to keep hidden, like trouble of an official nature involving my French-speaking colleagues. Drugs, theft, or the like. Can it?"

"No reason I can think of," Max said slowly.

"I'll get in touch with our friends in Belgium. If anything emerges of great interest, we may have to send someone over there." He smiled. "Strange, but it's always easier to find volunteers to travel over to Europe than to — oh, say, Milton Keynes, for example."

Max held up the bottle, offering the last few sips, which Cotton accepted.

"Your instincts are good," Cotton said. "Who do you suspect?"

Max could only shrug — he suspected everyone. He supposed it was a legacy of his MI5 days. The Major, Lily Iverson, Frank Cuthbert — the list was long of people who were at the Fayre, but whose exact presence was not accounted for at the crucial noon hour? No matter how suspicious he might be, he could not see any of these people committing murder. And yet it must be one of them, or someone just like them. The Fayre attracted every sort of person from miles around, but no one who would have stood out as a homicidal maniac. More was the pity, of course. It was going to make finding whoever was responsible deuced hard. *And* finding proof that they did it.

"I told you I saw the Major the other day," said Max, "and he told me his wife was not using the local GP."

"Right. And he showed you that letter from his son. The contents of which we verified, by the way: he was where he said he was. Which reminds me: along with the calendar, we found a stash of letters to Mumsie from the son, Jasper. I have them here."

"Really. Could I see them?"

Cotton fished for the briefcase at the side of his chair.

"Go carefully, there," he said, handing over a small stack of letters inside a clear plastic bag. "We didn't bother to bag them all separately. Here, put these on."

He handed over a pair of disposable plastic gloves for Max to wear.

The letters, Max saw, were nearly identical in style and type with what Jasper had written to the Major — asking for money or thanking for money, effusively — and addressed to only one parent, not both. The last was dated in May.

"The husband hid them from the wife and vice versa — is that it? More strangeness in that family," commented Max. "We're absolutely sure, are we, that the son is in the clear?"

Cotton nodded emphatically. "Passport control confirms it. The media in Argentina confirm it. No way he was anywhere near the scene."

They chewed over the evidence, the inconsistencies, and the possible motives for another few minutes, but little of useful note emerged.

"Where to now, Max?"

"I need to think a bit," Max replied. "And I do that best at St. Edwold's. Right now, there's a pile of images and puzzle pieces in my head — nothing quite fits together.

"But it will. If I sleep on it a bit, and pray on it a lot. For the first time, I'm starting to believe it will all come together."

CHAPTER 23
ST. EDWOLD'S

The next day saw a return of a brisk wind, this time from the south, pushing before it heavy white clouds. It gave the illusion, as Max approached, that St. Edwold's was moving, somehow being born aloft against the clear blue of the sky.

Words from the Book of Common Prayer similarly floated across Max's mind: "We have followed too much the devices and desires of our own hearts." Was some similar selfish impulse — so often a precursor to murder — behind Wanda's death? The words mirrored those in the sermon he had been working on, so long ago it seemed now — James's "You want something and do not have it; so you commit murder."

His late conversation with Cotton had raised more questions than answers, although with so many facts to tie together, Max felt he must be gaining on the killer. He had the fanciful idea he was stepping on his or her shadow.

DCI Cotton appeared just then, coming from the direction of the Horseshoe. He paused just long enough to wish Max a good day. Frank Cuthbert, accompanied by the faithful Sadie, came into view as Max parted from DCI Cotton at the lich-gate to the churchyard.

Frank lurked (it was the only word for it), watching closely and waiting as Cotton crossed the High to the police pod near the Village Hall, where the ceramic shepherd and shepherdess peered blindly out on the scene from their respective windows. Max, wanting to hear Frank's own version of his run-in with Wanda at the Fayre, could see no sideways approach to the matter, but Frank, as if reading his mind, saved him the trouble.

"I was just on my way to see your DCI," Frank told him. "Best to make a clean breast of things."

It would be too much to hope, thought Max, that Frank was confessing to the murder — things were never that simple. As it transpired, Frank only wanted to be sure the police heard of the incident with Wanda before a version reached them — a version that tainted his silence with suspicion. It seemed Wanda had tried to get Frank moved to a less prominent spot, saying the public had seen enough of his "stupid books."

"Stupid!" Fairly spitting, a flush of remembered anger washed over Frank's already hectic complexion.

"It's a minor thing," said Max soothingly, "but I do feel telling Cotton up front would stand you in good stead."

Frank, with a tip of his beret, said, "Minor, is it? Damn the woman. As much trouble in death as in life. Always the corrosive influence around here. And she wouldn't know a good book if it bit her."

But, seeming to gather together the shreds of his authorial dignity, Frank turned and followed in Cotton's steps over to the pod.

Max opened the lich-gate, which was rusting about the hinges and making an unnerving, Boris Karloff–type creak whenever anyone touched it. He'd have to get the sexton on it. Even though such things were best left to Maurice, there was a weird proprietary game being played between the two men with regard to the church, and Max wasn't sure he knew all the rules as yet.

Skirting the churchyard, Max opened the church door and stepped through the narthex and into the nave. The murk was at first blinding, and he nearly tripped on the flagstone floor, which had been scooped and worn into a veritable pothole by centuries of worshipers. It was as good a reminder as any of life "everlafting," as the old plaque inscriptions in the church would have it.

Visitors who took the trouble to find Nether Monkslip never failed to be amazed when they stumbled upon the jewel of a church that was St. Edwold's. To all appearances, from the outside it was just another squatty little Norman church of not particularly inspired execution. Inside, the stained-glass windows caught and scattered light in a way designed to transfix. The few entries in the church's guestbook usually fell back on words like, "awesome," "breathtaking," and "peaceful," invariably followed by a row of exclamation points. For while England had many lovely old churches, St. Edwold's, through some divine trick of light, or cunning artifice of its builders, seemed to shimmer and glow in the patina of centuries. People swore it was a holy place on holy ground, and Max could only agree.

In the days and nights that followed his "conversion" in Egypt, he had puzzled to pick out the thread in his reasoning. Why the Church of England? Why not go the whole hog and join, say, a Tibetan monastery? It was not merely the pull of the familiar, although that played a part: one of his aunts, his father's sister, had become an Anglican nun. He could recall, as a small child, walking between his parents on the way to church, each of his small hands clasped in one of theirs, his body nearly suspended, his feet barely touching the ground. This was before his siblings had come along. Like all only children, he gloried in having his parents to himself. As much as they had traveled during his nomadic childhood, the Anglican Communion, the local church with its predictable rituals, had been his consistent home.

Even in adulthood, when he was an occasional churchgoer at best, he would have questioned his own sanity had he suddenly taken up a religion about which he knew next to nothing. It seemed to him it almost didn't matter, the outward form a religion took — the prayers and rituals. What mattered was the near-universal agreement throughout mankind's time on earth that we weren't here, on this lonely planet, alone. These were views he kept quiet about while reading theology, especially from the more kneejerk conservative of his instructors. Like a magpie, he selected from their teachings what made sense to him, what brought him comfort, and hid from them his more elastic views.

There was beyond all this, of course, the question of joining an institution that to all appearances was foundering, rocked by scandal and nearly toppled by indifference. Why the C of E, beyond habit? Perhaps because at the end of the day it was Max's church — the selfsame church that had taught him right from wrong, however far he might later have steered from the path.

He looked about him in the glowing silence of the building that had awed and humbled so many strangers, of all faiths. It helped that the sexton who maintained the church building (and did double duty in the office of verger, assisting at services) was a punctilious and conscientious man who seemed to regard the place as his own property and its care a divinely appointed task — hence the open rivalry with Maurice. Mr. Stackpole was a dour, humorless man Max had inherited from his predecessor. While the sexton was always polite — just — he seemed to regard Max as an upstart interloper; his narrow figure, like something out of Edvard Munch's *The Scream,* exuded condemnation for the way the world was turning. He was one of the staunchest preservationists in the village, and while Max agreed in theory with much of what he stood for, his inability to see both sides of any issue made him a difficult person to deal with.

Max always felt that he himself was on trial with the sexton — a normal ordeal for any incoming parish priest to go through. But in this case, Max believed that no matter how exemplary his conduct and personal habits, Mr. Stackpole would always find him wanting when measured up against the conduct of Walter Bokeler of sainted memory.

The truth, Max suspected, was that Mr. Stackpole (he insisted everyone address him as "Mister") had trouble categorizing Max theologically, and the lack of easy labels made a man like Stackpole uneasy. Especially in an age where it was felt the church was circling the drains, some people clung to whatever looked certain and solid, making them less able to handle ambiguity and apparent contradiction. Stackpole wanted firm answers. Max did not have firm answers to give, only hope and abundant good will. This, Mr. Stackpole seemed to feel, was simply *not good enough.*

The former vicar of St. Edwold's had been

High Church in his views; Max was determined to follow a more inclusive, middle road. Some, like Wanda and the Major, had been outraged at the change, going so far as to travel to Monkslip-super-Mare for services. This lasted until poor weather, and a growing sense of their isolation from the rest of the village, had driven them back (rather, had driven Wanda, the Major remaining ever pliable). Wanda's sense of her place in the village was her prize psychological possession.

Although Max had that rock-star status from the start, the trust of the parishioners had to be earned daily. He wouldn't really have wanted it any other way, as frustrating as their suspicions (inborn in the case of the long-term native villagers) had been — even though it was like being watched over by the head of a particularly snotty public school. Several heads.

Max walked in silence now through the jewel-lit darkness of the nave's main aisle, the heels of his shoes ringing against the floor, a sound magnified as it ricocheted against the high ceiling. The church building was always left unlocked, vandalism being almost unheard of in Nether Monkslip. And cold-blooded murder even more so.

Would Wanda's death change all this — make his parishioners fearful, contaminate them with the urban fears and prejudices and phobias they had come here to escape? Max sighed at the thought of the worm in the apple.

As he approached the chancel steps, he heard a slight pattering sound and, on turning, saw he was not alone. Little Tom Hooser was sitting in one of the pews, rhythmically tapping the toes of his small feet together. He was so small the top of his head with its springy dark hair could not clear the pew in front of him. Max wondered not only how he had managed to crawl up into the pew but also how he had slipped the bonds of the all-seeing Tildy Ann — possibly he was here because it was one of the last places his sister might look for him. Max had been uncertain until this moment that Tom could function without her, but Tom seemed to be managing well.

Max, greeting him, sat in the pew in front.

"There's something growing there," Tom informed him. Slowly, dramatically, he lifted one small hand, a bit the worse for what looked like the remains of a peanut butter and jam sandwich, and, like Scrooge's ghost, pointed a finger at the wall directly to his left. Max followed the spectral-like directive. Together, solemnly, they gazed at the wall.

Where there was, no question about it, a moist stain of some kind, a dark nimbus forming on the white plaster, like a solar eclipse in reverse. Max barely suppressed an oath: damn and double damn it all forever. The roof must be leaking again, water seeping down through the old cracked walls. Another item for Maurice to assess, and probably well beyond his capacity to fix. Max had the sudden, mean realization that Wanda's murder had probably truncated the profits that had been earmarked to flow from the Fayre toward the church restoration fund. He looked at Tom, who seemed to sense the gravity of the situation, and sympathetically shook his head. Duty done, he said his good-byes and left, the Vicar wondering what on earth it was going to cost to repair his incandescent little church — this time. Why the child was not in some sort of school or day nursery he also stopped to ask himself. He would have to ask Tom's mother. Or Tildy Ann, who was more likely to know.

He breathed deeply and deliberately, trying to calm and clear his mind, but before long the problem of the roof was replaced by the questions that had assailed him in the night. They crept back, all part of the same theme: who could have killed Wanda? Max was not enamored of the passing-stranger theory, if only because one felt one had to know Wanda rather well before being inspired to see her removal as a blessing for all mankind. That might be a rough sentiment for a vicar, but it was a realistic appraisal. The same applied in the case of the tradesmen and various farmers involved somehow with the Fayre. Dislike on such a massive scale, Max felt, had to have taken some time to accumulate, with repeated infusions of ill will, to set the killer's mind on slaughter.

He suddenly had the odd sensation of seeing himself from the outside, as a passing visitor would see him, a tall, dark-haired man sitting surrounded by the beauty of the solemn old church. He decided to do what he long had done for direction — and he smiled, knowing Awena did the same, although her name for it was guided meditation: she would choose a picture or a phrase at random and go with the flow of whatever ideas emerged. Max would open a Bible at the Book of Common Prayer at random for guidance, although the meaning sometimes took a lot of sifting. His eye more often than not fell on phrases that seemed nonsensical, unrelated to the topic that perplexed him. As happened now, he could not see the guidance as the book fell open to Psalm 51, in which David asks to be purged of his sins and made "whiter than snow."

David's were sins of murder and adultery. Max's thoughts turned to betrayal — how murder was the ultimate in that line. Betrayal by an enemy or a trusted friend; Judas's betrayal. He turned to find the psalm he was reminded of, the one he thought of as the Betrayal Psalm, and finding it, he read:

For it is not an open enemy, that hath done me
this dishonour: for then I could have borne it;

Neither was it mine adversary, that did magnify
himself against me: for then peradventure I would
have hid myself from him;

But it was even thou, my companion: my guide,
and mine own familiar friend.

He pulled out the small notebook and pen

he carried everywhere with him, used for jotting down dates and reminders — also random thoughts, ideas, and inspirations, most of which ended up in his sermons. He began trying to marshal his thoughts. He wrote nothing for a long while, but it was like doing the crossword puzzle — without pen in hand, he never felt the answers would come to him.

After a while, he wrote "Elka," followed by "Betrayed? Would lie to protect son? To avenge?" It was one of those moments when his subconscious seemed to have taken over, because rereading this he had no idea from where the thought had emerged. After another minute he added, "Grief-stricken? — the Major." And: "Lily. As frail as she seems?" Now he was forcing the issue, he realized, so he crossed all of this out and sat, quiet and still, waiting.

And what came to mind, of all things, was the vicarage study — those awful curtains. Queen Victoria's knickers. And a phrase he had heard or seen recently, or that reminded him of something someone had said. Something to do with an envelope. Pushing the envelope, perhaps — a phrase that had long lost its original meaning, given it by test pilots, of pushing the limits of a plane's capabilities. The Major had shown him an envelope, and told him there had been a delay in receiving his son's letter. Max thought of all those letters found in Wanda's house, read and presumably treasured and stored away. The lyrics of a treacly old song came to mind, a song of innocent summer times, summer memories: "So let us make a pledge / To meet in September." "Sealed with a Kiss" — that was it. She had died in late September. He tried to catch the memory or idea that now danced tantalizingly out of reach. And could not. It seemed significant now.

Drat.

CHAPTER 24
ACOLYTE DOWN

The night before Wanda's funeral, Max dreamt he was solemnizing a wedding. The couple stood before him at the chancel steps; in the way of dreams, it made perfect sense to him that both bride and groom had their faces swathed in heavy black veils. Wanda, mother of the bride, was there, her face wearing its accustomed mask of displeasure. He began to read aloud the lovely and age-burnished words, "Dearly beloved, we are gathered together here in the sight of God . . . to join together this man and this woman in holy Matrimony." But when dream-Max turned to ask the man if he would have the woman as his wife, he saw his mistake: this wasn't a wedding. This was a funeral, and the man and woman now stood before him wrapped together in a white shroud. How could he have got it so wrong? The banns hadn't even been published, he suddenly realized. Wanda would be furious. Desperately, he began to search the prayer book for the Order for the Burial of the Dead. All he could remember of the words was that we brought nothing into this world. "We brought nothing into this world," he told the couple. "Nothing!" The shrouded bodies began to stir, and again Max knew in the way of dreams that whatever the white cloth covered was decayed and no longer human. Terrified, his heart pounding, in a cold night sweat he awoke to a room bleached gray by moonlight.

The next morning, Max, who had been up since before dawn reworking the funeral sermon, looked out blearily over his congregation. The vestiges of his dream hung over him, lending a dreary pessimism to the already distasteful task of laying Wanda to rest.

An open verdict had been returned at the reconvened inquest, and the body freed by the coroner's order for burial; the Major, far from barring its release, had begun agitating for it. The Major was the type of man to chafe at any uncertainty — to need official opinions and renderings and judgments — and this uncertainty regarding his wife's fate was surely the greatest test of any man's patience. The open verdict — the verdict of last resort — meant the jury found the circumstances of Wanda's death suspicious, but they could definitively say no more than that. On a fact-finding mission only, they could legally make no accusations. They had been nothing if not earnest and thorough, but the law as they were allowed to apply it was narrow in scope, a verdict of unlawful killing too far a reach with the evidence at hand. Max had felt the palpable suspicion, as well as frustration, hanging thick in the air that day, and not all of it emanating from DCI Cotton alone. The truism of any investigation was that as the trail grew colder, the chances of the culprit's going free increased, even if the culprit were caught eventually.

At the rendering of the verdict, the Major had retrieved a large handkerchief and let into it a loud snort of either grief or disbelief. Perhaps both.

In the interim, St. Edwold's had continued to enjoy a boost in attendance, which would reach its apex with Wanda's funeral, where Max knew he would play to a packed house. Murder had either put the fear of God into the villagers, or (far more likely) they didn't want to miss out on any developments. It was interesting over the days to watch when the time came to exchange the peace — it was like a live illustration of shifting alliances in the antechamber of a medieval court. Suspicion fell on first one villager, then the other; the Major was first out of favor (wasn't the husband always guilty?), then back in (surely, he wouldn't have had the nerve).

He wished he could take credit for this measurable spurt in the village's spiritual rebirth. More than that, he wished Wanda had not been murdered. Her passing had torn the fabric of the place. And the fact that he was not much closer to discovering who had killed her rankled as a personal and professional failure, no matter how he tried to look at it as something beyond his scope and control.

There was one measurable change: as Max had gone from house to house, trying to suss out information about Wanda's death, he had been relentlessly plied with little sandwiches and cakes. Word of his movement through the village, like that of a king on stately progress, had preceded him everywhere, to the point where he had added some noticeable bulk to his carefully monitored weight. By the end of each day he felt he could not stand to see another starchy, sugary confection, however well made or beautifully presented. And certainly no more liquids.

"Tea, Vicar?" some well-meaning soul would ask, and it was all he could do not to recoil in horror.

A lot of nonsense is spoken at funerals, especially when the deceased had not been well liked in life. Many euphemisms are called into play: "vital," "energetic," and (repetitively) "full of life." And frequently, these funerals of the unpopular are sparsely attended, many people suddenly recalling another engagement of critical importance elsewhere.

This was not the case with the funeral of Wanda Batton-Smythe. As expected, attendance at St. Edwold's hadn't reached such dizzy heights since 1980, when a baseless rumor had gone round that the vicar's wife was having it off with the verger. Now the fact that a villager had been murdered added a frisson of danger to the attraction. The sudden and suspicious death of Wanda had outstripped even the draw of the handsome "new" vicar.

Besides, people wondered whether *not* appearing might not be taken as a sign of guilt. So in they all packed, cheek by jowl, necks craning, and friendly little waves being exchanged when they momentarily forgot the solemn reason they were there.

As the organ wheezed its way to the concluding chords of "Amazing Grace," Max's gaze took in the elaborate coffin and the congregation arrayed before him. The squire's pew in front was left empty — by old tradition and unspoken agreement, although there was no reason, earthly or otherwise, for this undemocratic holdover from the past to persist into the twenty-first century. These worthies — the squire and his family — were in any event not yet returned from holiday (and would be most distressed when they learned they had missed the most exciting event to befall Nether Monkslip in many decades, if not centuries, although the affair did have about it the air of serfs misbehaving, which is never quite as interesting, it was felt, as murder among the upper classes).

Suzanna Winship was looking her usual ravishing self in vintage Chanel — beige wool trimmed in black, with a black chiffon scarf draped gracefully over her hair. Her skin was dappled green by light from the stained-glass window near which she sat, her brother at her side. Max had been hearing that the passing of Wanda had left a vacuum in the bossy busybody department;

it seemed nature did indeed abhor a vacuum, if the bright light of excited ambition in Suzanna's catlike brown eyes were any indication. The Women's Institute would not long suffer from lack of leadership.

Max gained the strong impression that wardrobe for the occasion had been given a great deal of thought by many of the women apart from Suzanna. Awena Owen was resplendent in a dove gray robe accented with amber at her ears, wrists, and throat; on her feet were embroidered slippers with small, transparent heels. Tara Raine sat beside her, looking transcendental in a dress of dark saffron and a short netted veil springing from a black bow atop her head. Elka Garth had put aside her usual workaday, flour-dusted clothes and found an old dress for the occasion; it might have been a dress better suited for a tea party on the lawn, but Elka, judging by her expression, felt her presence at the service was sacrifice of time enough. Miss Pitchford wore a deep lavender suit, the matching plumed hat tilted at a rakish angle over one eye. Lily Iverson was dressed somewhat festively in a knitted navy blue suit embroidered at the neckline with bluebells and cherries. Mrs. Hooser, having left the children with a sitter, wore a confection of beige lace that Max knew had been purchased for the recent wedding of a cousin. He supposed it was as well she had not been the bridesmaid, or something even more clingy and inappropriate might have made an appearance.

Max also spotted Guy Nicholls, and Frank and Lucie Cuthbert, but it was hard to see everyone in such a crowd, and some were half hidden behind the church pillars.

However, the young man and woman sitting by the dark-suited Major in a front pew were impossible to miss. The word that best summed up the young man was trendy: he wore glasses with rectangular lenses and thick frames, and sported a soul-patch beard. The eyes behind the glasses, however, were rimmed red as if he had been crying earlier. His dark hair, slicked back, accentuated the square angle of his jaw, although the child he once had been still shone clear on his face. This had to be Jasper, the son of Wanda and the Major. Many, unabashed, turned fully round in their seats for a better view when he walked in, late, to join his father.

There was a sardonic cast to the young man's features, despite the red eyes. Max repressed the instant doubt that rose within him, knowing that prejudging never created anything but obstacles. Perhaps the fact that this was his first sighting of the young man was an irritant in itself — surely he could have arrived days earlier? He feared Jasper might be a supercilious little snit, given normal circumstances. A Sebastian Flyte of Brideshead — spoiled, but lacking the charm that had saved that fictional character, at least for a while. Now he simply looked awkward and out of place — probably, at his age, unused to funerals, and looking very much as if he wished to be elsewhere, a not-uncommon and understandable reaction.

Next to him and holding his hand sat a wisp of a girl with stringy blond hair that looked as if it had been randomly glue-gunned to her scalp. This must be the girlfriend with the unusual name. Clementia. The one on whom the Major had pinned his hopes of being able to settle his footloose son down at last.

Clementia looked to be as different from Wanda as could be imagined, and perhaps that was the attraction. But the pair seemed somehow ill-suited, and Max wondered if it would last.

As he intoned the age-old words from the Book of Common Prayer, he had the illusion of his congregation caught in a freeze-frame. There was Mrs. Hooser, pulling surreptitiously at a bra strap. And Clementia, trying to look grief-stricken or at least interested in the proceedings, but succeeding only in looking bewildered; Clementia was, he decided, possibly not the sharpest knife in the drawer. Frank Cuthbert, scribbling a note onto his hand, and probably hoping there would be a few stiff rounds in the Hidden Fox afterwards. In the midst of life . . .

Suzanna was thinking: The flowers are all wrong. Too jammed together in the vase. I've never liked mums, anyway. They remind me of funerals — that mothbally smell. Of course, this *is* a funeral, but still . . .

Awena thought: White chrysanthemums. They stand for truth and honesty. I wonder whose idea *that* was? Well, Wanda was nothing if not truthful, even if it was like being hit over the head with a claw hammer.

Elka thought: I shouldn't have come. I feel like a fraud. A hypocrite.

Lily thought: Is it warm in here? I'm going to faint. I know I'm going to faint . . . I hated her so, but now . . .

Max thought: How quickly and easily I fell back into my old role of investigator — just when I thought my life had changed, that *I* had changed. Now, instead of trying to empathize and comfort, I'm looking at all of them for flaws, second-guessing them, viewing everyone as a suspect.

Suzanna leaned over to her brother and whispered, loud enough for Max to hear, "Did you see his face?" Dr. Winship nodded. "I'm thinking: Banquo's ghost."

They rose to sing "Let All Mortal Flesh Keep Silence." Again, without Wanda's strong voice to carry the congregation, the song meandered. For the first time some were moved to realize the gap her passing had left.

Then Awena got up to say a few words. She had offered to speak because no one else was willing or able to find a few empathetic words for the deceased, and Wanda's husband and son had declined to do so. She spoke with moving generosity and forgiveness of Wanda, transforming her faults, in death, into virtues. It was a virtuoso performance.

Max was in the middle of his sermon — on the words "life beyond death" — when he heard, following a faint gasp, the most amazing *thunk!* as of something fallen onto the floor from overhead. He turned and saw Lydia, the young acolyte, fallen into a heap of cotton robe just behind him and to his left. She had dropped sideways — fainted dead away. He gestured to Mr. Stackpole to go to her aid, and, distracted, tried to continue. The parishioners all twisted their heads toward the disturbance like a flock of turkeys.

The acoustics of the church were excellent, and Max could hear someone whisper, "Happens every summer."

But it wasn't summer.

Several people ran to scoop up the fallen Lydia, and Max returned to what he could remember of his prepared remarks.

At the end of the service, he thought, *Go with God, Wanda.* Then he surprised himself by adding, in a sudden rush of anger, *I'll find whoever did this to you.*

For he had a sense just then of a shadowy figure out there, in the congregation, gloating, remorseless. And the thought made him livid. No one should be allowed to get away with such a sneaky crime. The jury could return all the open verdicts it wished. This was murder.

He wasn't sure he subscribed to Dr. Winship's view that a killer, having once killed, would find it easier to kill again, like someone on a slimming regime being increasingly unable to resist the fried potatoes.

What was it he had said? That a murder prompted by hatred was likely to be repeated? Surely, in most cases, murder would only become *harder* to commit — the killer burdened with a sense of pressing his or her own luck in getting away with it even once. But here he realized he was thinking of the more "intelligent" breed of killer, not the professional thug who had too often been his quarry during his days in MI5.

So Max was at the moment less interested in preventing another crime than possessed by the creeping, disagreeable sensation of a killer out there exulting in his or her cleverness — *that* he couldn't abide.

But what if, after all, Winship were right?

He came to himself with a start. His parishioners all gazed up at him from their pews like obedient children, expectant, trusting, mildly concerned that their normally dynamic pastor stood before them blank and unmoving. Favoring them with a weak, apologetic smile, he pulled himself together and said the words of dismissal. The organist struck up "I Vow to Thee My Country" (a special request of the Major's), and the church began to empty.

CHAPTER 25
AFTER THE FUNERAL

"Man that is born of a woman hath but a short time to live, and is full of misery."

Max stood at graveside in the St. Edwold's churchyard, intoning the words intended to bring Wanda to peace at last, and to bring some comfort to the Major, who truly looked to be close to a nervous breakdown. All trace of the hearty, inane bluster that was his signature trait was gone, subsumed by a stark, whey-faced despair. Jasper Batton-Smythe did not look as if he would be much of a prop to his father in the coming days; distracted, he was all but checking his watch as the lengthy service wound on. It might be just as well, thought Max, if Jasper returned to his peripatetic life as soon as decently possible — if not before . . .

". . . earth to earth, ashes to ashes, dust to dust."

He spoke the familiar words, tossing earth upon the casket, his mind in two places . . .

". . . this thy servant, whom thou hast delivered from the miseries of this wretched world . . ."

Why did the acolyte faint?

". . . in the place where there is no weeping, sorrow, nor heaviness . . ."

Why did Lydia faint? Max's mind kept returning to the question. Although it was close inside the church, it wasn't summer, when the trapped and stifling heat could make the young and old drop like flies. Nor, although the weather had taken a sudden plunge in temperature, was the church overheated against the chill — given the age of the heating apparatus, there was fat chance of that ever happening.

He concluded the burial service and left the body in the care of the gravedigger. The crowd of mourners began to disperse — Elka Garth had organized an informal wake at the Cavalier. Max went over and spoke a few words to the Major, who nodded, clearly not hearing. Max turned to Jasper and said, "Your father needs tea, hot sweetened tea, and lots of it. Probably something to eat as well, if you can talk him into it." But Max had little hope that Jasper had taken in the seriousness of his father's condition, or cared overmuch. He still seemed mentally to be checking his watch

— more so now that the service had concluded and freedom beckoned. It was an impression confirmed by his next words: "Actually, I'll be leaving soon," he said, adjusting his glasses. The jewelry that adorned his hands and wrists gave off an expensive, platinum glitter. "Obligations elsewhere, you know. Plane to catch. So . . ." Just then, a young man approached him, and Jasper, barely bothering to hide the rudeness of the act, turned away, brushing past to speak with another mourner. The choice of this mourner seemed to Max entirely arbitrary, the person randomly glommed onto. Incidentally, this sudden move left Jasper's friend, Clementia, rather at a loose end as well.

Max was wondering what to do. He hadn't planned on going to the Cavalier, but someone needed to stay with the Major. Clementia didn't look responsible enough for anyone to leave a cat in her care. Fortunately, Lily Iverson had overheard the exchange.

"I'll take care of it, Max," Lily said, at his elbow. She took the Major by the arm and murmured something inaudible but soothing as she led him away.

Max, meeting her eye, nodded his thanks and set off to change in the vestry, planning to go and make sure Lydia was all right. He had taken only a few steps when a tap on his shoulder waylaid him. He turned and saw a sturdy, well-built man, perhaps in his thirties, tanned and good-looking, if beginning to run to a slight paunch. He had an open, honest countenance that could be the sign of an easy conscience, or of a born con artist. It was the young man who had just now tried to capture Jasper's attention and been brushed aside.

"Father," he said, holding out a hand, "my name is Lawrence Hawker — Larry. I wonder if I could have a word?"

"Really, I'm in . . ." Max started to make an excuse, but he was caught up by the name. Where had he recently heard it before? He allowed himself to be sidetracked: Lydia was undoubtedly safe at home now with her mother; a few minutes more wouldn't matter.

"Miss Pitchford," Max said, with the air of a man having solved a difficult puzzle. "You were one of her pupils. She mentioned you the other day."

"As a friend of Jasper Batton-Smythe's, I would imagine. Yes."

"Come along into the vestry for a moment, then. We can talk there in private. I gather this is a private matter?"

Max couldn't in all honesty have said why he felt that, but there was something diffident about Larry's manner. "Furtive" would have been too strong a word. But he was not in any event surprised when Larry nodded in the affirmative.

The vestry was within the church, and was one of the oldest portions of the original building to have survived completely intact. The church as a whole had escaped the mania for gothic ornament that had gripped the Victorian age, for which mercy Max had daily to be thankful. Now he led Larry Hawker into the room, which was lined with cabinets, drawers, and shelves for the various vestments and other items used in worship, and indicated a chair for him to sit on. Max himself perched on top of one of the low cabinets.

Larry looked as if, having initiated the conversation, he needed prompting.

"It's about Jasper," said Max.

"Yes."

"I noticed just now he seemed in no hurry to speak with you."

"Yes."

"Have you seen or heard from him since you both were in school?"

"No. We both went our own ways soon

after. Of course, my family moved away. Jasper went on to bigger and better things than Nether Monkslip."

Max looked at him.

"I gather your parting wasn't amicable?"

Larry gave him a smile of rueful remembrance. "No, it was not. But that's not what I wanted to talk with you about. Or rather, that is why I hesitated to talk with you. It's just that, I want someone — someone in the village — to know my thinking here. And you look like a sound chap."

"Thank you, but if you have anything in mind that has to do with the . . ." (he hesitated to say murder) ". . . the demise of Mrs. Batton-Smythe, the police are the people you should talk with."

Larry shook his head decisively.

"Going to them would be gossip, pure and simple. And worse, seen as spiteful gossip, designed purely to cause trouble for him. Here is the thing: I feel I knew Jasper, at the time, and his relationship with his mother, better than anyone. I always sort of knew what he was thinking. I read how she was murdered in the paper — some papers were cagey about it, but they as good as said it was murder. And . . ."

"And?"

"You see, it's just this. He hated her so.

365

From the moment I heard, I felt Jasper had something to do with this."

Max, knowing Jasper had been put in the clear by various disinterested eyewitnesses, just looked at the young man. His face and his manner were vehement, full of conviction.

"But that is not evidence," Max said mildly.

"Exactly," Larry replied. "My certain knowledge is not evidence. I wasn't here. I haven't lived here for years. How could I go to the police? I'd look like I was just fanning the flames of some old rivalry. Some old jealousy."

"I see. A friendship gone wrong. Yes, the appearances could —"

"No, it's not that. It's more than that, Father. We were lovers."

The day had grown overcast, the sky purple with heavy dark clouds. They squatted soberly on the horizon like a hung jury as Max set out to check on the well-being of Lydia Lace.

Max reflected as he walked that while what Larry had told him was interesting, it had nothing to do with Wanda's death. Larry spoke of Jasper with a livid dislike he barely bothered to conceal — a dislike that seemed to have its roots in Jasper's belief that he was socially a cut above a poor farmer's son. "One day," Larry had reported, "he just stopped talking to me. There was no quarrel, no rift. He'd simply had enough — it was 'time to move on.' I suppose he'd taken up with someone else. But . . . I was crazy about him, as you are at that age. Crazy. You don't just dump people who care about you. But Jasper did. That was Jasper all over."

But Jasper had been in Argentina around the time his mother died, being interviewed on live television about his art in advance of an exhibition there, a fact DCI Cotton had confirmed. It had been a live, not a taped, appearance — an unbreakable alibi. There was no question that Jasper could have been anywhere near the United Kingdom at the time of his mother's murder. Max was glad the young man had come to him, not to DCI Cotton, for Larry's instincts were right: his opinion regarding Jasper and what Jasper was capable of was no more than that — opinion — and opinion tainted by a failed love affair that Larry admitted had ended in poisonous rancor on both sides.

Max wondered if Miss Pitchford had been alluding — in her blushing, genteel, old-world way — to the true nature of the relationship between her two former pupils. Looking back, he realized that what she had expressed was skepticism regarding the existence of a girlfriend in Jasper's life. Max was not of the school that felt love between adults could or should be regulated, and he got by in his profession by actively avoiding debates on the subject. There was so little in the way of real and abiding love in the world that it seemed to him a miracle if two people of whatever persuasion found each other and formed an attachment.

But Larry — disgruntled and disillusioned though he may have been by the end of his affair with Jasper — had been unwavering in his opinion.

"I know him, you see. I know what he's capable of, the greedy, sewage-minded little — I know what he's capable of, that's all.

"And I know he did this."

Lydia Lace lived not far from Miss Pitchford in one of the old cottages along the river, converted in the 1990s into an estate agent's dream. The prospect of selling such an abode frequently led said agents to their most orgiastic levels of praise (the word "stunning" was often evoked). Still, there was no escaping the fact that such dwellings, while as charming as something out of a fairy tale, were little more than doll houses barely large enough for two modern adults, however small.

Max tapped at the door knocker of Trout Cottage and Mrs. Lace appeared in the open doorway. She smiled as she invited him in. He remembered just in time to duck his head — he had on more than one occasion in visiting the cottages nearly knocked himself silly on a low lintel. Stunning, indeed.

"Could I have a brief word with your daughter, Mrs. Lace?"

"She's having a lie-down in her room. I'll just fetch her."

"Let me talk with her alone, please. I'll leave the door open but I'd rather you let me speak with her in private, at least at first."

Mrs. Lace, seeming to understand there were things a girl would tell Max Tudor but would not say with a mother present, and not resenting this fact in the least, merely nodded.

He was shown into a room covered in taupe wallpaper with a green design, like mold viewed under a microscope. Lydia was at that awkward age, torn between idolizing teddy bears and rock stars. Her room reflected her interest in both, with Kid Rock edging out Paddington Bear at two-to-one.

She was currently covered up to her eyes in a duvet. Those eyes were closed, although Max could tell she was not sleeping. Her brown hair, held back in a band that circled the crown of her head, was fanned out on the pillow — she looked like a Pre-Raphaelite illustration of the Lady of Shalott. As he pulled up a chair beside her, she looked up at him, relief at his presence written plain on her face.

"I was worried," he said simply. "Are you all right?"

An explanation for Lydia's sudden faint had occurred to him, one which he hoped very much would turn out not to be the correct explanation. It was a concern she immediately put to rest.

"I'm not — you know."

"Pregnant?"

Embarrassed, she seemed to look everywhere in the room but at him.

"Tha's right," she mumbled. "I'm fine. It's not that."

The words hung in the air so long he wondered if she had said all she was going to say. But suddenly she burst out, "I remembered him, you see. And I'm so frightened, Father."

"Him? Him who?"

But the direct approach seemed to have been a mistake. Eyes wider than before, she stared at him, clearly wrestling with the question of whether to share what she knew. Would it make her safer, or more vulnerable? She liked Father Max, everyone seemed to, but . . .

"Maybe I should tell the police?" she asked tentatively. "But . . . could they really protect me?"

A cold fear clutched at his heart. She could only be referring to something in connection with Wanda's death. What did the child know?

"Lydia, absolutely, positively. If you know anything, you have to tell." Thinking of his talk with Larry just now, he said, "If you don't feel comfortable telling the police, if you think they won't believe you, perhaps, tell me first. Then we'll decide together what's best to do."

She mumbled something into the duvet.

"Speak up, please, Lydia."

"They'll believe me — why wouldn't they?" she asked, with the hubris of the very young. "It's not just me, you see, though, who'll be dragged into it. And my mother . . . my mother will kill me."

Max doubted that, but there was a killer loose in the village who might very well kill the child. "Tell me," he urged. "We'll get it sorted out with your mother. But tell me."

And here the story came tumbling out. It seemed that Lydia had a boyfriend who lived in nearby Chipping Monkslip. He had come to the village of Nether Monkslip to be with Lydia during the Fayre — her disapproving mother being otherwise occupied, Max gathered, reading now between the lines.

"Greg was to meet me by the Plague Tree in the graveyard, which he did. There was no harm in it, Father. We were just talking."

Max, going by her demeanor and the deepness of the blush that flooded her face, wondered about that.

"Never mind," he said. "Go on."

"That was it. We met in the graveyard, and we . . . we talked. Greg had to get back home — he'd just snuck out for a bit. His father was punishing him, see, for staying out late the past weekend. Greg's father is really such a prat, he —"

"Greg left you in the graveyard and was heading home to Chipping Monkslip," Max prompted. "And . . . ?"

"He had to pass near the Village Hall as he left the village."

"What time?"

"Noon. Just around noon."

Max was struck by a sudden image from the day of the Fayre. Recalling the moment of Wanda's distraction as she stood with him by the trestle table, and the trajectory of her distracted gaze, he took a guess.

"Did Wanda by any chance spot the two of you together, earlier?"

"Yes," said Lydia. Her mouth set in a thin line at the memory. "And she wasn't half shirty about it. Like it was any of her business. She threatened to tell my mother. 'It takes a village to raise a child,' she said. Pompous silly cow."

He left a suitably long pause, allowing for the flush of outrage to pass.

"Sorry," she said at last. "I just didn't like her. But I'm sorry she's dead."

"What were you going to do?"

"I hadn't decided yet. Then . . ."

"Then she was killed."

"Father Max, I'm scared."

"Why, exactly?"

"Because as I was starting to walk back toward the Fayre, I looked back — I was, you know, hoping for a last look at Greg. Hoping he'd turn and wave. He's ever so handsome and I really think he —"

"And you looked back and saw . . . what?"

"Yes, I looked back. And that's when I saw . . . I saw a man coming from the Vil-

373

lage Hall. I didn't know who it was, and I didn't actually see him leave the hall, just come from that direction. It wasn't anyone I'd ever seen before. I thought nothing of it then — I thought it was just someone from another village coming to see the Fayre — you know how many strangers were in the village that day. But then, this same person was in church today, at the service — and he recognized me. You could tell he recognized me. And you should have seen the look in his eyes. Stared right at me, he did — for a flash second, looking like a devil, I swear it. And then I recognized *him* — I might not have noticed him otherwise, you see. And I knew. This was the man who killed Mrs. Batton-Smythe."

She began to wail. "The person who killed Mrs. Batton-Smythe saw the look in my eyes, and *knows*. He knows I know. What am I going to *do?*"

"How can you be so sure of that? That he killed her?"

"Because Greg heard a shout."

"Greg heard a shout," he repeated. "An argument?"

"Might have been," she replied. "He said he wasn't sure — just that he heard a shout. He told me this after, you see. It didn't mean anything at the time. We didn't put it together, you see. He heard a shout — so what? People were shouting all over the Fayre that day, half of them drunk. *I* didn't hear anything — I couldn't, not from where I was. But I saw a man coming from the area of the Village Hall. Even then, so what? When I saw the man today, it was the way he looked at me — that shocked look on his face. Only for a second, but he recognized me all right."

"No harm will come to you," said Max. "I promise you. Calm yourself now."

"But don't you see? The only reason I'm alive is I didn't tell anyone. I didn't know there was anything to tell. Now I do know something. How can I ever leave the house now? Even to go to school?"

School was the least of her worries, but Max didn't tell her that.

Still, there was something odd about her story. The murder had been the talk of the village, and she and Greg were only now reliving it?

"Why did it take so long for you two to compare notes? Any particular reason?"

She sniffed. A down feather escaping from the duvet seemed to capture her rapt attention.

"Lydia-a-a? You're telling me the whole story, aren't you?"

She sniffed again, and looked up at him from under her lashes. "Sorry. He started seeing another . . . another woman, didn't he?" she said, with one of her odd forays into the adult world.

Oh, for the love of —

"You mean you had a lover's quarrel, so you didn't see him to talk to?"

"That's right. I have my pride, you know. *Now* he says he's sorry. We're trying to work it out. But he told the police at the time what he'd heard, he says. So that's all right."

Really. OK then. That's all right.

Greg could only, he reflected, be the kid who heard a commotion coming from the Village Hall — the one DCI Cotton had told him about earlier, at the beginning of the investigation.

Max stood up, restless, seized by a desire to pace the room. I've been around Cotton too much, he thought.

He then asked Lydia a pointed question, to which she replied firmly in the negative.

"No. I know who Noah is. Everyone knows Noah. This man had *white* hair."

The beat of his heart quickened. *Oh, my good Lord.* "Tell me. Everything you remember."

She complied as best she could, but with frequent, lurid reference to the evil and

376

devilish aspect of the man she had seen. Max patiently sifted through the embellishment, then proceeded to issue a string of warnings, all of which Lydia swore she would heed.

After he left, Mrs. Lace went into her daughter's room with a cup of tea. She sat waiting until she had Lydia's full attention. No question about it — Lydia had been hiding something. No doubt to do with that no-hope boy from Chipping Monkslip — the boy Lydia fondly believed her mother knew nothing about. Finally, she asked Lydia what she'd told Max. At Lydia's reply her mother looked satisfied, as if some of her worst suspicions were confirmed, but also very frightened. How much did this put her child in danger?

Outside the cottage, Max was doing what he could to keep his promise to Lydia that she would come to no harm. He walked over to the river to a spot where he was sure he could not be overheard, and put in a call on his mobile to DCI Cotton. He got his voicemail and asked that the detective call him back immediately.

As he waited for a response, he reflected on what a short time it had been since he had found Wanda dead, and had witnessed the — as it transpired — already hopeless attempt at mouth-to-mouth resuscitation. The kiss of life, a technique discovered centuries before for reviving drowning victims.

Kiss of life. Kiss of death. Judas kiss.

Sealed with a kiss.

He felt his skin prickle.

At Oxford, he'd met many theologians who were at odds with the new ways of the church — the place tended to be the strangest combination of innovation and clinging to tradition he'd ever come across. He thought now of a particularly unruly professor he hadn't thought of in years — a peculiar man even by the standards of Oxford dons, many of whom seemed to revel in their reputations as lunatic crackpots. This man would blow his nose before offering his hand for the exchange of peace, as a way of showing his contempt for all the "newfangled tampering" with the service. In a different century he might have been burned at the stake, but as it was his fellows merely gave him a wide berth, as if he were the walking embodiment of contagion.

Contagion. Now, why . . . ?

Just then, his mobile rang — Cotton returning his call. They had a tense, wide-ranging conversation that lasted several minutes.

But the first priority, both agreed, was getting a guard posted at the front of the Laces' house.

CHAPTER 26
REVELATIONS

The church that had so recently held the mourners and the curious at Wanda's funeral was hauntingly empty that afternoon. Max sat in a pew near the altar, to all appearances deep in thought. Unlike DCI Cotton, Max had an endless capacity for the still, silent vigil. His notebook and pen rested at his side. He needed all his attention focused outward.

In speaking with Cotton outside Lydia's cottage, Max had relayed the suspicions of Jasper's old school friend.

"Evidence, Max. We need evidence," said Cotton.

"That," Max told him, "is precisely why we're setting a trap. I'll draw off the poison — direct it away from Lydia and her friend Greg. Whoever shows up is by definition our man, frantic to know what Lydia told me. Agreed?"

They argued, but in the end, Cotton could

380

hardly keep a priest from sitting in his own church — all night long, if he felt like it.

Max had come to this point in his reflections, with a sure and growing conviction as to how Wanda had been killed, when he heard the main door into the church open, and the whispery sound of soft-soled footsteps brushing the stone floor. Max didn't have to turn to know who was there.

And he was certain it wouldn't be Jasper.

"Guy," he said. " 'Rhymes with High.' Or would you prefer to stick with the French pronunciation?"

That threw him; the slow, confident steps halted for a moment. Then Guy resumed his walk up the center aisle.

"Exactly what stories has that girl been telling you?" he asked.

"Lydia saw nothing," Max told him, his gaze still on the altar. "I thought perhaps she had, but she was preoccupied that day, the day Wanda was murdered. What a shame she couldn't help us: Lydia would have been the only witness to who had gone near the Village Hall when they should not have been there — when they had pretended not to have been there."

"You're lying," said Guy at last. "Padre, you really need to learn not to meddle." He sat in the pew directly behind.

After a brief internal struggle, for he hadn't thought the try-on would work, Max turned to face him, one arm resting on the back of his pew. "I'm out of practice," Max acknowledged. "I thought it was worth a shot to try to protect her from you, but lying is an art that requires frequent rehearsal. I've been away from MI5 too long. She saw you that day, at the Village Hall, where you and I know you didn't belong, but she didn't recognize you until the funeral. She'd never seen or met you before then. She'd have been in school on many of the occasions when you'd come to Nether Monkslip for supplies. She thought the man she'd seen that day of the Fayre was just a visitor from another village. Which, as it turns out, he was."

No need to mention Lydia's boyfriend, thought Max. At least he could keep one of them out of it.

"If you hadn't come to the funeral," he went on, "this might not have unraveled for you so quickly. But how were you to know Lydia would be assisting at the service, and would have a front-row view, as it were, of the entire congregation? What really threw her was that she recognized your face, but when she saw you at the Fayre you had *white* hair. A wig, of course — a disguise to hide your distinctive haircut and color, just in case you were seen. A wig long since consigned to the fire, I'd be willing to bet. From a distance, the disguise worked. But only from a distance."

Guy might not have been listening. "MI5," he said. "I didn't really believe the talk about your background, you know."

"That was wise," said Max. "It is all much exaggerated. They like to have a little story to tell about their vicar. Gives them bragging rights in the other villages, I would imagine. So, let me tell you what I know about how you pulled this off. You can fill me in on the why. How's that? Fair enough?"

Guy just looked at him steadily. Only a slightly ragged edge to his breathing betrayed his agitation.

"When we found Wanda," Max said, "you raced over to give her mouth-to-mouth resuscitation. Thus obscuring your role in causing her death. Should anyone have thought to test the saliva in her mouth there was a perfect explanation if your DNA was found. You thought of everything, didn't you?"

Could they separate his DNA from Wanda's? Max was certain they could.

Scientists could do almost anything these days. What was important was, Guy had thought so. He'd thought of every way to eliminate any trace of his involvement — just in case.

Max said, "I knew with near-certainty she was dead beyond hope but I have . . . a familiarity with death. It didn't occur to me that there was another reason for your persistent attempts at revival. I just knew in good conscience we had to try. Miracles do happen." He smiled. "I have it on the highest authority."

Guy's rapid breathing was becoming more pronounced, but Max judged that his adversary was not ready to strike — yet.

"When I asked myself what had happened in Nether Monkslip in recent weeks or months, what had altered, at first I drew a blank," he went on ruminatively. "Nether Monkslip is what it is — unceasing, unchanging. That's why we like it. But in fact, one inhabitant had experienced a life-changing event — a loss, in fact, of the most basic kind. Wanda. Her mother had died. And as a result Wanda came into a substantial amount of money and property. That is what had changed."

There was a gaping, Pinterish pause as Guy evidently considered his options.

"Okay, look," Guy said, looking incrementally less sure of himself than before. "It was an accident. I didn't know about her allergy."

"That is a lie," said Max, all traces of cordiality gone from his voice. "You knew perfectly well she was allergic. She was planning a catered dinner party and you were to be the caterer. The chances were nil she wouldn't mention she was deathly allergic to a particular type of food as you were going over menu choices with her. People who had practically never *met* Wanda knew of her allergies, that's how obsessively she worried about an accidental ingestion. The Major has already confirmed this — he was there — so you can stop lying and start telling me the truth."

"All right," said Guy, with the air of a man making a huge concession. "You may as well get the full picture before you go." This was said softly, the threat only implied. "I don't want you to get the wrong idea. That would be . . . creepy."

You might well be the authority on creepy, thought Max.

Guy said, "We weren't having a full-blown affair — are you kidding me? With Wanda? — but a rather heavy-handed, old-fashioned flirtation. It pleased the old cow to engage

385

in this coy, tortuous type of romance — the kind of thing women's magazines peddle by the page. Moonlight and roses. It was 'our first kiss.' Touching, eh? Actually, it was disgusting. That old woman. That silly, stupid old woman. I could hardly bring myself to touch her, let alone —"

He used several Anglo-Saxon words and phrases to express his revulsion for Wanda. Max could forgive any witticism, however crude, however sprinkled with four-letter words, so long as it was actually witty. This was not. His face hardened with distaste.

"If you were finding it all so distasteful, so upsetting to your aesthetic sensibilities, you could have backed out of the scheme. You could have let her live in peace, talked her son out of this. You're the strong one in the relationship, after all. The brains. Not Jasper. You. Anyone can see that."

Flattery, in Max's experience, often worked. The stupider the criminal, the more likely it was to work. What was more, Max believed what he said to be true. The older man of the pair had a talent for deception that required a mature intelligence — an emotional intelligence that Jasper, less able to mask his feelings, lacked. No doubt this failing had contributed to the decision to keep Jasper well out of the picture until the deed was done. Guy was the leader of this folie à deux.

But the expedient of flattery was not going to work this time, Max realized.

"Do you have any idea how much money is really involved? Don't *you* be stupid. Father." The last word came out as a scornful sneer — familiar to the believer confronted by a nonbeliever. Too much to hope, thought Max, that he'd have stumbled across a murderer with some vestiges of childhood religious training — relics of some superstition, even, that might make him hesitate to attack.

Guy moved suddenly, and Max saw he was carrying a knife, sharp from his kitchen. On his face, a vicious smile.

"Kilo!" Max shouted, standing. The agreed-upon code word for the choice of weapon. "K" for knife. Max had known there would be one.

Suddenly there was a huge crash, the sound of a dozen votive candles tumbling against the stone floor, and DCI Cotton and several of his team erupted from the Lady Chapel. Guy turned momentarily in the direction of the distraction. A moment was all Max needed.

The pew stood between him and Guy, otherwise Max would have grabbed his wrist

387

and twisted his own body around, using the momentum to force the knife from Guy's hand. As it was, he could use the pew for leverage: Max grabbed the arm holding the knife, and used it to pull Guy toward him until he was hinged over the back of the pew. A knee to Guy's nose took him out, but still he clung to the knife; a chop to the wrist made the knife clatter to the floor.

It was over.

CHAPTER 27
AT THE HORSESHOE

"Imagine the cavernous rage required to plot this murder," said Max. "A murder at secondhand against one's own mother." Did the distancing make it more or less cold-blooded? Max couldn't decide.

"Followed by a carefully calculated display of public, crocodile-tear grief," added Cotton.

Max nodded. They sat before two pints of ale in the Horseshoe's saloon bar. It was midafternoon on a cold day, and they — along with Thea, who napped at Max's feet — had the run of the place. The landlord had served them at their table by the fire and discreetly slipped away. Then, just as discreetly, he had slipped back. Max had rather thought he might: this was too good a chance to be in on the ground floor of the scoop villagers would crowd in later to hear. Cotton had politely but firmly told him they needed to be left completely alone.

"That's the worst of it," said Max. "Jasper did it rather well. He probably rubbed something like salt in his eyes to make them red. I can just picture him rehearsing his demeanor over and over, in front of a mirror, or with Guy. Going over his lines, the body language. Suzanna said something about Banquo's ghost. I thought she was intimating that Jasper was a manifestation of his father's feelings of guilt or something like that. But she now says Jasper reminded her of an actor she and her brother had once seen on the stage. She had picked up on the fact that what we were watching was a *performance*. As a former stage actress herself, even amateur, she saw what we missed. It was all a performance by Jasper, and by Guy."

"But really, there was no disguising Jasper's core personality. It was Guy who was the real performer here."

Max nodded. "They must have realized they were in dead trouble when they saw Lydia's reaction in church, and saw me going to see her. If I'd realized the danger at that point, of course, I'd not have gone there. Afterward, I knew you'd need to station your people in front of her cottage. We couldn't risk either of them trying to eliminate this witness against them. But that couldn't go on forever. Of course, her boyfriend, Greg, would also need to be eliminated, if they learned he was also a witness. Where it would have ended, heaven knows."

"She was in the wrong place at the wrong time — at the right time for us, as it turns out."

"Meeting her young love by the Plague Tree, long a village courting spot. She saw Guy coming from the Village Hall. If what Jasper's old school friend said were true, and Jasper was behind this, Jasper had to have had an accomplice. But we didn't know for certain who that was until I asked Lydia to describe this man she saw.

"She only later realized in comparing notes with her boyfriend that because of the timing, Guy had to have been leaving Wanda — leaving her body, that is. At the Fayre Lydia had been, for one thing, too preoccupied with her own assignation, and with not getting caught herself, to have been paying much attention. When she saw Guy in the church congregation she recognized his face, and being so young she wasn't able to mask her reaction quickly enough. His own look told her he had caught her start of recognition. I had my back turned, but it was impossible in any event to say what or *whom* she was staring at before she fainted. It could have been any of the suspects — the people who had some sort of history with Wanda — who were all sitting more or less in the same area."

Max glanced around him. The pub, living up to its name, sported a horsey theme — whips, saddles, and similar equine paraphernalia hung on the walls, along with a few hunting prints and a staggering collection of old horseshoes. The place always had the not-unpleasant smell of polished leather mixed with hops.

"I'm not sure what it was that chummed the water for me," Max went on, "but in thinking of the crime, I felt the psychology of it was striking. There was something sneaky about it, as I think you and I discussed. A betrayal of trust, on a large scale. It was several things, really, that set me off, beginning with the thought of contamination and poison. Which is really what happened to Wanda, of course, a form of poisoning."

"This is one for the books," Cotton said, settling back into his chair, fingers woven together across his flat stomach. "Literally the kiss of death. He was hoping to make it look like accidental ingestion, he says. He's singing like the proverbial down the nick, and happy to drag his partner in crime, Jasper, into the frame at every step. That plan — to make it look like an accident — fell apart almost immediately when she struggled, but, undaunted, I think he hoped — they hoped — to pin the crime on the Major if it came to that. Jasper could tick two boxes that way — get rid of two people who stood in the way of what he wanted."

Max nodded and said, "The Judas kiss is what really put me on the trail to Guy. Thinking of that. Perhaps it was what inspired these two, also. One thought led to the next step of wondering where she was most vulnerable. Of course, Jasper knew all about where his mother was most vulnerable.

"The aggravating thing is," he continued, striking one fist against the arm of his chair, unintentionally disturbing Thea's rest, "a copy of Caravaggio's *The Betrayal of Christ* hangs in my study. I'm kicking myself because it's something I see every day, that painting, where Judas Iscariot greets Christ with a kiss, to point him out to the soldiers waiting to capture him." It was, he realized, a classic case of what he *thought* had happened not having happened at all. Had he really forgotten so much of his life in MI5 — that hall of mirrors where almost nothing was ever as it seemed?

"Once I began to suspect how the poison was administered, I looked around for likely partners for Wanda, including the Major, of course. At least I felt certain I could eliminate the women of the village, which narrowed the field considerably."

"What made you suspect Guy?" Cotton asked.

Maybe it was years of pretending to be someone I was not, Max thought. I could spot a phony; I was one. That he nearly hadn't spotted *this* one bothered his pride more than he cared to dwell on. He may have hoped that in coming to Nether Monkslip, he could simply throw off his past, like shedding an old garment. But Guy's deceit — nearly successful — chilled him. He had vowed he would never again be the reason anyone walked into danger . . .

It was so routine a matter — so beneath their skill levels — that he and Paul relaxed. Nothing to worry about: we're covered. If anything, Max was annoyed by the assignment, while easygoing Paul just accepted it as part of the job. And now Max was even leaving early to meet a date, having taken over part of the earlier shift from Paul, who was on night duty at home with his newborn son. They would sort it all out later. Then it would be the weekend, and the Russian was leaving, to go back to his unsuspecting family in Moscow (the man seemed to have half a dozen mistresses in London). He and Paul could handle this with their eyes closed.

It was his own arrogance that he later found so appalling, so unforgivable.

Paul earlier had flipped open his wallet and turned the photo in its clear plastic frame toward Max: a red-faced gnome in a blue hospital hat, eyes not quite yet fully open, fists clenched in outrage at the many liberties taken.

"Paul II," Paul I said, proudly.

Max made the required noises of wonder, although Paul II, like all newborns, had the look of something that had been soaked too long in beet juice.

"That's great, man. Really great. How proud you must be. Look, I'll see you back at the office. Get Randolph to spell you if need be — that lazy sod owes us."

Paul, gazing transfixed at the tiny photo, might not have heard him.

"What?" Paul said at last. "Sure thing." He turned to get into the official, anonymous silver car Max had left parked in an alley. "You need a lift? Drop you somewhere?"

Max shook his head and, thumping his stomach, said only, "Exercise." He turned, and the last thing he heard before the blast threw him on his face was the sound of Paul starting the car.

After the explosion, he could remember very little through the haze of his concussion to help the investigation in any real way. There had been, five minutes earlier, a man standing around wearing sunglasses. They had white frames and blue lenses, making him look like an alien visitor from Hollywood or Mars, and Max remembered thinking he had appalling, juvenile bad-boy taste. But none of this was much help to the investigators. They suspected who was to blame — and one group of jackals had taken credit for it. They'd probably let them get away with it for now: that happened to fit with the policy of the moment.

He had tried to carry on as usual. Then he noticed, days after his release from hospital, a tiny stain as he pulled the linen shirt he'd been wearing that day from the laundry hamper. A pinprick of color against the white collar. It might have been anything, come from anywhere. He'd probably cut himself shaving. Or it might have been the catsup he tended to spray all over himself when opening one of those individual tear-packets for a sandwich. It probably was that, he told himself. Of course, no more than that. One of life's daily little irritants. But he knew with a terrible certainty that it was Paul's blood. He couldn't wash the garment, or even throw it away, knowing that. He didn't see what use the lab would have for it even in their grim task of re-creating what had happened, so he couldn't somehow turn the horror into a useful tool to ram it home to the murdering bastards. In the end he folded it into a plastic bag and stuffed it into the furthest recesses of his closet. But first he wept into the fabric, as lost and heartbroken as a grieving child.

The loathing for the terrorists who had killed Paul consumed him except in his sleep, which was dreamless, a total, rapid, and welcome descent into unconsciousness at the end of each day. Clearly the only sane response, he told himself, was to sleep as long as possible — to escape the memories that awaited him, like something alive and coiled to strike, from the moment he woke. Asleep, he couldn't hear that explosion and the looping play of his last, everyday conversation with Paul leading up to it. Sleep he did, as much as he could, for days stretching into weeks, for in the end, he had taken an extended leave of absence, after first using up all the time off coming to him. Whether he ever intended to return, he was not even now certain. Tough-guy Max, as he'd thought of himself, inured to everything brutal the job could throw at him, simply wanted to pull the covers up over himself, curl up into a ball, and forget.

He nearly said something of all this to Cotton, but found he could not. His throat tightened at the thought. Maybe one day. Maybe one day he could break out of the emotional straightjacket that held him fast.

In becoming a priest, he had made a conscious choice to head down a path where he could connect with others. Where he could do good on a human level, rather than on a political one. The rational part of his mind resisted the information that "sharing" the most fraught and terrifying of his memories was possibly the first step toward making that human connection.

He merely answered, "I didn't suspect. Because of Lydia, we knew something Guy had told us was wrong. An innocent man would — probably — have told me and the police that he'd been in the vicinity of the Village Hall at a crucial time. He did not. Why not? I wondered. An innocent forgetfulness, like Noah? Or something else?"

"Even so, that alone is not evidence. People lie to me all the time, and for the stupidest reasons," said Cotton. "Some lie to the police just on general principles."

"I know. But then Guy came to the church to find out what I knew, and he dug himself in deeper when he tried to pretend he didn't know about her allergies. He had told me himself he'd discussed catering a meal for Wanda. The chances she wouldn't mention this allergy, as I told him, were zero."

"A fact the Major confirms," said Cotton. "He says that of course Guy had been told, 'had been warned repeatedly' were his words."

"Anyway, as I say, Jasper of course knew all about his mother's vulnerability — that includes her emotional vulnerability, as well as her physical susceptibility. But Jasper was not on the scene. He could not be on the scene, as suspicion would fall on him immediately, especially if she died soon after he'd returned from his long absence. So . . ."

"So, Guy moved here, set himself up, and began ingratiating himself with Wanda," Cotton finished for him. "Moving in for the kill."

"Not long ago," said Max, spinning his glass between the palms of his hands, "I read of a case where a child nearly died from anaphylactic shock simply by being exposed to molecules of peanut in the air of a café. People who are susceptible can be very susceptible."

"And not just to allergies. I wonder," said Cotton, "how Wanda ever fell for this setup in the first place?"

"That's the easiest part for me to understand — now. Imagine her loneliness. She had no friends in the village, and few elsewhere, to all appearances. Her marriage had become a formality at best. Her son, vanished, for all intents and purposes. I should have sensed her aloneness but frankly it was well hidden under all the bombast and busyness. Still, it's my job to notice these things. I feel that I failed her. I did fail her."

Cotton merely looked at him, then shook his head.

"I don't think being perfect and all-knowing is in the job description. Leave that to your boss upstairs, why don't you?"

Max smiled wanly, looking into the dregs of his beer. As it happened, that was good advice, if very difficult to follow.

"Let's see," Max said. "What else? Oh, yes. That diary of hers. Why put a star in your calendar by some dates — for the dentist, for example — and not others? Some of the dates were a blind. Some were real. As we now know, a star in her diary or calendar meant she was visiting Guy at his place over the restaurant, so seeing the doctor or dentist or hairdresser in Monkslip-super-Mare wouldn't necessarily and didn't always match up. Sometimes she would see both the doctor and Guy on the same day. Some days she would have no appointment on the day she said she did; some days she would. Only the star told the truth about her Guy meetings."

"Beneath that formidable exterior beat the heart of a romantic," said Cotton. "She did seem to enjoy the intrigue. Perhaps she saw it as harmless fun. After all, it was a flirtation, a younger man paying her the attention she craved — not really an affair. Guy is adamant about that, and I believe him — I think the whole idea of Wanda as paramour offends his ego."

"Poor Wanda. I think you're exactly right. She was a romantic with a highly developed sense of drama. It was a weakness to be exploited, and exploit it these two did."

"There was another romantic touch," said Cotton. "The figurine on the windowsill at the Village Hall."

"He confirmed that, did he? Yes. I noticed

it was facing in a different direction from the usual. I can see it from the churchyard, you know. MI5 uses that sort of signal all the time at safe houses. A safe house being, as you know, an ordinary place used by officers to meet agents. Each safe house has a system of signals to indicate whether it is clear to enter — something like an ornament in a window pointing left or right. Sometimes the direction of the ornament indicates the time of day for a proposed meeting, like a clock. If the ornament or figurine is pointed straight ahead, the meeting time is noon. If pointed with its back to the window, that means six o'clock. And so on."

Cotton laughed. "No one but you, Max, would have noticed, or attached any significance to it."

"But I didn't piece that bit together until very late in the game — and even then, Guy's actions were what drew my attention to it: he made a move to straighten up the shepherdess figurine when we discovered Wanda's body. Wanda and Guy used it as an all-clear signal on the occasions they met up in the Village Hall. It was frequently deserted, at times Wanda would know all about, and so ideal for one of these passionate — or rather, passionless — little trysts she so enjoyed."

"You must be right about her loneliness."

Max nodded. "I imagine he would flatter her, soften her up. Playing up to her vanity, he made her fall in love with him by painting a picture of the life she thought she was cheated of via marriage to her boring husband. It was a courtly courtship: no doubt she saw his impeccable manners as part of his deep and abiding respect for her and their timeless 'love' for one another. Her ego would blind her to the fact that these corny, courtier-like manners masked his repugnance. Maybe even, in his heart of hearts, there was a feeling of self-loathing, knowing what he was going to do to her."

"What heart?"

Max said, with sad resignation in his voice, "You may have a point. Anyway, her son wanted to be rid of her because it might be years before someone of her vitality might die of natural causes, and he wanted *all* the money she inherited from her parents to go to him. He had begun to fear she might change her mind, and her will, the longer the years of estrangement went on. She might even be able to put an entail on his inheritance via his father. Guy probably got out of her how much money was involved in her inheritance — making sure all this trouble was worth their while."

"We have learned one interesting thing on that score," said Cotton. "There was a young man hanging about the widowed grandmother before her death — your hunch may have been right there. From the description, it might have been our friend Jasper — a neighbor lady didn't like the looks of things she saw going on across the lane. Funny that if it was Jasper he wouldn't introduce himself as the grandson, isn't it? We'll ask him a few questions on that score, too. Having an eyewitness will be of inestimable help there."

"Is the thinking that they hastened the old woman's death?"

Cotton nodded soberly.

"Good heavens. Even though it occurred to me . . . it's diabolical if they really did that. The level of planning involved . . ."

Cotton asked, "Do you think there's a chance Guy may initially have planned simply to convince Wanda to reconcile with her son?"

"No," said Max flatly. "I don't. I think he and Jasper both realized that was a non-starter — and anyway, it didn't carry the guarantee of inheritance they craved, even if she had agreed to reconcile. Wanda's mind made up was . . . well, a mind made up. Ut-

404

terly unchangeable. No, I think her death was in the cards from the moment the grandmother died and Wanda safely inherited. Oddly enough, the Major intimated to me that things might have swung quite another way. The 'old lady' was going to leave much of her wealth to the church but then became disillusioned by her new rector. Wanda's coming into the lot was almost a fluke."

"Unfortunately," said Cotton, "it was a fluke she broadcast to her son in a moment of braggadocio, perhaps thinking she could dangle wealth in front of him as a bribe, a way to bring him round to being the devoted kind of son she wanted. But all it did was, as they say in melodrama, seal her fate."

Max drained his glass, declining Cotton's invitation for a refill.

"The more I thought of it," Max said, "the more the oddest small things fit together. The change in the usual direction of the bibelot — the shepherdess ornament — suggested an assignation. A way to say, 'I'm here, waiting — the door is unlocked.' More playing to Wanda's sense of the drama of the thing, no doubt. As I say, I watched as Guy made a grab for the figurine, to switch it back into position, that day we found Wanda's body. I thought nothing of it."

Cotton said, "Wanda and Guy would always have bolted the door from within for privacy — they were both inside when Maurice tried the door, although Wanda may have been dead at that point, with Guy still there just making sure he'd not forgotten something. But, why was a signal even necessary that day? Why not just murmur a time and place in passing?"

"As Dr. Winship said," replied Max, "there was a 'mash' of people at the Fayre. Even if you'd had one eye out for Wanda you might not have spotted her to pass a message, to arrange an assignation. This is why the prearranged signal was necessary. There was no way to whisper in her ear or pass notes because finding her was challenge enough. And this was the day Guy had settled on for her death — nothing must go wrong, no slipup in the timing.

"So, he had her do what they had often done in the past: the direction of the shepherdess indicated the all clear," said Cotton. "Brilliant."

"I do think diabolical is the word," said Max, a distraught, hard edge to his voice. "Those two, Jasper and Guy — they planned and plotted this crime, literally for years. Probably as sort of a game at first. Then, the more they talked about it, the closer they came to acting it out in reality."

"Tampering with the auto-injector was a particularly nasty touch," said Cotton. "Guy says he did that a few days before, at some other meeting with her."

"Yes. Guy stole the auto-injector in advance from her handbag and replaced the contents with water. He had to do it that way because she was never without her handbag with the auto-injector inside. He couldn't steal the thing outright because she would undoubtedly notice it was missing. Then, once she was dead, he removed the fake auto-injector from the handbag. He later threw it in the lake, where Constable Musteile was instrumental in its recovery."

Cotton reached into his ever-present briefcase.

"I thought you might want to see this," he said, handing Max a small, flat, square package wrapped in brown paper.

CHAPTER 28
JOLIE LAIDE

Max unwrapped the parcel. Inside was a painting of a woman with tightly curled hair. Max immediately thought of the term *jolie laide* — it was a face both pretty and ugly. Although abstract in execution, it was unquestionably Wanda's face — even without the curly hair it would have been recognizably her.

Max had once visited the Lady Chapel of Ely Cathedral, which had been vandalized by the Puritans in the sixteenth century. The faces of the statues had been mutilated with a criminal ferocity. Of course, in that case, obliteration was the goal, but a few had escaped with their features "merely" damaged, not hammered off entirely. Max wondered how well those men, the destroyers, had slept at night. Probably well. The smug self-righteous always did.

Wanda's face in the painting reminded him of this. It was a work of genius, stark and vicious, executed in bold, unhesitating strokes. An evil genius, in this case.

"Jasper's work, of course?" he said.

Cotton nodded. "It was found hidden in Guy's flat above the restaurant. A gift from Jasper — a picture of their intended victim. Bizarre, is it not?"

"Everything about these two is bizarre."

Max gazed at the painting, at the audacious slashes of black and gray mixed with violent shades of red and deep purple.

"And Wanda — her reaction to the setup, as well, had the taint of a pathology, don't you feel?" asked Max. "I think it is possible that Guy reminded her a bit of her son on some unconscious level. There is a logic to that, since Guy has spent many years in the company of her son. His mannerisms, patterns of speech: it's a commonplace that longtime couples grow to be alike. Her reaction was unconscious, and probably as much maternal as anything else — a reaction to the familiar. This goes in part to explain her unreasoning devotion to a man too young for her, apart from the fact he played to her vanity and her ego. One clue I missed was that she had taken to wearing a great deal of makeup lately. It didn't necessarily mean she was having an affair, but it suggested *something* in her life had changed to make her overly concerned with her appearance."

Cotton said, "Jasper had at one point been on the receiving end of a smothering love from his mother. He told us this at great length. A more self-involved, sniveling little nub of humanity it would be hard to find. Anyway, smothered he was. At least in the beginning, he was showered with anything it was in Wanda's gift to give the boy. But her 'gifts' of money were always conditional. Jasper's father, meanwhile, intuited that he had not exactly fathered the prototype of the macho man, but he could not, *would* not accept that he had fathered a gay man. Don't ask, don't tell? Don't even allow the possibility of opening a discussion of such a topic, in the Major's view, and in Wanda's. I think Jasper's exile may have been self-imposed, but it was also encouraged. Neither of his parents could begin to cope with Jasper's sexual orientation. His looks, talent, and undoubted gifts were never enough to reconcile them."

Max asked, "Has that anything to do with Guy misleading me about Belgium?"

"Yes. That was a minor thing that loomed large in Guy's mind. Guy's specialty seems to be panicking over the details, even though he's cool as can be when it comes to the big picture. Guy and Jasper were legally married in a ceremony in Belgium some years ago. In Belgium, as of 2003, there are no restrictions regarding nationality in entering into such a contract. Naturally, this formalized relationship is a matter of public record. Guy didn't want you to put us onto searching records in Belgium, which is where they lived together. So he pretended to you to be most recently from France. It was overkill, really. Clearly he is one to believe the devil is in the details. There was little reason for us to start questioning his orientation, or Jasper's, and it is irrelevant to the murder, but just in case . . . He wanted as much opaqueness with regard to their relationship as he could manage."

"I did wonder why he felt Belgium was something he should conceal from me. Why do people lie about where they've been recently, I asked myself? To get a job, perhaps, when their former employment didn't end satisfactorily? That's understandable if a man is desperate for work, to feed his family. I understand that kind of desperate, and wouldn't try to parse the morality of it. But Guy was the restaurant owner, so why lie to me — and then tell you, the police, the truth? Only one reason: because he knew you could and would check what he said about his places of residence, and what he told you had to match up."

Cotton nodded. "He didn't appreciate the danger: you had the old connections to do some verification on your own, if you took it into your head to do so. He thought the MI5 gossip, when he came to hear of it, was just that, and he also didn't realize at first you would be so involved in the investigation that I would confide in you." He smiled. "I didn't think so, myself."

"Ordinarily," said Max, "you would not have shared the background details about a suspect with me or with anyone. As it happened, you didn't tell me Guy was from Belgium until I asked."

Max looked into the fire, casting his mind back over the days of the investigation. Thea nudged his hand until he began gently to scratch her ears.

"It really was the unrelated details that tripped them up, although I nearly missed their significance, every time. There was an odd moment or two in my conversation with Miss Pitchford — her unusual emphasis when she told me about Jasper's school friend. I misread her, and thought she was being a social snob — that she felt a friendship with a poor farmer's son was slumming it for the son of a military family, which in

412

her fine scheme of things would be just a rung above, socially. But no, she was trying to tell me their relationship was outside the limits for her generation — that it went beyond schoolboy friendship. Educated a woman as she was, Jasper's orientation was not spoken of directly by her age group. The habits of a lifetime are not easily broken."

" 'The love that dare not speak its name.' "

"Certainly not as far as Miss Pitchford is concerned. What I barely noticed in all this was Miss Pitchford telling me that Bombay was a favorite place of Jasper's. She was using the name she'd grown up with, rather than its modern name of Mumbai. Mumbai, where Guy told me he had lived awhile."

"They met in Mumbai originally," Cotton told him. "Guy was traveling about, and Jasper was simply looking for a cheap place to live where he could stretch out the money his parents sent. Interesting, that. He would play one parent off against the other, at least until Wanda pulled the plug, and neither parent knew the other was sending him money. It's a game you might call 'Double Your Money.' Double-dipping — hitting both parents up for money, and swearing each parent to secrecy about it."

413

"The cynicism is breathtaking," said Max.

"Isn't it just? Apparently, he hated both of them. I have the idea — a dead certainty, in fact — that the Major might not have lasted long after he inherited from Wanda. Not long at all. I'm sure the Major was their next intended victim, after Jasper's mother. The rich pathology of this family hardly bears scrutiny."

"I'm afraid you are quite correct about that," agreed Max. "What no one told me was how much both parents adored Jasper — each, perhaps, in their own way. And in Wanda's case, up to a point. But the sentiment wasn't returned."

"No, it was not," said Cotton. "The whole point being the money he and Guy coveted so much — for this restaurant of Guy's, for one thing, to keep it afloat. And for their travels, for another. I gather they'd run through quite a bit of cash, via one scheme or another — never thinking two days out, especially in Jasper's case. Guy, with his business experience, seems to have been somewhat of a stabilizing influence. Jasper was always the dreamer. And the big spender."

"So," said Max. "Mumbai is where Guy met up with Jasper in his travels. Possibly where their evil plot was conceived. Certainly where like soul called out in recognition to like soul."

"Guy described it to me as being hit by a thunderbolt," said Cotton.

"He went out of his way to present himself to me as heterosexual to almost a parodic degree — ogling the waitress, drooling over Suzanna. Tara says he went out with her a couple of times, but there was nothing doing, and she rather wondered why he'd bothered. And Jasper's coming here, dragging that poor Clementia with him, was more of the same kind of blind."

Cotton nodded. "We never thought in terms that were not stereotypical. Jasper, we were told, had a love interest. That love interest must, therefore, be female. How hard it is to think outside of these stereotypes."

"A drawback in both my profession and yours, I would say."

"You were right about the key business, by the way," Cotton said. "Guy says Wanda always preferred to use the more romantic French pronunciation in addressing him. *Guy* — rhymes with *key*."

"So what Miss Pitchford heard — or rather misheard — as 'oh, key' was Wanda saying his name: 'Oh, Guy.' Presumably in some breathy, adoring, distracted way. She

415

was probably looking for her compact, her lipstick — it could have been any number of things. But Miss Pitchford heard 'key' — or thought she did — and linked the word, quite naturally, to the sight of a woman scrabbling around in her handbag. I sat there in Miss Pitchford's sitting room, where the works of Guy de Maupassant are ranged on her bookshelves. Something about the name caught at my mind at the time — 'Guy' pronounced in the French manner of course rhymes with 'key.' It wasn't until much later that I made the connection."

"Is it possible," Cotton asked tentatively, "that Miss Pitchford is a bit hard of hearing, as well?"

"I suppose it is. She's somewhere in her eighties. And when I spoke with her the other day, she did ask me to repeat something I'd said. She'd misheard 'food' as 'mood.'"

"I really never thought to ask her about her hearing. She is so completely sharp and canny in every respect."

"Something tells me she might not have 'fessed up to it if you had asked. She's rather proud, our Miss Pitchford, and I don't suppose she likes getting older any better than the rest of us do."

"Still, it sure beats the alternative."
"You think?" Max asked. "Not in my book."

"Still, it sure beats the alternative."

"You think," Max asked. "Not in my book."

EPILOGUE

Max sat at his desk sipping hawthorn tea as he ruminated over his next sermon. Mrs. Hooser came in with the vicarage mail, which had arrived several hours before. Although it was not raining, and had not rained for days, she had managed to get the circulars, bills, and assorted rubbish soaked through with water.

Water, he thought, sighing, was becoming a recurring theme in his life.

The water stain, painted over twice now, had reappeared on the wall of the church, despite all Max's attempts to fix the leak in the roof, or to at least divert the tide that would descend at the next rainfall. During a recent Sunday service, little Tom Hooser had said loudly, "Looks like Jesus," only to be shushed immediately by his sister. All heads swiveled to look, and an excited buzz rose from the congregation.

Max, walking over after the service, joining the others for a closer look, saw what the boy had seen: The stain, growing darker, its outlines and contrast more pronounced, was beginning faintly to resemble the face on the shroud of Turin, something the boy had no doubt seen on a recent telly documentary. A negative image of a gaunt, bearded man with longish hair, eyes closed as if in sleep. The resemblance was slight, but definitely it was there. Max, far from being enthusiastic, felt immediate twinges of panic. This was not something he would welcome at St. Edwold's — the rubberneckers, the curious, the devout, and the crazy would all crowd in if word got out. He had seen this kind of thing before — crying statues that turned out to be crying because of some weird, one-off juxtaposition of the atmospherics, the climate, a malfunctioning boiler, and the humidity in a church. He'd have to get it repainted. He reached for his phone to call Maurice again.

He thanked Mrs. Hooser now and she turned to leave; the broom she carried just missed sending all the magazines and papers on a table near the fireplace to a fiery death.

"Oh," she said, turning again, and doubling her chances of leaving chaos in her wake. "I nearly forgot. She's here. The witchy woman."

She could only mean Awena. "Please show her in, Mrs. Hooser. And whatever you do, don't call her that."

Awena bustled slowly in, swathed in folds of brilliant fabric, as always looking like a queen on a stately progress. Thea, knowing better than to jump, instead threw herself in a rapturous heap at Awena's feet. She seemed to consider Awena something of a soul mate.

"I'm on my way to tonight's Women's Institute meeting," Awena said, briefly bending down to caress the top of Thea's head, "and thought I'd drop in and say hello. We haven't really spoken since you rounded up those two cretinous thugs."

"Good heavens. Is it that time again? I did hear Suzanna had taken up the reins of power."

Awena nodded. There was a glint of mischief in her eyes that should have forewarned him.

"Big changes are afoot," she said.

"Really?" Refusing to be drawn, he started to turn back to his sermon.

"Don't you want to know?" she demanded.

"Don't you want to tell me?"

"Very well. If you insist. Be among the first not on the distaff side to hear: the

Nether Monkslip Women's Institute is going to make a calendar."

"They do that every year, I thought. So you can only be saying . . ."

"That's right. A nude calendar. Well, not *completely* nude, but . . ."

"You mean, like the North Yorkshire women in *Calendar Girls?*"

"Exactly. Miss Pitchford is positively scandalized."

This could only be Suzanna's idea, he thought. Suzanna, with her pinup looks.

"Who else is involved?"

"Oh, you know. Elka. Lily."

Lily? "That is supremely hard to imagine," he said aloud. "How did she ever get talked into it?"

"Talked into it?" repeated Awena. "She's one of the most avid supporters. She's a changed woman, since she's started seeing the Major. She'll be posing with her spinning wheel."

Good heaven. "I'm going to have to start getting out about the village more," Max said.

"He's been 'squiring her about,' as only the Major could do," Awena told him. "It's a real old-fashioned courtship. He calls her 'Little Lady.' "

"He actually called her that? Good Lord.

421

It's like a line from a bad John Wayne film."

"Which one? All his lines were bad. Anyway, she seems to like it. She has come into her own, our Lil. She worships him and his accomplishments, as she sees it. Love is strange."

"Ah," said Max. There seemed no other possible response.

"But she's playing the field, in the most genteel way imaginable," Awena assured him. "Keeping her options open. Smart girl."

"So. Who else is going to appear in the calendar?" Max asked.

"Oh, you know. Me, for one." She practically shuffled her feet, examining one beaded shoe, then another. "I've agreed to pose wearing a witch's hat, stirring toil and trouble in a black caldron."

Really. "That's . . . nice," he said.

"It's for charity," she told him. Her eyes were gleaming; clearly, she couldn't wait for the opportunity.

Max reflected that the last time he'd heard the phrase, "It's for charity," things had not turned out well. This time, he felt in his heart, would be different.

The employees of Thorndike Press hope you have enjoyed this Large Print book. All our Thorndike, Wheeler, and Kennebec Large Print titles are designed for easy reading, and all our books are made to last. Other Thorndike Press Large Print books are available at your library, through selected bookstores, or directly from us.

For information about titles, please call:
    (800) 223-1244

or visit our Web site at:
    http://gale.cengage.com/thorndike

To share your comments, please write:
    Publisher
    Thorndike Press
    10 Water St., Suite 310
    Waterville, ME 04901